Paula Gosling was born in Detroit and moved permanently to England in 1964. She worked as a copywriter and a freelance copy consultant before becoming a full-time writer in 1979. Since then she has published fifteen novels, has won both the John Creasey and Gold Dagger Awards from the Crime Writers' Association, and has served as the Association's Chairman. When she isn't committing murders by typewriter, cooking or reading, she can be found in her sewing studio, creating abstract embroideries and patchwork quilts. She has a wonderful husband, two beautiful daughters, two lovely cats, and a pet overdraft which she is grooming for Gold in the Banking Olympics.

RICOCHET

PAULA GOSLING

timewarner
paperbacks

A *Time Warner* Paperback

First published in Great Britain in 2002 by Little, Brown

This edition published by Time Warner Paperbacks in 2003

A CIP catalogue record for this book
is available from the British Library.

ISBN 0 7515 3469 2

Typeset by Palimpsest Book Production Limited,
Polmont, Stirlingshire
Printed and bound in Great Britain by
Mackays of Chatham Ltd, Chatham, Kent

Time Warner Paperbacks
An imprint of
Time Warner Books UK
Brettenham House
Lancaster Place
London WC2E 7EN

www.TimeWarnerBooks.co.uk

To Liz
the very best friend

RICKY SANCHEZ IS A GOOD person.

He loves his family.

He works hard.

He studies hard and gets good grades.

He is ambitious.

Almost everybody likes him.

And yet he has a problem.

If he's right, he could save a life.

If he's wrong, he could destroy one.

But he knows what he saw.

And he knows what he heard.

And he knows he should do something about it.

What he doesn't know is that he has less than forty-eight hours to live.

ONE

IN KATE TREVORNE'S OFFICE IN New State Hall the phone rang. Absent-mindedly, her concentration on the essay before her unbroken, she reached for the receiver. 'Yes?'

'I know about you and Michael Deeds,' said the voice at the other end. 'You should be ashamed.'

She sat up straight, her mind suddenly focussed. 'What?' she asked, not quite sure what she had heard.

'You heard me. I know about you and Michael Deeds.' The words came in a metallic, nasty, pinched little voice. If a cockroach could talk, she thought, it would sound like that.

'Who is this?' she demanded.

'Aha . . . wouldn't you like to know. You are a slut, did you know that? You are a disgrace to the profession. If you don't stop poaching students, I will take what I know to the Dean. And you know what that will do to your chances for tenure, don't you?'

'I haven't the least idea what you are talking about, and I resent the impli—'

'I've had him here in my office. He told me all about it. Your tender little relationship. The money you paid him to keep quiet. Oh, just everything. I must admit I was very, very shocked.'

'You are insane,' Kate snapped. 'There was no "relationship".'

'That's not what Michael says.' There was now a singsong kind of glee in the voice. Childish, smug, savouring it all.

Kate stared at the phone with distaste.

Michael Deeds.

Her partner Jack hadn't liked him at all and told her so at the time. But the boy was so promising, had such talent for writing. And she had felt sorry for him. When he was thrown out of his digs for non-payment of rent, she had taken him in, temporarily, only for a few nights. Until he could find alternative accommodation.

But the few nights had become a week, much to Jack's annoyance. Then there was the night that Jack was away on duty, and Michael came in drunk and had made a pass at her. Not a big pass, an almost sweet little-boy pass, but he had turned a bit nasty when she summarily rejected him. He hadn't hurt her and was easily evaded. Indeed, she had ordered him to bed like a naughty child, and he had gone, eventually. She had locked her bedroom door, much to Jack's confusion when he came home in the early hours.

She had been rattled, but had handled it, and the next morning she told Michael he had to leave. When he pleaded that he couldn't find a place without a rent deposit, she had given him some money just to get rid of him. She knew she had made a mistake allowing the boy to stay so long and she wanted him out of her private life. He went. Sorted.

If Jack had ever found out about the pass, he would have . . . would have . . . well, she didn't quite know what Jack would have done, but she preferred to deal with things herself. She and Jack were partners, she was not a wife, not a possession. She had her own professional life, quite apart from their relationship.

But if she was truthful, she was ashamed of the episode, too. She could have handled it better, more maturely. She had just panicked and made the boy get out of the house immediately.

What the voice on the phone was accusing her of was nonsense. True, Michael had dropped out of her course after that – for all she knew he had dropped out of university. She was sorry, but there were many reasons students left – and money was a big one. She had simply thought he had been unable to continue for financial reasons and had written off the loan as money unwisely spent. Certainly when he had left that morning he had shown no sign of acrimony. On the contrary, he had been shamefaced and apologetic about the incident.

Now this. What had the voice said? 'I have had him in my office and he's told me everything'? What everything? There had been nothing to it, nothing at all, and certainly no 'tender relationship'. Had Michael's talent for creative fiction been extended?

The threat was a real one, though. Sexual relations between a faculty member and a student were strictly forbidden, and the threat of charges of sexual harassment hung over female faculty as well as male. She was vulnerable and the voice on the other end of the phone knew it.

Without saying anything further, she hung up the phone and went back to the essay she was marking, trying not to think about what the voice had said.

Two minutes later the phone rang. She picked it up.

'That wasn't very nice,' said the insinuating voice.

In nature, autumn is a time of ending. Leaves change colour to blaze briefly and drop. The air turns colder. Night comes sooner. In scholastic and academic circles it is a time of beginning: new term, new notebooks, new pencils, new textbooks, new subjects.

In law enforcement, however, it is no different from any other time of year. People rob, cheat and kill each other just the same. All it means to a cop is more paperwork. Or, in this modern world, computer time. Detective Lieutenant Jack Stryker was up to his ears in it and getting nowhere.

He was muttering balefully to himself when Sergeant Toscarelli came through the door. 'It's not healthy to grind your teeth,' Tos informed his friend and superior officer. 'You could get temporal mandibular misalignment and you wouldn't like it. My cousin Ralph has it and he can make his jaw click like a castanet, plus he gets headaches—'

'I already have a headache, thank you,' Stryker growled.

'Well, there you go, it's probably already started,' Tos said, settling down in the chair facing the desk. 'Just goes to show.'

Stryker looked up. 'Show what?'

'What?'

'Just goes to show what?'

'What does?'

'Funny, you don't look like either one,' Stryker said.

'Who?'

'Abbott or Costello.'

Toscarelli sighed and inspected his socks, pulling one back up. 'You need a break. Some action.'

Stryker closed his eyes briefly as he leaned back in his chair. 'What do you suggest? A murder? Nice talk, wishing someone dead.'

Tos shrugged. 'It happens.'

'It's a terrible thing to admit,' Stryker said, 'but catching a shoplifter or a crooked accountant would be infintely preferable to sitting here staring at this damn thing.' He pushed the keyboard away from him and scowled at Toscarelli. 'Are you working on anything I should know about?'

Toscarelli stood up. 'My chest expansion. I'll be in the gym if you want me.'

Stryker sighed as Tos went out. He was on call; he had to stay at his desk.

And wait for the phone to ring.

Out in the bull pen, footsteps heralded something coming, but it was only Pinsky.

'Hey, Pinsky, where you been?'

'Following up that old lead on the Carson case,' Pinsky said. He threw himself into a chair and nearly knocked

6

it over. 'Whoa, old paint,' he muttered, rebalancing the chair, then raised his voice. 'Not that it went anywhere; there's nothing at that witness address at all but a vacant lot.'

Neilson came over and looked down at his partner. Ned Pinsky was tall, skinny and seemed badly put together, as if by an amateur. But the look was deceptive – he was athletic and fit, ate like a horse and never put on an ounce. 'You ask around, in case we got the number wrong?'

'Of course I did,' Pinsky growled. 'Nobody knew anything – like you'd expect in that neighbourhood.'

'Bummer,' Neilson said sympathetically. Neilson was handsome, lazy and not overly bright, but amiable. 'There was a call for you.' He held out a scrap of paper. 'Sounded like a kid – Ricky Sanchez. Know him?'

Pinsky sat up, frowning. 'Sure I know him. He's been dating my eldest girl – they're both at the university now. Did he sound OK?'

'What do you mean?'

'Like did he sound worried or scared or anything?' Pinsky was instantly concerned about his daughter.

'He sounded . . . young,' Neilson said, shrugging his shoulders. 'I asked if I could help, but he said he wanted to talk to you. He'll be at that number until three.'

Pinsky looked up at the pale-green smoke-stained wall. The old clock was always ten minutes slow. 'Damn,' he said. Adding in the missing ten minutes, it was almost three thirty. 'Did he say where he'd be after three?'

Neilson shook his head. 'Don't worry about it, it's probably nothing.'

Pinsky wasn't so sure. 'No, it's something. He's not the kind of kid who rings up to pass the time of day. He's a serious kid, pre-med student, very smart, very . . . cocky. Did he sound cocky?'

Neilson considered. 'No. He just sounded kind of in a hurry, is all.'

'OK, thanks.' Pinsky reached for his phone. 'Maybe I'll

call back, just in case.' He rang the number, but when someone answered it turned out to be a payphone in the hall outside the Student Union cafeteria. Whoever it was said Ricky had left. Pinsky hung up slowly, wondering why Ricky had called, why he had been in a hurry. It didn't sound good. He wondered if something had happened to Denise on campus and Ricky was trying to tell him in order to get him to the hospital or something. He considered ringing home, but realized his wife would still be at her part-time job down at the library. And if it was that bad, Ricky would have said so to Neilson. He wished he knew Ricky's cellphone number. Why hadn't he left it?

Neilson sat on the edge of his desk. More compact than his partner, he was a snappy dresser with an eye for the female of the species. Where Pinsky was dark-haired, Neilson was dusty blond, with a face like the late Alan Ladd. 'He reliable, this kid?' Neilson asked.

'Oh, sure,' Pinsky said. 'You remember that neighbourhood shooting we had about three years back – guy got into an argument with a neighbour over hedges or something and the neighbour shot him?'

'Sounds familiar – like maybe I've done nine or ten like that.' Neilson grimaced. Like all cops, he hated 'domestics' – there was never a right answer to them.

'No, this was in *my* neighbourhood,' Pinsky said, implying it was a little different from the ordinary. Which was fair enough: the Pinsky family lived in a very nice neighbourhood, not rich, but very respectable. 'Guy who was killed was named Leo Sanchez.'

'Any relation?'

'He was Ricky's father. Damn shame. It's a nice family. Mother works in the mayor's office, all the kids are decent kids. Ricky sort of took over his father's place. Made sure the younger kids stayed in school, didn't get into trouble – you know how a shock like that can send kids off in all directions.'

'Yeah,' Neilson agreed.

'Well, Ricky . . . he sort of steadied things down. The

8

neighbour got sent away for manslaughter.' Pinsky frowned again. 'Maybe that's it – he might be getting out soon if he's behaved himself. Maybe Ricky's worried about that.'

'What makes you so sure he's worried?' Neilson wanted to know. He picked up a letter opener, examined it, put it down, picked up a rap sheet, glanced through it, put it down, picked up an apple, bit into it.

'Because he's never called me at work before,' Pinsky said. 'He's never seen me as a cop, just as Denise's father. I took an interest, you know – Denise had just started up with him then. Ricky sometimes would sit and talk with me, waiting for Denise to get herself ready to go out. Like I said, a serious kid if a little cocky. Very, very smart, knows it; sometimes that rubs people the wrong way, but it's not intentional. I think I'll ring home and see if Denise is back from classes – she must have his cellphone number.'

'Maybe he's even there,' Neilson said, chewing a mouthful of apple. 'With Denise.'

'Maybe.' Pinsky nodded. 'Maybe.'

'You don't want to interrupt anything.' Neilson grinned.

'Very funny,' Pinsky grumbled. 'Denise is no angel, but she's no fool, either.' He leaned forward and dialled.

'I don't know where he is, Dad,' Denise told him when she answered his call. 'I haven't seen him all day, because our classes don't match. And he has to be at the hospital by four.'

'At the hospital?'

'Yes – he has a part-time job as an orderly at the hospital. It's real good experience for him, you know.'

'Yes, I guess it would be. Is that City Hospital?'

'Yes. He usually works in the ER, I think. You could try to get him but I don't think they much like people getting calls at work, in case like if someone is trying to get through with an emergency? And they make them turn off their cellphones while they're in the hospital because it causes interference with some of the machines or something.

He'll be back by ten tonight and he usually rings me when he gets home. You could talk to him then.'

'I guess that will have to do,' Pinsky said slowly.

'How come you want to talk to him, anyway?' Denise wanted to know. 'Does it have anything to do with my birthday, maybe?'

Pinsky grinned. She was a sly little thing. 'Not as far as I know, sweetheart. And stop trying to find stuff out, my lips are sealed.' They were sealed because he had no idea what his wife's plans for Denise's birthday actually were. 'Ricky's not . . . he hasn't been worried about anything special lately, has he?'

'Just his grades, like always,' Denise said. 'And his mother because she works too hard. And his little sister because she's getting interested in boys . . .'

'I get the picture. A born worrier.'

'That's Ricky,' Denise agreed. 'Oh, I know – his kid brother got a speeding ticket the other day. That's probably it.'

'OK, then. See you tonight.' He hung up, feeling a little better. As far as he recalled, Ricky's 'kid' brother should be about seventeen now. So as Denise said, that was probably it. Although he was a bit surprised – Ricky didn't seem the type to try to get a ticket fixed. Well, he'd wait until this evening, then, rather than disturb the boy at work. He hadn't realized Ricky was working at the hospital. That was a good break for a pre-med student. Maybe that was why Denise was home more nights than usual these days, which was not a bad thing.

He looked across at Neilson and said, 'I think we should check out that other address, over on Hayes. What do you say?'

'I'm free.' Neilson flapped his wrist like that of a popular television character. He tossed the apple core into the nearest wastebasket. 'Let's go.'

Lieutenant Jack Stryker looked out through the glass wall of his office and watched Pinsky and Neilson depart. The only one left in the squad room was the new rookie, Joe Muller, who was reading old cases to get used to the routine. He seemed like a bright prospect and was very eager. What was against him was his appearance – although he was twenty-four he looked about sixteen: lightly built, blond hair cut tight to his skull, big brown eyes that seemed as innocent as a faun's. He might be bright, but he would find it difficult to impose himself on witnesses. They would treat him like a child.

Stryker narrowed his eyes. Mind you, if Muller played it right, that could work for him. He wondered if the boy was bright enough to use his audience. It was an unusual way to gain information, but it might work. It might work very well, especially with women. He was going to watch Muller's progress with interest. Reports from his former bosses said the boy was good and he had been effective on the street, particularly with adolescents. Time would tell.

All the other detectives were either hard at work or across the street eating doughnuts at the coffee shop that had become a second home for the off-duty officers and men of Police Central. The owner, a big Italian woman with a heart of gold and teeth to match, made them all welcome, reasoning that a constant police presence in what was, admittedly, a criminous part of town gave her coffee shop a measure of protection against nutsos and robbers. And besides, her doughnuts were fabulous, home-made and very, very fresh. She closed at six, where-upon any idling police customers decamped to their favourite bar. It made getting in touch with men easier, he figured, and Captain Fineman agreed, so they didn't come down on the men for 'wasting police time' in these places. In addition, it was preferable to have the men get fat during the day rather than drunk. Not that any of them had that much spare time these days.

Stryker leaned back in his chair, ignoring the blinking cursor on the screen. Early on in his career he had earned the nickname of Jumpin' Jack Flash, always on the move, but he had slowed down a little as the years passed. His curly hair was slightly receding, and both it and his moustache showed considerable amounts of silver. It ran in the family, he insisted, this tendency towards premature grey. He was a compactly built, highly strung man for whom leisure was just a matter of breathing slightly slower than normal.

He certainly didn't feel comfortable behind a desk. But that desk had been one of the things that had eased his relationship with his girlfriend, Kate. She said she would live with him, love him, but not marry him, because she knew how cops' wives waited during the nights and days, waited for that phone call, or the visit from the superior officer who told them their man was dead. Worse, that the father of their children was dead.

For some reason, avoiding the final commitment of marriage made a difference to her. It seemed almost a superstitious attitude on her part. He didn't understand it, but he reluctantly accepted it. And she was very much caught up in her career at the university, which she found very fulfilling. The university was so different now from when he had been a student there himself. Then it had been made up of a few buildings and some big old houses converted to offices for the various departments. Now it was a state institution, with a modern and quite elegant campus, some prize-winning architecture and a landscaping department second to none. Part of him was pleased but most of him regretted the loss of those big old houses where he himself had taken his degree in pre-law. Then his parents had died and he had gone into the police. Getting his law degree was still a dream and he occasionally found time to take the odd course for credit, but it was a sometime and long-time thing. Since he had been living with Kate, he begrudged losing any time with her and it was only when she herself was teaching in the evening that he matched a class with hers. This autumn he had been studying torts while she taught nineteenth-century American literature. It meant two evenings

12

together lost, but there was the nice advantage of being able to go out for a drink together or even a meal after classes finished. Sort of like being an undergraduate again. He smiled to himself. *And at our age*, he thought.

So the fact that he was more desk-bound also meant he was better able to regulate his life. He wasn't sure if it was an advantage or a disappointment. Just because a person was old enough to consider slowing down didn't mean he had to, did it?

The phone rang in the squad room and he punched the button to take it, Muller apparently having gone to pick up more files. 'Major Crime.'

'Is Sergeant Pinsky there?' asked a young man's voice.

'Sorry, he's out on a case. Can I help?' Stryker leaned forward and punched a couple of keys to move the cursor down to the next line of the form he was filling in.

'No . . . I don't think so. I really need to speak to Mister Pinsky,' the young man said. 'Would you tell him Ricky called?'

'Ricky what?'

'Oh – sorry – Ricky Sanchez. He knows me.'

'OK.' Stryker scribbled the name down. 'You sure I can't help?'

'No . . . it isn't really about homicide, see.'

'We don't only work on murder, son,' Stryker said. 'Are you quite sure I can't help?' The boy sounded stressed.

'No, sir . . . it's . . . personal.'

Stryker raised an eyebrow. Sir? That degree of politeness was rare these days. 'OK. I'll tell him as soon as he comes in. Has he got your number?'

There was a strangled laugh. 'Oh yeah, he's got my number all right. But I'm at work now . . . I'll speak to him tonight.'

'OK.' Stryker hung up thoughtfully. He'd speak to Pinsky about it when he came back in. Something about the boy's voice worried him, but he couldn't have said exactly what it was. He shrugged, dismissing it, and went back to the computer. All he had to do was get through

13

this report and ten others like it, and he could go home at a reasonable time for once. No classes tonight – he and Kate had a whole evening to themselves. He hoped.

Tos Toscarelli was working out in the gymnasium in the basement of the municipal building, but his beeper was placed conscientiously nearby. A big man naturally, he had a constant battle with his weight and the only way forward he could see was to turn fat into muscle. Italian through and through, he had black curly hair and snapping black eyes. He had finally decided that if he was going to be big, he might as well be big and hard. And, too, the department had high standards of fitness – standards he not only wanted to meet, but beat. It was better than going home.

For all his size, Toscarelli was a downtrodden man. He lived with his mother and sister – the former a mistress of hypochondria, the latter one of those seemingly shy people who hide an iron will behind a velvet demeanour. He was the breadwinner for them and they guarded him zealously. No matter that he was much in love with a woman named Liz Olson, a colleague of Kate Trevorne's, and she was in love with him. They wanted to marry, but every time Tos brought up the subject of Liz at home, Mama Toscarelli always managed to produce a 'heart attack' and his sister a crying jag. They 'needed' him, this Liz woman wasn't Italian, they would be unsafe alone etc. etc.

It was really beginning to get him down.

He knew Liz was losing patience. She, too, was a big person, in more ways than height. She was a professor of French and Spanish ('Why not Italian?' his mother kept asking) and carried herself proudly – six foot of her blonde, shapely self was a noble spectacle around the campus. When she and Toscarelli got together, it was an inspiring sight. The trouble was, they didn't get together often enough for either of them.

'I feel like the Other Woman,' Liz had complained last

14

week. 'Like you already have two wives and I am something on the side.'

He knew she had every right to feel that way.

It was his own cowardice that left the situation unaltered. He stared at himself in the mirror and sneered. He could build up his muscles all he liked, but he had a chicken heart.

Something would have to be done, and soon, because Liz was not going to wait for ever. She was an independent woman, she said, but since falling in love with Tos she yearned for the safe harbour of marriage. He had made her realize she was lonely, she told him. Well, he was, too. And now, at her suggestion, they were 'giving each other space'. That meant that she did not want to see him again until he made up his mind.

He wondered if there was a body-building machine that duplicated the sensation of being between a rock and a hard place. Maybe he could practise on it. He loved his mother and he loved his sister, but . . .

But.

Families are funny things. They bind with ties nobody else can see or understand. They weigh you down with responsibilities you never asked for and you wonder how you got into that particular corner. But if he was not careful he would get to be an old Italian bachelor, looking after his spinster sister and his elderly mother, and nobody would be happy. Especially not Liz – and he wanted Liz to be happy. He wanted them to be happy together.

He added a weight to either end of the bar and continued with his compressions and lifts. Steel on his chest and Mama on his back. And, any minute, a call to get dressed and follow up on some new case, because that was his job. It was for times like these that doughnuts were invented, he thought. Where else to find solace?

It seemed he spent all his time being pressured from two sides and tripping over dead bodies.

A hell of a life for a grown man.

TWO

'DADDY, RICKY WANTS TO TALK to you.' Denise was standing outside the bathroom, calling through the door.

Pinsky, woken from a comfortable doze, gave his head a shake. 'Tell him I'm in the bathtub,' he called back. There was a moment when he could hear Denise mumbling into her cellphone.

'He says it would just take a minute.'

Pinsky was exhausted and his brain was in a very low gear. 'Do you know what it's about, Denise?'

'No. It might be his brother getting a speeding ticket the other day. But it could be something else. He's kind of upset.'

Pinsky sighed and dragged himself up out of the bath. The water had cooled anyway. Wrapping a bright-red towel round himself, he opened the bathroom door and reached for Denise's cellphone. 'Hey, Ricky,' he said. 'What's happening?'

'I got kind of a situation, Mr Pinsky,' came Ricky's voice. He did sound a little strained.

'I hear your brother got a ticket for speeding.'

'Oh. Yeah, well, he deserved it. This is something else.'

'OK, shoot.' Pinsky shivered as his wet body cooled in the draught from the half-open door.

'Well, I think somebody I know is doing something wrong. I don't know for sure, it's only something I've suspected, and I don't know what to do about it. If I go off half-cocked, I could destroy a person's whole career. If I'm right, I get called a sneak. Nobody likes a sneak.'

'I think whistle-blower is a better name.' Pinsky smiled.

16

'Yeah, well, whatever. What do I do?'

'Find out more,' Pinsky said promptly. 'Get as many facts as you can, then go to the authorities. Would that be us or somebody else?'

'I'm not sure. Probably somebody in administration to start with. Should I talk to the person concerned?'

Pinsky thought for a minute. 'That would be the honest thing to do, but it could backfire on you. Could even be dangerous.'

'Oh, I don't think he would be dangerous,' Ricky said. 'He's all talk, really.'

'Well, then, talk to him. Ask him what he's doing. Say you're worried, but admit that maybe you're wrong.'

What in the hell was bothering the boy? He was being so careful in what he said that he seemed more like a pre-law student than a pre-med one. Was it a professor at the university? Something at home? Someone where he worked? An election was due next year – was it something to do with that, something his mother had mentioned in passing that he had picked up on? A question of morality, of ethics, not law? *So why call me*, Pinsky wondered wearily. Of course, with Ricky's father no longer around, maybe he just wanted reassurance that he should act. That it was all right to act. Maybe he just wanted support. Or permission. He leaned against the door jamb and wiped a drip from his nose.

'Are you sure you don't want to tell me more?'

'Not yet,' Ricky said. 'I don't suppose it's anything, really. It's kind of weird. But I didn't know ... well ... how to proceed.'

'You could phone the person if you're worried about talking face to face,' Pinsky suggested. 'But either way, be as sure as you can about your facts. If you told me more ...'

'Not yet,' Ricky said. 'Not until I'm sure. I'm not even sure what laws are involved. If any.'

'OK, then,' Pinsky agreed. 'Listen, I'm freezing my ass off here in the bathroom ...'

17

'Oh. OK. Sorry.'

'No problem. Ring me tomorrow if you're still worried.'

'Will do.' There was a pause. 'Can I talk to Denise?'

'Sure.' He handed the phone out through the door to his daughter who was standing in the hall, trying to figure out what was going on from what she could hear of his end of the conversation. Pinsky closed the door and began to rub himself dry. Kids. They got all worked up about the damnedest things. Still, Ricky was a good kid. If he was worried about something there might be good cause. On the other hand . . . he *was* only nineteen. Things can look big and bad at nineteen. And, if anything, Ricky was overcautions and over-conscientious, verging on the righteous. Pinsky shrugged and reached for his toothbrush. He'd get Ricky's cellphone number from Denise, talk to the kid tomorrow. Get more information. Ricky needed to come up with more facts, but he just wasn't in the mood to deal with it tonight.

Stryker was asleep on the hideous couch that Kate could never convince him needed re-covering or dumping. He loved it. It fitted his contours. It understood him. Kate came in from cleaning up the kitchen after dinner and gazed at him affectionately, but with a touch of exasperation. 'Well, this bodes well for the rest of the evening,' she said with a grin.

He opened one eye. 'Do you want me to get up and dance?'

'Oh *yes*, please,' she enthused. 'I'd really like to see that.'

'You and a hundred others. I do not perform for small audiences.' He stretched and reached for her. 'Come and join me in my slothful bed.'

'That's not a bed, it's a horrible old sofa and I have things to do,' she said, avoiding his grasp.

'Name one.'

'Checking some essays.'

'Name two.'

'Preparing a lecture.'

'Name—'

'Oh, shut up,' she said, pushing his legs aside and slumping down on the far end. 'What did you do all day that's made you so tired, anyway? I thought you said you'd had a quiet day.'

'Yep. That's what did it. Paperwork, meetings, phone calls, lunch, then more paperwork, meetings and phone calls.' He scratched his nose. 'One in particular kind of bothered me.'

'Oh?'

'Some kid trying to get hold of Ned Pinsky. I don't know what it was, exactly. Sounded upset.'

'One of his informants?'

'I don't think so.' He shrugged. 'Probably nothing. We get a lot of funny phone calls.'

'Tell me about it,' Kate said, looking at a fingernail and rubbing a rough spot. 'I deal with teenagers, remember?' She stood up abruptly. 'Now I really have to get to those essays.' She started towards her desk in the dining room.

'How about a compromise?' he called after her.

She turned and raised an eyebrow. 'What did you have in mind?'

'Come to bed and I promise not to bother you for an hour while you mark the essays. I'll just read quietly beside you.'

'Oh yes? And then what?'

'Let's just say you'd better be quick about those essays.'

THREE

SOME TIME DURING THE NIGHT eleven people died in Grantham, seven of them in hospital. Of the others, two were traffic deaths, already dealt with by uniformed officers. The remaining two were the death of yet another homeless man on French Street and a domestic homicide.

Concerning the latter, neighbours had heard shouting and what sounded like a gunshot, shortly after which they had heard a car drive away fast. It had taken them a while to talk themselves into calling the police. When patrol officers arrived at the house in question, they found a woman lying dead on the floor in the bedroom. There was no sign of the husband. The house was empty aside from the body.

The detectives arrived at the house in question soon after coming on duty next morning, went to the open door of what was obviously the master bedroom and peered in. The bed was made, but the cupboard doors were open, revealing some empty hangers among the clothes. Bureau drawers gaped, their contents scrambled and tumbled.

'Guy must have been a fast packer,' Neilson said, carefully keeping his hands off the woodwork.

'Or he was already packed and that's what the argument was about,' Pinsky suggested, looking down at the dead woman on the carpet. Behind them in the hall a Scene of Crime crew waited impatiently, convinced the detectives were going to waltz into the room and destroy

20

vital evidence, which was not true – they all had sufficient experience not to trample on anything that might be useful.

'Has the ME been here yet?' Stryker asked one of them. He felt guilty about longing for action the previous day – now a woman lay dead. She was young – early thirties at a guess. As they say, be careful what you hope for because you might get it. He doubted she had ever hoped for death. The thought of it had probably never entered her head. Unlike the bullet.

'The ME's office is backed up, but they said they were on their way,' the technician answered, shifting his heavy case from one hand to the other.

'Better get on with it, then,' Tos said, stepping aside. He glanced again at the woman and looked away quickly. The gaping wound where her left eye had been pretty much indicated there was no sense in asking her anything. There was no sign of a weapon, although if it was still in the room the SOC techs would find it.

The dead woman was wearing jeans and a crumpled sweatshirt, and her blonde hair was straggly and unwashed. Because of the wound it was difficult to tell whether she had been attractive or not. Her feet were bare and the soles were dirty, as if she were accustomed to going without shoes or slippers. She didn't match the house, which was well-furnished and well-kept.

They moved into the next room, obviously used as a study. In the corner was a desk with a computer on it, still turned on, a screen-saver flashing stars. In front of it a chair was overturned – the only sign of anything being out of order. 'Looks like it might have started in here,' Stryker said. 'I wonder which one of them was on-line?' He went over to the desk and moved the mouse to turn off the screen-saver.

Up came a chart with words and figures concerning some kind of scientific data. None of them had the least idea what it really was, except confusing. Obviously they would have to call in the experts – there was a department downtown that dealt solely with computer concerns. It had become necessary because office break-ins, computer fraud and other cyberspace crimes had increased so dramatically. The rest of the force viewed them with some dismay and not a little wariness, but the officer-technicians had already proved their worth many times over.

Stryker looked at the books above the computer and on the other shelves. Mostly scientific, predominantly to do with archaeology, anatomy, history and biology, with a small section of detective paperbacks at one end of a bottom shelf. 'First guess – the husband was working here,' he said. 'Maybe she started nagging him, interrupting his work. An argument blew up, he decided to move out, she followed him into the bedroom, maybe threatened him with the gun not to leave, he lost his temper, grabbed the gun and turned it on her.'

'Or maybe he just went in there, got the gun and shot her cold when she followed him in,' Tos suggested.

They moved into the kitchen. Nothing there was out of place. It was an almost antiseptic room, all white and gleaming. The refrigerator held ample supplies of food. 'They ate well,' Stryker commented, fumbling his way through packets of meat, fresh vegetables, full-fat milk, butter. 'Neither one on a diet from the looks of things.' He straightened up. 'Plenty of cookbooks, too. Very domestic.' The dishwasher was loaded and had run – obviously from a meal the evening before. Two plates, cutlery, a couple of saucepans and a grill pan. Plus lots and lots of coffee mugs.

'Either she had a coffee morning with her friends or she drinks coffee all day long and likes a fresh mug each time,' Pinsky said. 'Pat does that – our dishwasher looks just like this at the end of the day.'

They looked around the rest of the house: one other bedroom, obviously a guest room, rather sterile and sparely decorated. 'So they slept together, anyway,' Neilson said.

'Yeah, but they had separate bathrooms,' Pinsky called

out. 'This one is all his stuff – she must use the one off the master bedroom.'

'Interesting. She didn't look like she used it much,' Tos said. 'Did you see the state of her feet?'

'Maybe she likes to walk in the yard,' Pinsky responded, coming back into the hall.

There was a big family room, with further well-filled bookshelves – novels, more detective fiction and quite a few general science titles. There was also a stereo unit and a shelf of CDs – a mixture of jazz and classical. The furniture was ultra-simple – a couple of huge recliners with small tables beside them and one of those cinema-screen television sets.

'Everything for the leisure life,' Neilson observed. He liked the room. He would have enjoyed having one just like it. Unfortunately, his apartment was too small for such spacious luxury and self-indulgence.

'This is getting us nowhere,' Pinsky finally grumbled. 'Let's talk to the neighbours for crying out loud.'

They stopped at the bedroom door on their way through. 'Find a weapon?' Stryker asked the SOC team.

'Yeah, under the bed,' one said, holding up a plastic bag. 'Saturday night special, fired once.'

'Fingermarks?'

'No – wiped clean.'

They looked at one another. 'Interesting,' Stryker said.

'TV has a lot to answer for,' Neilson said.

'Yeah, and Ed McBain, too,' Stryker replied. 'Come on.'

Mr and Mrs Koslewski, the couple who had called the police, were both fascinated and horrified to learn that their neighbour had been murdered. 'My, my,' said the woman, a large, comfortable personage in a flowered muu-muu. 'Poor Professor Mayhew.'

'What's he a professor of?' Neilson asked, with a glance at Pinsky. This would settle the question of the data on the computer screen.

'Oh, *he's* not the professor, she is,' Mr Koslewski said. He was a round man with a bald head and the combination reminded Pinsky of a billiard ball balanced on a beach ball. Koslewski wore a large moustache as if to make up for the emptiness of his pate. What little hair he had left was dark, but his moustache was rusty red. 'He's just some sort of travelling salesman. She teaches at the university – but I don't know what she teaches. Some kind of "ology" – or it could be chemistry or something like that. Some kind of science thing. But lately this summer she's been working real hard on something.'

'A book,' the wife put in. 'And she's an anthropologist.'

'My goodness,' the husband said sarcastically. 'How do you spell that?'

'With difficulty,' she responded. They didn't look at one another, their sparring obviously automatic and of long standing. The living room was filled with large furniture, with every piece upholstered in a different pattern. The carpet and the curtains were also differently patterned, and combined with the design on Mrs Koslewski's muumuu the effect was both kaleidoscopic and headache inducing. Tos wanted very much to close his eyes, but managed not to. It was the red moustache that kept him alert – it wobbled and fluttered when Mr Koslewski spoke, and Tos had a fleeting thought that it might be a false one. But why, he wondered to himself, why?

'Would you say they got on together?' Neilson asked.

'Sure,' said Mr Koslewski. The moustache blew out like a small flag.

'No,' said his wife. 'Not at the moment. He was away a lot of the time and she was all wrapped up in her work. She had someone in every day to clean and make the meals while she was working on this book, hardly stopped for anything lately. We used to have chats but during the last few months she's kept her head down on this theory of hers. She told me what it was, but I didn't understand a word of it.'

'That's a relief,' Mr Koslewski said, rolling his eyes. 'I was afraid you were going to tell us.'

'So the fact that he's gone could mean he's just on one of his selling trips?' Stryker asked.

'Maybe. Why – you think *he* killed her?' Mr Koslewski sounded eager. 'He sure doesn't look the type.'

'Why not?' Neilson wanted to know.

'No bigger than a fly,' Mr Koslewski said.

'He's a shortish, slender kind of man,' Mrs Koslewski put in. 'But very good-looking. *Very,*' she repeated for emphasis.

Mr Koslewski turned to view her with surprise. 'I didn't know you went for little men,' he said.

'I don't,' she told him, 'normally. But he's cute as a bug's ear.'

Mr Koslewski scowled. 'You ever *seen* a bug's ear? Ugliest thing you can imagine.'

'Well, he isn't,' Mrs Koslewski said complacently. 'She wasn't a real big woman, either, but she was taller than him. When they first moved here, about two years ago, they were real cute together. But lately . . .'

'Yes?' Stryker prompted.

Mrs Koslewski spread her hands apologetically. She had short fat fingers, festooned with large rings. 'She's kind of let herself go, what with all the studying and all. I told her she should do something about her hair, but she just looked at me like she didn't see me. Well, maybe she didn't, she was *real* near-sighted. Wore big glasses for a while, then got them contacts finally. Changed her whole appearance, made her look almost nice. She wasn't *real* pretty, but without the glasses and if she'd done something with herself instead of just . . .' She shrugged. 'You know what I mean.'

'So we have a man who is away a lot of the time and a woman, an educated woman, who is wrapped up in her work,' Tos summed up.

'That's them all right,' Mr Koslewski confirmed. 'You got it.'

'And no kids?'

'She couldn't have them,' Mrs Koslewski said sadly. 'Real shame. I think it was one of the reasons she worked so hard at her stuff, her science stuff. And I think she worked with students a lot. Filled up the gap.'

'So, would you say they were happily married?' Neilson asked.

'No,' Mr Koslewski said this time.

'Yes,' Mrs Koslewski countered. 'Just . . . not lately is all. It was temporary. As soon as she finished that work she was doing, I think everything would have been fine again. She was just – real tired.'

'Too late now,' Mr Koslewski said with a kind of triumph. 'All done now.'

Mrs Koslewski looked as if she were going to cry. 'I can't believe he would shoot her,' she said plaintively. 'We thought it was an intruder, some druggie or something. So many guns everywhere – you don't know who to trust.'

'You think you know everything but you don't know everything,' Mr Koslewski told his wife with a degree of satisfaction, his moustache flapping for emphasis. 'No matter how hard you try, Eva, some people in this neighbourhood still got secrets from you.'

'Including you?' she snapped.

He literally backed off. 'Now, I didn't say *that*.'

FOUR

KATE TREVORNE AND LIZ OLSON had been friends from adolescence. Although Liz had gone straight through to her professorship, BA, MA, Ph.D., tenure, Kate had taken a side turning into advertising, making a very good living as a copywriter but not finding satisfaction in her work. Her old professor, Dan Stark, now head of the English department at Grantham State University, had persuaded her to come back and pick up the threads, which she had done and found, to her delight, that the scholarly life suited her beautifully. She was only an associate professor and did not have tenure yet, but was hopeful it would come along in due course, fingers crossed. Perhaps not a very intellectual attitude, but one she was stuck with. She needed to publish more.

She and Liz had shared a duplex house until Stryker had entered Kate's life, whereupon she had decamped to his house, leaving Liz on her own. Liz understood and cheerfully tolerated the various graduate students to whom Kate rented out her old upstairs apartment from time to time. Liz's life was steady, but Kate's had recently suffered a further upheaval. The English department had just moved into a brand-new building near the old Science Hall, and the shifting of books, files and attitudes had been exhausting. As had been the case throughout their friendship, Kate depended on Liz to provide a well-grounded centre.

The two friends regularly met for lunch to maintain their friendship, keep up on campus gossip and exchange pleasantries or gripes about their respective men.

To give themselves some perspective, they usually met at nearby restaurants rather than face university cuisine. Today it was Joe's Diner and they were indulging in a little cholesterol binge. It was a chilly day, they reassured one another, and one needed fuel to stay warm.

Kate eyed her Eggs Benedict with anticipation . . . just looking at all those calories was a pleasure in itself.

Liz, who had been a little more abstemious, eyed her with amusement. 'Are you going to eat that or have it bronzed?' she asked her friend.

Kate sighed and picked up her fork. 'Every bite I take leaves less to enjoy,' she said, digging in. 'It's like reading a really good book – you hate to come to the end.'

'There's always ice cream afterwards.'

'True.' They ate companionably for a while, ignoring the hustle around them. Joe's was a very popular place and even here they couldn't totally escape the students of GSU – a group of them were crowded into a rear booth, hilariously enjoying their break from routine too.

'Anybody we know?' Liz asked, when a particularly loud burst of laughter emanated from behind her.

'I don't think so,' Kate said, peering around her friend's shoulder. 'They look like engineers.'

'Ah.' Liz nodded. 'That explains everything.'

After another pause, Kate looked at her friend. 'Have you been getting any strange phone calls lately?'

Liz seemed startled. 'I'm sorry to say, no. My phone calls are universally dull. Why, have you?'

'Yes.'

'Really?' Liz's blue eyes widened. 'At work or at home?'

'At work.' Kate pushed a bit of English muffin around her plate.

'Well, let's hear it,' Liz said impatiently.

'I think I have a problem.' Kate told Liz what the caller had said and threatened. They both loved a mystery, but this was too unpleasant, Liz decided. Mysteries were best enjoyed in books.

'And you think it's someone in the university?'

'He told me to stop poaching students.'

'Did he give you names?'

'Just Michael's. I don't know what the hell he's talking about. I don't "poach" students. They switch majors all the time.' Kate blinked. 'I hung up; he called back. I hung up again and he called back again. I've shouted at him, begged him to stop, become outraged . . .'

'That's just what they want.'

'I know, I know . . . so this morning on the way to work I bought myself a great big whistle. I plan to eventually deafen the little bastard.'

'Now, see, you're defining him already. How do you know he's little?'

'I don't. I just like to think of him as a little bug.'

'Be serious. This isn't just a dirty phone call. This is something a lot more. I don't think needing a new eardrum is going to stop him, frankly.' Liz finished her omelette and pushed the plate away, retrieving a few chips to nibble on. 'Listen, it could be a student. Could be Michael himself, after more money.'

'No, he sounds older.'

'Old older, or just older? Could it be some pathetic little old man, for instance?'

'No, not that old, just . . . mature.' Kate finished her meal and put down her knife and fork. 'And he called me Katie,' she said reluctantly.

Liz frowned. 'Nobody calls you Katie.'

'My dad does.'

'Oh – that's nasty.' Liz frowned.

'Yes – especially since most of my contact with my parents is by phone these days, what with them living out in Arizona or gadding about the world the way they do. We only see them a couple of times a year, if that. This guy's voice isn't the same as my father's, but even so, I don't like it.' Suddenly Kate shivered.

'I don't see why you should,' Liz commiserated. 'Has he e-mailed you at all?'

'No.' Kate looked surprised for a moment. 'I guess it's the voice thing he's after. That gasp of shock . . . isn't that what they like?'

'I think so. At least, ordinary dirty phone callers do. This is a little different, don't you think?' Liz reached for the menu and tugged it out of its holder, opening it to the desserts. She regarded her friend over the top of the menu and pitched her voice gently. 'Has he got a case?'

'*No!*' Kate said, more loudly than she had intended.

'Then tell Jack about it,' Liz said firmly. There was a silence. 'Kate?'

Kate flushed. 'I don't want to.'

'Then there *is* something to it,' Liz said without judgement. 'Come on. Tell.'

'It's just . . .' Kate picked up her fork and laid it alongside her knife on the empty plate, very, very carefully aligning them just so. 'I might have unconsciously encouraged Michael,' she went on slowly. 'He might have assumed that as I made an exception and took him in . . . he might have thought . . .'

'Did you think of it?' Liz asked.

Kate ran her fingers through her hair, making the curls stand up in disarray. 'No. At least, I don't think so.' She leaned forward. 'But I might have, subconsciously. He is a very handsome boy. Tall, beautifully put together, dark hair, blue eyes . . . navy-blue eyes . . .'

'Well, navy-blue . . . makes all the difference.' Liz smiled.

'And Jack and I . . . I've been very edgy lately, for some reason. Restless. Could I have flirted with Michael without realizing it?' Kate asked plaintively. 'He was a wow with the girls, any number of them would have given him houseroom. But he came to me . . .'

'Ah,' Liz said. 'Flattery got him somewhere, then.'

Kate sighed. 'I guess so. It was a pretty stupid thing to do, but I was afraid he would drop out . . .'

'And he did.'

'Yes. But was that because of me or . . .?'

30

'What's the difference? The point is, at some time this creep who is calling you got it out of him. Or got something out of him that sounds bad enough to threaten you with. You say the boy was sorry, or said he was, when he left.'

'Yes, he was sweet about it. Very contrite.'

Liz cleared her throat. 'How much money did you give him?'

'Well, he would have needed a deposit . . .'

'How much, Kate?'

'Five hundred dollars.'

'My God . . . you keep that much cash around the house?'

'No . . . I . . . I wrote him a cheque.'

Liz sank back into the leather seat. 'You absolute fool.'

'I know. I know,' Kate whispered. 'But how could I know he would tell lies about me?'

'Oh, Kate . . . you used to be in advertising. You ought to know all about lies, damn lies and spin. My guess is he was trying to get money out of this guy who called you and told a sob story to strengthen his position. The real point here is not what is truth and what are lies, but whom he talked to and who called you. And what is more, why? If you heard a story like this about another faculty member, would you use it to threaten them?'

'No, of course not. There's always gossip . . .'

'Sure. Always. And for the most part the Dean listens but does not hear – or he couldn't run the place. But an official accusation is quite another thing. You've got to find out who this bastard is. If you won't tell Jack, then tell the phone company. Jack doesn't have to know about it . . .'

'That makes it official too,' Kate said. 'I would have to tell them what was said . . . they would hear . . . it would go on record . . .' She stopped. 'I can't do that. It would be like telling on myself.'

Liz took a deep breath and let it go slowly. 'It's aural rape and you shouldn't have to put up with it. I still say tell Jack. He could find out who it is in a nickel-plated minute and keep it confidential, too. What is the point of being married to a cop if you can't take advantage of the system?'

'We're not married.'

'My point is the same,' Liz said repressively. She found it difficult to understand Kate's reluctance to marry Jack, but never openly criticized her friend on the matter. 'Jack would understand.'

'I don't think so.'

'That doesn't say much for your relationship, kiddo,' Liz said. 'You didn't do anything wrong. Surely he'll see that.'

'He didn't like the boy. He was irritated with me for taking him in. We had a bad fight about it. This would only bring it up all over again ... I was stupid, Liz. Very stupid. But it's my problem. I don't want to make it his, too. I can look after myself.'

'Balls,' Liz contradicted uncompromisingly. 'I believe you, why shouldn't he?'

'I don't sleep with you,' Kate pointed out. 'It's complicated.'

'It isn't, Kate. It really isn't,' Liz insisted.

'OK, OK, let's leave it,' Kate said impatiently. She knew Liz was right, but the thought of Jack's face, his disgust at her stupidity, his inevitable moment of wondering whether there was fire where there was smoke ... she couldn't bear it. 'I need some ice cream to calm my nerves. Even talking about it upsets me.'

'Sure it does,' Liz said wryly. She knew her friend well enough to back off – for the moment. 'And exactly how much ice cream will you require to assuage your raw nerve endings?'

'Oh, about a gallon.' Kate began to review the flavours on offer.

Liz sighed. 'Then I guess I'd better join you. I am very empathetic, you see. I suffer when you suffer.'

'Up to the point of chocolate sauce?'

'Oh, *way* past that.' Liz grinned. 'Maybe even to the point of chopped nuts and whipped cream.'

Pinsky, caught up in putting out an APB for the missing husband of the dead lady professor and writing up his notes, kept reminding himself to call Ricky Sanchez. He had his cellphone number from Denise, but the time never seemed to be right. While he waited for the results of the Scene of Crime investigations, he made a list of people they should interview about the late Professor Mayhew and various other avenues they could pursue in the case. The husband looked the most likely suspect, of course, but there was no guarantee that it had been he who had been doing the shouting and the shooting – he could be away on business, some other man could have been in the house. The Koslewskis hadn't actually seen anyone, just heard the shouting, the shot, and the car driving away. Neighbours on the other side were out of town. Across the wide suburban street nobody had heard anything, apparently. It was early in the investigation and it already looked like being a complicated situation. Nine times out of ten things were obvious, easy to assess, easy to solve. This was apparently going to be one of those other times. Pinsky was not happy.

Stryker and Tos were unhappy too. Stryker, because he was perplexed about the new case, and about Kate. In the past day or two she had been very snappy, very much on edge. In fact, she had been more moody than ever lately, but when he asked what was wrong she would just shrug and say she didn't know what he was talking about. He supposed it would be easier if she were just some little housewife who would do his bidding, but he would have hated that. He was proud of her. He liked her being a strong woman, an individual. But sometimes it was a problem.

Tos was unhappy for more basic reasons. He was also perplexed and annoyed, because he wanted a big lunch and had to have a small one, due to calories. He hated calories. They loomed too large in his present existence, they ruled his every meal, the numbers haunted him and made him mad. Salads made him even sadder. 'I am so sick of being healthy,' he muttered as he gazed on to the plate before him.

'Then you've certainly changed your tune.' Stryker grinned. 'Usually you're yelling at me to eat better.'

'Yeah, but that was when I could have a steak now and again. Or a doughnut. I haven't had a doughnut in weeks.'

'Thereby negating the common stereotype,' Stryker said.

'There you go again,' Tos said. 'Talking like a professor.'

'Ain't it the truth,' Stryker agreed. 'It's Kate's fault; she uses big words all the time, deafens me with grammar, drowns me in verbiage. I keep having to go to the dictionary when we have an argument, kind of slows down my side of the thing.' He spoke with affection, however. As a once-aspiring lawyer, he, too, had a respect for proper language. It was just that working day to day with other cops, he tended to talk in their terse jargon and defend himself with their black humour in difficult situations. The terrible things they saw and heard were enough to send anyone nuts. They needed barriers to insanity. Swearing and joking helped. Almost.

'The trouble is my mother doesn't understand that I want to get in shape again,' Tos complained. 'She puts out the same big meals and sits there glaring at me until I clear my plate. If I don't she sulks and says I don't like her cooking.'

'Leave home,' Stryker said for the umpteenth time.

'Easy to say,' Tos snapped, also for the umpteenth time.

'Shut up and eat your greens,' Stryker advised.

'It would help if you didn't order stuff like that,' Tos said, gesturing towards Stryker's plate of cheeseburger and fries with a side order of macaroni salad.

'I have the opposite problem from you.' Stryker was

talking around a mouthful. 'Kate is into healthy eating too. I don't think we've had butter in the house for months. I'm getting damn sick and tired of grilled skinless chicken breasts, believe me. And as for broccoli . . .'

'My mother serves broccoli,' Tos said. 'With tomato sauce and a thick layer of melted cheese.'

'I suggest we change partners,' Stryker said. 'I will eat at your house and you can eat at mine.'

'Deal.' Tos glumly began on his salad.

FIVE

THE ANTHROPOLOGY DEPARTMENT OF GRANTHAM State University was located in one of the few old houses remaining on the campus. It looked very odd, wedged as it was between the science building and the new English and arts building, both of which were modern in design and loomed over the two-storey anachronism between them.

The cramped premises contained the combined studies of archaeology, paleontology and anthropology. The department had been promised space in the new cultural sciences building that was currently in a state of becoming, but for the present made do with a warren of tiny offices and an insufficient number of bathrooms. This gave rise to much compromise, bringing about in equal measure conflict, constipation and exaggerated good manners. One of the instructors had observed that if their skeletal remains were dug up centuries hence, there would be many questions as to the wear and tear on molars due to the grinding of teeth. No doubt some future scientist would write a monograph on it, attributing the phenomenon to diet or religion, when really it was a result of workplace claustrophobia and the strain of being polite to one another.

Pinsky, Neilson and Muller found the old house rather intimidating, as it seemed to be full of people arguing – although the arguees would have called it brisk academic interchange. The walls were covered with oddities such as African masks and casts of dinosaur bones and, in one memorable display, sepia photographs of many naked-breasted women in native dress. Overburdened shelves were filled with books, pots, shards, bones, raffia structures of indeterminate origin and purpose, fearsome-looking weapons, leaning stacks of periodicals, and lots and lots of half-empty coffee mugs. Some of the latter contained mould that would no doubt interest the department of biology, were it offered to them.

The computers on all the desks in all the rooms seemed like alien invaders, humming to themselves, largely ignored and occasionally decorated with ethnic art of mixed origins along with cartoons clipped from magazines, some of which were so old they had yellowed and curled at the edges.

They finally located the man they wanted to talk to – a Professor Winchester. He was a large, balding man wearing a very loud Hawaiian print shirt and chinos, and he inhabited a corner office that actually had a brightly coloured Mexican rug in front of the desk, indicating true status. It was a very small rug, though, for the desk took up most of the space. Its owner was stretched out in a reclining office chair, glaring at the computer screen before him. As he glared he played with three polished stones of a brilliant blue, turning them over and over in his palm rather in the manner of Captain Queeg of *Caine Mutiny* fame.

'What can I do for the local police?' asked Dr Winchester with a beaming smile, when they had identified themselves. That is, Pinsky and Neilson flashed their ID. Muller, who was shadowing them, hung back and stayed quiet, watching, listening. 'Not another student in jail for drunkenness?' He seemed delighted to be distracted.

'It concerns a member of your staff, sir, a Professor Mayhew.'

'Associate professor,' Winchester corrected them. 'A very able young woman; I expect great things of her.' His beam suddenly changed to a frown. 'She is not in any difficulty, is she?'

37

'Well, in a manner of speaking,' Neilson said. While he couldn't be said to enjoy being the bearer of bad news, he admitted to himself that he got kind of a kick out of the startled look on people's faces when he laid it on them. He found that everybody reacted differently and so he considered his observations to be a study of humanity. Also, occasionally, they were funny. He told himself it was wrong to be amused, but he couldn't help it sometimes. 'She was found murdered at her home this morning,' he announced.

'Good God!' Winchester said, straightening up so abruptly that his chair nearly went over. Neilson added that absurd wobble to his fund of observations, but managed to keep a straight face. Of course this 'study' of his only applied to people who were not emotionally involved with the victims. He was not a monster. He understood grief. It was shock that interested him, shock and the invariably revealing reactions to it. It exposed people, told things about them that might be useful to an investigation. In this case it told him that Winchester was the kind of person who loved drama.

'You're not serious!' Winchester continued, rolling the polished pebbles ever more rapidly in his palm. His eyes were wide with astonishment and, sadly, the excitement that often accompanies such revelations. Here was a Moment in his otherwise dull life. Here was Something Out of the Ordinary. Terrible. And fascinating.

'I'm afraid so, Dr Winchester,' Pinsky said. 'We believe the assailant escaped by car. There was no sign of robbery. The husband is missing.'

'Good Lord.' Winchester put down the stones and passed his now-empty hand across his balding pate. 'I hardly know what to say.'

'Could you tell us something about Professor Mayhew?' Pinsky asked, pulling up a chair and sitting down. Neilson did the same. Winchester waved his hand as if giving them permission to do what they had already done. 'Did she have any enemies? Did she have any particular friends on the staff? Was she popular with her students?'

There was a pause. 'I'm sorry,' Winchester finally answered. 'Give me a moment to take this in. I've never known anyone who was actually murdered before ... I can't seem to get my thoughts together.'

'Take your time,' said Pinsky patiently, as he got out his notebook. He glanced at Neilson, who was watching Winchester closely. Behind them, leaning against the door jamb, Muller also took out a notebook. He was trying to look official and almost succeeding.

Finally Winchester took a long deep breath and let it out slowly. 'What a damned shame,' he said. 'She was good, you know, she was a very good teacher and getting better all the time. I liked her, we all liked her, although she was a bit serious for some. A bit intense, sometimes. But that's not a bad thing in an academic. She was interested in physical anthropology, you see. Bones, mostly. That was her particular speciality and she was writing a brilliant book on it. Elise was not one to get out and mix with primitive tribes – there are far too many of us who are happy to do that and avoid having to teach in order to eat, which is what happens to most anthropologists. She was particularly interested in diseases of the bones – tracing patterns of disease in the bones that were found in mass graves. She didn't like to dig herself, preferred lab work, but she put ideas and theories together brilliantly. What we call a synthesist. A born researcher. She was full of ideas ... Damn!' He struck the desk with a fist. 'She was going to do good things.' Glancing at them, he seemed to suddenly take in what they had said. 'You say the husband is missing?'

'Yes. We aren't certain yet whether he is out of town or—'

'Or whether he killed her himself,' Winchester finished for him.

'Yes,' Pinsky agreed. 'Until we locate him there's no way of knowing. She could have been killed as a result

39

of a domestic argument, or by some other person who broke in or was let into the house because she knew him. Or her, come to that.'

'She was . . . what? Shot, you said?'

They hadn't said. Muller leaned forward a little.

'Horrible, horrible,' Winchester continued. 'She was right. Our society *is* becoming more primitive, not less, gentlemen. And guns are at the heart of it. No time to discuss, no time taken to use reason, oh no. Shoot first and win the argument, that's the way it goes now, doesn't it? I just can't take this in. Her teaching schedule—' He caught himself. 'Sorry, sorry. So many things to consider. A terrible loss to us, you see. We are a small department, fighting for our very existence and certainly for our funding. She was going to do great things for us . . . we had hopes, we had definite hopes.' He shook himself. 'Never mind that, never mind. You came for my help. What can I do?'

'Enemies,' Pinsky said succinctly.

'None,' Winchester said firmly. 'At least none in her work here. She was a pleasant woman, extremely competent, extremely encouraging of other people's work – and that's an important trait, believe me, the jealousy that can . . .' He trailed off, brought himself back to the question. 'No, no enemies here. As for her personal life, frankly, I knew little about it. I knew she was married, but we never met the husband, not at any faculty functions when he might have come along. He never did. We deduced he was either uninterested or possibly even resented her career. It does happen, you know, with women academics. I think his name is Donald Mayhew, if that's any help, and he's a salesman or something like that, not academic at all.'

'You tend towards suspecting the husband, then?' asked Pinsky innocently. They already had Donald Mayhew's name and place of employment – an office supply company. They were attempting to work out where he might be if, in fact, he was on a sales trip and not running scared.

40

Winchester was not stupid. 'How could I know?' he asked. 'I don't know him or anything about him. From what you say, it might have been, or it might not have been. Surely there were clues, some indication . . .?'

'The gun was registered to Professor Mayhew herself,' Neilson said. 'So it wasn't brought from outside. But she might have gone for it to defend herself and the assailant took it from her. We just have no clue, no actual clue, as to who fired the shot. One shot, to the face. It could have been an accident, a struggle for the gun. But the gun was wiped clean of fingermarks, so it wasn't suicide.'

'Suicide? Good Lord, no. Never. Not Mayhew. Too curious. Too interested in life. Intense, yes, but never depressed. Never defeated. Buoyant, gentlemen. She was a buoyant person, loved her work.' He paused. 'Perhaps too much?' he added slowly.

'That's what we're trying to find out. You say she was working on a book?'

'That's correct. Working very hard and nearly finished, I believe. I have seen the work in progress. Not my particular field, you understand – I'm primarily a cultural anthropologist – but there was no doubt that it was original and insightful. She would have been published easily. Easily.' He looked up at his own well-filled bookshelves.

'So you know of no one who would want her dead, no competitor for position, no one jealous of her work, no emotional involvements with other members of the faculty, or with her students . . .'

Winchester was startled. 'What do you mean?'

'Well,' Pinsky began carefully. 'People do have affairs. People who teach often are troubled by students who get crushes or become obsessive or even begin to hate because of poor marks, say, or—'

'Good Lord, what an idea.' Winchester reflected. 'No affairs with the faculty, I'm afraid. I would have known about that, we are very close-packed in here, no secrets. Students – she never mentioned any problems. And she was not very ... how can I say this ...?' He thought a moment, then leaned forward. 'She was not very sexy,' he confided in a low, almost embarrassed voice. 'She was all mind, you see, all analysis and deduction. Possibly even cold, to some degree, although affectionate towards her students, I understand. She had a lack of interest in her appearance, for example. I don't mean she was slovenly, but she dressed for comfort, as they say, not style. One was rarely even aware that she was a woman, to be perfectly frank. It was the mind one engaged with, always the mind. Do you understand?'

'I think so,' Pinsky said. 'She wasn't sexy.'

'No,' Winchester agreed rather sadly. 'Shame, really. We get kind of fusty and musty in here ... could have used a bit of femininity about the place. Even our secretaries are ... sensible. Just as well, of course, just as well. But ...' He smiled wryly. 'Bits and bones, that's physical anthropology,' he said. 'Dead bones, dead civilizations, all rather ... dead.'

'Like Professor Mayhew,' Muller said abruptly, behind them.

Pinsky and Neilson turned to look at him and he blushed. 'Well,' he said defensively. 'She is.'

And they all thought about that for a while.

There were actually a few men on the force who enjoyed attending autopsies. Neither Jack nor Tos was among them. Tos, especially, had a delicate stomach and the merest whiff of the chemicals in the morgue would make him go pale. Nevertheless, rules were rules and there they were. Tos focused his attention on Bannerman, the Medical Examiner.

'She was basically a healthy woman,' Bannerman was saying. 'But I'd say she'd been neglecting herself lately. Not eating right, that sort of thing. Her skin was loose, her flesh dehydrated. Her nails are chewed right down, toenails, too.'

'You mean she chewed her toenails?' asked Muller in

amazement. He had joined them, leaving Pinsky and Neilson to continue their questioning of the other teachers in Mayhew's department.

'No, I mean she picked at them,' Bannerman said. 'She had a couple of scabs that she picked at, too, and some heavy scratches on her scalp. The woman was nervous is all I'm saying. Sort of nibbling herself away.'

'Are you saying it was suicide?' Jack asked.

Bannerman came around the long table on which lay the sheeted figure of the late Elise Mayhew. As was always his unconscious habit, he squeezed her toe affectionately as he passed. It always amused Stryker.

'No. Angle of the wound is rather awkward for that. Could have been, but she would have to have been a bit of a contortionist.'

'Well, if she chewed her toenails . . .' Muller began in a nervous attempt at humour.

Bannerman just glanced at him impatiently. Bannerman was a serious man and felt himself to be an advocate on behalf of the victims he analysed. They didn't complain or cry out like live patients, but he felt sympathy for them, whoever they had been. Even hardened criminals got kindly treatment from Bannerman. But he was thorough. Very, very thorough. 'I understand there were no prints on the gun.'

'None. Wiped clean.'

'Well, funnily enough, there were some faint traces of powder on her hands,' Bannerman said.

They all looked at one another. 'Then she was holding the gun?'

'Maybe. At first I thought she might have been holding it with some sort of barrier between her hands and the actual weapon. I looked to see if there were powder burns on the hem of her sweatshirt, for instance . . . she could have held the gun using the bottom of her sweatshirt.' He demonstrated by gathering up a handful of his scrubs, showing how he might hold something in that way.

'Why?' Tos asked.

'Well, exactly. It's a rare suicide who tries to make it look like murder. Too caught up in their own escape to think of what comes afterwards. Cruel, really – they never think about who is going to find them and it is usually a loved one. Anyway, there weren't any powder burns on her clothes. Did they find any towels or handkerchiefs or scarves near the body?'

Stryker picked up the Scene of Crime report and went through it. 'No,' he said. 'Nothing like that.'

Bannerman shrugged. 'Well, she might have put up her hands when the assailant pointed the gun at her . . . there was no real pattern in the powder deposits. It was just something I noticed.'

'Anything else?' Stryker asked.

Bannerman shook his head. 'No bruises on the body, no signs of a violent struggle. Nothing under her finger-nails but household dirt, her own skin cells and so on. Have you gone over the house yet?'

'About to do that,' Tos informed him.

'State of mind,' Muller said. 'Right?'

Bannerman nodded. 'We don't know much about her yet. But she was worried about something, that's clear.'

'She was writing a book,' Tos said. 'Some serious kind of book. Neighbour woman said she was wrought up about it.'

'She also said – this neighbour woman – that she had "let herself go" and that maybe the marriage was going bad,' Stryker put in.

'I cannot totally rule out suicide,' Bannerman said. 'It's far-fetched, but it is possible.'

'The gun was found under the bed,' Muller said, eager to participate.

'Could have skidded away when she fell.'

'But—'

'I know, I know,' Bannerman agreed. 'The argument that was overheard . . .' He shrugged. 'Something was

44

going on in her life, something was going wrong . . . she was going downhill.'

'You care too much, Bannerman,' Jack stated.

Bannerman looked at the sheeted figure on the table. 'Somebody has to,' he said.

SIX

PINSKY AND NEILSON HAD ACQUIRED a list of Professor Mayhew's students from the previous term, and a list of her current students although, as Dr Winchester said, they had hardly begun the autumn term and most of them wouldn't know her very well, or vice versa.

They also picked up a faculty list, giving names and departmental numbers and extensions. These lists, they discovered, were like gold dust and it was only Winchester allowing them to photocopy his that secured them the information.

'What did you think of Winchester?' Pinsky asked Neilson, when they stopped for coffee after tiring of wandering around the campus trying to track down people teaching classes.

'Not sexy,' said Neilson in a vague imitation.

Pinsky laughed. 'I thought the shirt was an interesting style statement.' He tore off a corner of a sugar packet and tipped the contents into his mug. 'It said "I'm a regular guy".'

'But he isn't, is he?' Neilson asked. 'He obviously admired Mayhew's mind.' This was clearly odd to him.

'He noticed that she didn't dress up,' Pinsky pointed out.

'But he seemed to approve of that, I thought,' Neilson said. 'What kind of a person studies bones and rituals anyway? Never mind the shirt . . . a lot of them down there were dressed pretty casually, I noticed. Sort of a departmental look.'

'Anthropology,' Pinsky mused.

Neilson frowned. 'What?'

'I studied a bit of anthropology at college,' Pinsky said. 'They were all like that. Casual as hell, sort of lured you into thinking they were casual markers, too. They weren't.'

'I didn't know you went to college,' Neilson said.

'Two years, that's all. Flunked out. Not my style, really. Although I did like anthropology. Find it useful in dealing with perps. Primitive patterns, all that. Native impulses. Social responses. It's real interesting. Also, Denise is studying it as part of her degree, so it's kind of come up lately.'

'I don't have any idea what you're talking about,' Neilson complained. 'I went straight to the Academy from high school myself.'

'Not a bad thing,' Pinsky told him reflectively. 'A good thing. Sometimes I get distracted, see. By thinking of those things. If you start looking all the time at the Big Picture, which is what anthropology does, then you tend to trip over the little picture, like who shot who and why, you know? Better to be all cop, maybe. Jack, now. Jack has a legal mind and that gives him problems too. He gets caught up in what's permissible evidence, in legal ramifications, even in questions of good and evil . . . winds him up tight sometimes. He's another one who's mostly mind, like the late Professor Mayhew. Although he's a lot better since he met Kate, I will say that. She's loosened him right up. Are you going to finish that other doughnut?'

'No – have it.' Neilson pushed the plate across the table.

'I don't know,' Pinsky said around a mouthful of sugar, cinammon and calories. 'Maybe "all cop" isn't the best thing either. "All cop" narrows your vision a little too much, maybe.'

'Yeah,' Neilson agreed. 'Like, I was thinking maybe I should do some night school stuff. Broaden my outlook.'

47

'That would be good. Trouble is making the classes. We don't exactly have predictable schedules, right?'

'Right,' Neilson said glumly. He was depressed at learning Pinsky had two years of college, even if he had flunked out, which Neilson doubted. Got fed up, possibly, but not flunked. Not Pinsky. Ned was smart. He was learning a lot from Ned. But he did wish he'd gone to college too. He wished he'd done a lot of things, but there you go. Man has to work, man has to eat. You got on with what you did best. And he had made detective, hadn't he?

When they got back to headquarters Stryker and Tos were discussing the Mayhew case.

'Anything at the university?' Stryker asked them.

'Not much. She was a lovely woman, loved by all and everything was lovely. They are "very upset",' Neilson reported with appropriate gestures. He even bowed at the end.

'Hmm. Doesn't sound like any university department I've ever heard of,' Stryker said. 'There's always a lot of backbiting and infighting going on in these places.'

'Maybe anthropologists are different,' Neilson suggested.

'Maybe,' Stryker agreed. 'But it does seem weird. We'd better go at them again. You talked to the head honcho, right?'

'Right,' Pinsky said.

'Hmm. I think some more conversation with the lesser mortals of the department might be revealing.'

'I'll put it on the list,' Neilson said.

'We're going back to the house,' Stryker stated. 'I've been going over the photographs of the scene.'

'Here we go,' said Neilson. He was referring to Stryker's habit of asking the photographers who took pictures of the scene of crime to also print out the negatives back to front, so he would have two sets of each one. He maintained, and it had proved true on several occasions, that the eye often doesn't see what it is looking at. And a second look at the scene itself didn't hurt either. They all chuckled, but Muller looked confused.

Stryker explained his theory. 'Here.' He held out a pair of photos. 'Take a look yourself.'

Muller took the photographs. 'I don't see anything different,' he said, puzzled.

'You will,' Stryker told him. 'Come on, we'll go back to the Mayhew house and see what we can find.'

He called again.

Kate felt quite sick when she heard the thin, insinuating voice: 'Hello, Katie.'

She hung up, knowing it would do no good. Knowing he would call back.

And he did. 'I can go on with this as long as you can,' he said.

Kate gripped the handset so tightly her knuckles ached. 'What do you want?' she demanded. 'What is the point of all this?'

'In good time, Katie, in good time. I just want you to know that someone is watching you. Someone who knows all about you. Someone who will tell all about you. Eventually.'

'What does eventually mean?'

'It means . . . punishment, of course,' said the voice. 'Punishment for bad behaviour.'

'I'm going to tell the Dean myself.'

There was a chuckle. 'Oh, I don't think you mean that, Katie. I really don't. So embarrassing. And you'll never get tenure.'

'Still, it is better coming from me than from you. I can give my side. I can explain.'

'And will you be believed? That is the question, isn't it? Will you be believed? Or will they believe the boy? After all, I have the evidence of the cancelled cheque.'

'I've done nothing wrong, dammit!'

'Oh, but you have. Poaching students is not very nice, Katie. Taking students from what they should be doing

49

to what you teach – silly books and poems. So much easier. So very much easier.'

She frowned. 'Easier than what?'

Again, the chuckle. 'Naughty, naughty,' said the voice and then there was just the dial tone.

Stryker and Tos could almost feel the curious eyes behind every neighbourhood window as they approached the house and ducked under the crime scene tape that was still around the Mayhew home. Muller felt odd, following them. What the hell were they looking for anyway? Hadn't the Scene of Crime guys checked it all out already? Taking out the keys that had been found in the house during the initial assessment, Stryker opened the front door and they went in.

There was a light blinking on the answerphone and Stryker pressed the button.

'Hi, honey,' came a man's voice. 'Don't know where you might be at this time of night, but I just called to say I love you and will be home on Saturday. You have my itinerary and the numbers if you need to call. Goodnight, sleep well.'

Tos and Stryker looked at one another.

'The husband, presumably,' Tos said.

'And where would the itinerary be?' Stryker enquired and they both turned to the room that was set up as an office.

'He obviously doesn't know anything about what happened,' Muller said, as they searched the heaps of scattered papers on the surface and went through the drawers.

'Or he called as a bluff,' Stryker said. 'It would be a good cover, don't you think?'

'Kind of sick.'

'More calculated than sick,' Stryker observed. 'You or I might think of it.'

'We're devious,' Tos said with a wink.

'He might be, too.' Stryker straightened up, holding a

pad of Post-it notes. At the bottom was a company name. 'Dirkson Medical & Office Supplies' with an address and a website. '"Aha! said Holmes",' he said. 'This is where he works. They'll have an itinerary, they'll know where he is.' He put in a phone call to the office to get someone started on the trackdown. 'This will speed things up.'

They continued to search through the late Professor Mayhew's papers. There were a number of essays, heavily marked, obviously waiting to be returned to the students. Endless notes on everything from envelopes to the backs of supermarket receipts to the insides of toilet-roll wrappers.

'She obviously thought a lot while she was on the john,' Tos remarked. 'Me, too. Only place I can get any peace.'

Stryker shrugged helplessly. 'I don't understand any of this stuff,' he complained. 'We should really get one of her colleagues to go through it. I don't know what refers to what – her life or the lives of the people she was writing about. Look here – she says "misery is felt in the bones". Does that mean herself or . . .'

'"Aha, said Watson!",' said Tos, holding up two matching books, 'diary and address book.' But it was only a calendar diary, detailing meetings, assignments and other day-to-day notations. 'Thought I had it there for a minute,' Tos muttered.

'Well, that's an idea,' Stryker said. 'She might have kept a diary . . .'

'Too easy,' said Tos. 'Way too easy.'

'Well, you can always hope.' Stryker headed towards the bedroom, where the outline of the body on the rug made a ghostlike presence in the room, as did the darkened stain at the head. They stood quietly for a moment, looking around.

'What did the SOC investigators say?' Tos asked.

'Not much. The bed was sat on but not slept in. The bedside drawer was open . . . presumably where she kept the gun.'

'So she sat down, took the gun out, stood up and blew her brains out.'

'Through the eye? I never heard of any suicide who did that,' Stryker protested. 'Especially a woman . . . they sometimes go through a whole ritual of making themselves look their best before doing the deed. In the mouth, maybe . . . but to stare straight into the gun? No way, I can't believe that. And—' He pointed to the bed. 'Not so apparent now, but in the photographs you can see that two people sat side by side on the bed.'

'Really?' Tos was startled. 'I never noticed that.' He turned to stare at the bed, which was wrinkled on one side. 'So she sat there with her killer, all cosy like?'

'I don't know how cosy it was, considering she got a gun out at one point,' Stryker said. He walked around the room. No cigarette butts in the ashtray on the far bedside table, but it was there, so one of them presumably smoked. 'Which side of the bed do you sleep on?' he asked suddenly.

'I sleep in the middle,' Tos answered virtuously. Stryker just glared at him, knowing Tos was aware he meant when Tos slept with Liz. 'On the right side,' he added grudgingly.

'Me, too.' Stryker nodded. 'But there were cigarette butts in the ashtray in the office, so presumably she smokes. In which case she slept on the right side.'

'Which means?'

'Maybe it means she was the dominant partner.'

'Oh, come on,' Tos scoffed. 'You can't know that. I thought you didn't go in for all that psychological crap.'

Stryker nodded. 'True – just a thought. The gun was in the left-hand bedside table.'

'His side? But the gun was registered to her.'

'I know. Interesting, isn't it – other people's marital arrangements.' Stryker wandered over to look at the other bedside table, hoping to find a personal diary. But the drawer and shelves only held aspirin, antihistamine tablets and tissues. In the other one there had only been a nasal spray and a crime novel. 'If we really wanted to know they could do a DNA from skin flakes,' he mused.

'For crying out loud, do we really want to know?'

'It helps to know the victim,' Stryker said quietly. 'If she was dominant, was she a nagger? Did she patronize him because she was the intellectual? Did she make him feel small? Did he come to resent her? Did he cheat on her to get his own back? . . . All that.'

'Oh God,' Tos said in despair. 'You're going to come up with some theory.'

Stryker grinned. 'Actually, I'm not. Not yet. But it is interesting, isn't it?'

Tos shrugged. 'I prefer ballistics and fingerprints; facts, not fancies.'

'Then let's check out the names in her address book. We don't even know her maiden name, so it will be hard to tell who are relatives and who aren't. Her husband was down as next of kin at the university, but until we find him we'll have to do what we can.'

They went back to Elise Mayhew's office.

As they were making another survey, Stryker suddenly stood still. 'Oh, dammit to hell, the computer.'

'What about it?'

'All the stuff we want could be on there,' Stryker said. 'I forgot to check back with whoever downloaded it. Some people keep everything on their PC – appointments, notes, the whole shebang.'

'Do you think she would have kept a diary there?'

'A diary is too much to hope for,' Stryker acknowledged. 'But the husband's itinerary might be in there; her will could be in there, her insurance policies . . .'

'No, they're over here,' Muller said from where he was going through the two low filing cabinets that flanked a big bookcase. 'All nice and tidy.' He pulled something out. 'She left everything to him. No mention of anyone else, relatives, so on.' He extracted another folder. 'Not a very big insurance policy . . .' He continued to survey bank records etc. 'They had a lot in the bank, joint accounts, some savings, some investments. He'll do all right.' He paused, slowly straightened up with yet another folder, quite a thick one. 'She was an orphan,' he said in some astonishment. 'Her maiden name was Avery – look at this.'

Stryker came over. The clippings were yellowed and brittle, but the story was clear. Almost everyone in a small family named Avery was killed in a car accident in Michigan. The only survivor was a little girl named Elise. The man responsible, a drunken van driver, was jailed and – on the last clipping – they saw the little girl had been taken in to be raised by her maternal grandparents, Mr and Mrs Gunderson. The date on that clipping was just over thirty years ago. Elise had been eight.

'Do you suppose they're still alive?' Tos asked.

'I doubt it. Check out the address book.' They did. But no mention of Gunderson or 'Gran' or 'Grandad' appeared. The address book was fairly new and there were no others in the desk.

'So, just the husband – unless there are some cousins lurking somewhere,' Tos said, closing the book. 'Poor kid.'

'She did all right,' Stryker pointed out. 'People liked her, she was smart and hard-working. The grandparents did a good job.'

'And now look,' Tos said. 'Blown away.'

'Well, I don't know what else to look at,' Stryker said. 'I'll talk to the Crime Scene guys again, see if they came up with hairs or fibres that weren't hers. We'll have to wait to get the husband so we can eliminate him or his fingerprints.' He glanced at Tos. 'You know, there weren't any fingerprints on the doorbell, the door knocker, or the doorknob of the bedroom . . . none at all. Not even the dead woman's.'

'Wiped.'

'Not suicide.'

They looked at each other and simultaneously sighed heavily. Old partners, old communications. And a hard task ahead. Muller looked at them and felt very new on the job.

SEVEN

WHEN THEY RETURNED TO THE squad room after visiting the Crime Scene lab and talking to the computer techies, Stryker spotted Pinsky seated at his desk. Pinsky looked pale and dazed. And as they drew closer they could see that he was actually on the verge of tears.

'Jesus, Ned, what's the matter?' Stryker asked, going over to him.

'That kid,' Ned managed to say, his voice thick with emotion. 'That poor, dumb kid.'

Stryker glanced at Neilson, who sat on the other side of the desk looking worried.

He sighed. 'You know that kid who kept trying to get in touch with Ned?'

'What kid?' asked Tos.

'Name of Ricky Sanchez,' Neilson replied. 'He's been calling Ned here and at home – he goes out with Ned's daughter – but we've been so busy on this Mayhew homicide that Ned kept missing him.'

'I forgot,' Pinsky whispered. 'I forgot.'

'Well, they just reported finding him dead in an alley off French Street. We're about to go down there . . . when Ned is ready. We only just heard,' Neilson finished.

'I think I talked to the kid myself,' Stryker said. 'The other day he called. He seemed worried.'

'Yeah,' Ned confirmed, taking a deep breath. 'He was worried all right. And look where it's got him. I should have listened. I should have taken a minute, Jesus, just a minute or two to get back to him. I should have realized

55

it was more than just a little worry. Maybe he'd still be alive.'

'You couldn't know,' Tos said.

Ned looked up angrily. 'That's just it. I *could* have known if I'd taken the time to find out. But oh no, I had to go chasing around being the big homicide dick ... well, the "dick" part is true enough. This kid was calling out for help ... and I didn't listen. Not hard enough. Denise will never forgive me. Shit, I'll never forgive myself.' He stood up. 'Let's go. I want this case and I'm going to have this case.'

'You're too involved, Ned,' Stryker protested.

Ned turned and gave him such a look that Stryker actually stepped back. 'Let's *all* go,' he suggested. 'You blew him off too, didn't you?'

'I offered to listen,' Stryker said. 'I could hear he was unhappy.'

'He didn't know you from Adam,' Ned said. 'Why should he talk to you? I was the one he knew. I was the one he turned to. And I let him down. We all let him down.'

'Now, listen.' Neilson put a hand on his partner's arm. Ned pushed past him. 'Let's go,' he said.

Stryker looked after him. 'Fineman will never let him stay on the case.'

'I really don't think that will make any difference,' Neilson said. 'I've never seen him like this. I mean, I haven't known him for all that many years, but this has really hit him bad. It's kind of scary.'

'He's upset, he'll get over it,' Tos said comfortably. 'It just got to him, that's all. We all have weak spots and Ned has a big conscience. He feels too much.'

'Look who's talking,' Stryker muttered as they followed Pinsky out to the cars.

The alley was surprisingly neat for an alley off French Street. A building was being renovated and the area was being kept fairly clear by the builders. Rubbish was contained in large cardboard bins or dumpsters and there was almost no litter between them. The surface was pitted and rough, but looked as if it had been swept recently. The fact that a dead body was lying there seemed even more shocking as a result. A long line of blood snaked from beneath the tarp the patrol officers had used to cover the body and drained neatly into a manhole. Even in death, Ricky Sanchez seemed socially responsible.

Pinsky stood over the body, rocking slightly back and forth. After a minute he nodded to one of the uniforms and the tarp was pulled back. Ricky Sanchez had been killed with blows to the back of the head. One hard blow had shattered his skull, either the first blow, or the last, depending on whether the assailant had just wanted to bring him down or had wanted to make sure once he was down. Nearby lay the probable weapon, a length of pipe, already bagged and marked. They could even see where it had come from: the builders' dumpster, half filled with plumbing bits and pieces, outside the building undergoing renovation. Which might indicate it had been a spur-of-the-moment murder, the killer grabbing whatever was at hand to strike the boy down.

Pinsky knelt beside Ricky and reached out a hand to touch the side of his face. 'Sorry, kid,' he whispered.

Neilson, Stryker and Tos were busy talking to the patrol officers who had found the body, and pointedly ignored Pinsky's turmoil. 'It looks like a straightforward mugging, Lieutenant,' the patrol cop said, consulting his notebook. 'No wallet, scrapes where his watch was dragged off and ditto some kind of ring.'

'So when was he found?' Tos asked.

'About an hour ago,' the patrolman answered. 'The builders found him when they started work this morning. We found his ID – hell, it was pinned to his jacket – and called it in. If it weren't for that ID we wouldn't have known who the hell he was.'

Under his ski jacket Ricky was wearing green surgical scrubs. A plastic hospital ID was just visible fastened to

57

the left breast pocket. He lay on his side in what is commonly called the recovery position – but he was never going to recover.

'I wonder what the hell he was doing down here?' Neilson said, looking around. French Street was probably the least salubrious street in town. Lined with cheap bars and shops specializing in porn, it was the main drag for the homeless, the alcoholic and the drug abuser. It was patrolled more regularly than most areas, but to little avail. Cunning was the common feature of its regular inhabitants – clocking the patrols and timing their crimes was the least of their worries. It was a punishment patrol – you got busted down to French Street. As the citizens went, so went the police. Right to the bottom. But the patrolmen who had found the body were young and seemed eager. They had put up Crime Scene tape immediately and had been talking to the gathering crowd. A head start for which the detectives were grateful.

'We're not that far from the hospital,' Tos said. 'Maybe he was taking a short cut.'

'Even from here it looks like a hell of a blow,' Stryker said, looking over. 'Took some strength.'

'Yeah,' Neilson agreed. 'Got to be a man.'

'Women work out now,' Tos reminded them. 'You should see them down at the gym, they got muscles bigger than mine, some of them. It could have been a woman. He might have turned his back on a woman easier than a man.'

'He's not very tall,' Tos observed. 'Not much in the angle to tell us how big the assailant was.'

They were all being very precise, trying to ignore Pinsky's emotions, to remain distant, professional, neutral. But it was hard, because they felt for Pinsky, they felt for the kid and they felt guilty themselves. Not that they had anything to feel guilty about; it was just a generalized guilt engendered by Pinsky's personal agony. Although things like this occurred every day, they knew damn well they shouldn't happen, that they should be

58

preventing crime more than solving it, that there were gaps in the department, in their own lives, in society, allowing things to happen that shouldn't. They felt the guilt of omission, the helpless guilt that was inescapable but all-pervasive in a situation like this. Other homicides they had been investigating were problems to be solved, quite separate from themselves, a challenge, a duty, the kind of thing they were trained to do, did every day. But this one was going to be different, because of Ned and his pain. Otherwise it looked all too common.

The ME arrived then. Bannerman as usual – he loved to get out of the morgue when he could. He glanced at them and then at Pinsky, who was still kneeling by the body, and raised an eyebrow.

'He knew the kid,' Stryker explained, that far and no further.

'Shame,' Bannerman said. He went over and put a hand on Pinsky's shoulder. Pinsky looked up, saw who it was, and slowly stood up and stepped back.

The others waited a moment, then ducked under the tape and joined him.

'He worked at the hospital?' Bannerman asked over his shoulder after looking at the plastic ID badge on the body. 'Was he an intern or what?'

'He was a pre-med student. He had a part-time job as an orderly in the ER. It was a great chance for him; he got to observe a lot, understand things he might be up against himself one day, understand routines and procedures.' Pinsky took a deep breath. 'He tried to save his dad when he was shot. Kept him alive until the paramedics arrived, but he couldn't do enough and the old man died right on their own front lawn. It kind of marked him.'

Stryker frowned in puzzlement and Neilson explained the old shooting of the boy's father some years before. Stryker vaguely remembered it, then, and nodded.

'That made him want to train,' Pinsky said with an air of wanting to explain why the boy was different. 'It was

59

going to take him a long time, but he was determined and he would have done it, too. He really would.'

'Look, Ned, we've got to get on with this,' Stryker said. 'He was robbed. It looks like a straightforward mugging. Wrong place, wrong time. I'm sorry . . . but it wasn't your fault. It's just one of those things.'

'But the kid was worried,' Pinsky protested. 'It's got something to do with that. It has to.'

'Ned, he was robbed. The mugger probably didn't even realize he'd killed him.'

Pinsky shook his head. 'He was worried. Maybe scared. He talked to me once about something he felt was wrong, maybe even illegal, something he wondered if he should report on or not. He wasn't very clear, he was playing it very close to his chest. He was afraid he'd be called a whistle-blower and that it would affect his own career, because people don't like tattle-tales, especially in the medical profession. You know, doctors are supposed to stick together, that kind of thing.'

'Cops, too – but that's not always a good thing,' Stryker said gently. 'That's why we have IAD, damn their sneaky hides.'

'That's exactly what he meant,' Pinsky said with almost a smile. 'See? You hate tattle-tales, too.'

'Sure. But I know they keep most of us in line, aside from our own sterling qualities of honour and professionalism,' Stryker said with heavy irony.

'Was it to do with doctors?' Tos wanted to know.

'I'm not sure,' Pinsky admitted. 'Although he did say he might be destroying someone's career, come to think of it. If he was right, that is. The problem apparently was that he wasn't sure he *was* right.'

Stryker took a deep breath and laid his hand on Pinsky's arm. 'Look, Ned, you're just upset. There's no connection here. It's obviously a street crime and we've got other—'

'No,' Pinsky contradicted. 'I let him down. It's not just a mugging. There's more. There has to be.'

'No there doesn't,' Stryker said firmly. 'People worry all the time . . . and people get killed for no reason at all. It was random, it was chance. He was in a bad area, wearing a decent coat – it's a wonder they left that. And his shoes.'

'Well, there you are, then,' Pinsky said.

'It needn't have been a homeless – could have been a druggie,' Tos said. 'Didn't need shoes – just money for his next fix. Maybe he saw the ID, maybe . . .' He paused and turned to the patrolman. 'Any keys on him?'

The patrolman checked his notebook again. 'No, no keys.'

'Then somebody better notify the hospital – he might have had keys to drugs cupboards, stuff like that,' Stryker said.

'I'll do that,' Pinsky volunteered. 'I want to look around that hospital.'

Stryker shook his head. 'No, Ned. Leave it.'

'How can I?' Pinsky asked. 'He turned to me and I let him down.'

Stryker glanced at Tos. 'No, Ned. Neilson can go to the hospital. You go home.'

'His mother works in the mayor's office,' Pinsky said stubbornly. 'I need to tell her.'

'A secretary?'

'Hell, no, much more high-powered. Personal assistant to the deputy mayor,' Pinsky said carefully. 'She's a smart cookie, is Mrs Sanchez. The whole family . . . what's left of it . . . is smart.' His voice was bitter. 'The father was a lawyer. Ricky was going to be a doctor. He has a younger brother who is some kind of computer whizz and a younger sister who is going to be a concert violinist, or so he says. Said. But they're going fast, the Sanchez family. We'd better move quickly while there's still someone to talk to.'

Neilson hit him gently on the shoulder. 'Take it easy, Ned.'

'Yeah, sure,' Pinsky murmured, looking away to where

they were loading the body into the ME's van. Suddenly he stiffened. 'Denise,' he murmured and seemed frozen, appalled.

'OK, look, I'll do the prelim report. I'll go to the hospital,' Neilson said encouragingly. 'You go talk to Denise, she'll really need you.'

'If she'll talk to me at all,' Pinsky said. 'She's bound to blame me for not taking Ricky more seriously.'

'No point in blaming anyone,' Stryker told him. 'It won't accomplish anything, Ned. The kid was mugged. Move on.'

Pinsky looked at Stryker for a long time, his lean face unreadable. Then he turned and went back to the nearest car, his tall figure slumped, his head held low.

'He's taking this too hard,' Tos said. 'It's not healthy.'

'He had a relationship with the boy,' Neilson said. 'Since the boy lost his father, he's talked to Ned. Leaned on him a bit, I think. So in a way it's like Ned has lost a son. Well, a stepson, maybe.'

'I didn't realize they were that close.' Stryker was surprised.

Neilson gave half a laugh. 'Well, apparently Denise takes a long time getting ready to go out on a date, so they had plenty of time to get acquainted. And Ned caught the case of the father's shooting, brought the neighbour to court, got a conviction. The boy was grateful. He was only about fifteen at the time . . . rough time to lose your father.'

'Any time is a rough time to lose a parent,' Stryker said. He had lost both while in college, a car accident far away in England, a sudden wrench, the end of his own life in a way, for he'd had to abandon any hope of a law degree. His lively and adored parents had been antique dealers, never wealthy and with minimal life insurance. They always said they were grasshoppers, never providing for the future. In that, they had been prescient – their future never came. Stryker had become a cop out of a need for money and a need for justice. Practising law remained a dream, further away every year, for all his desultory night courses. He was a good police officer and even now was not certain he would have been as good a lawyer. Play it as it lays, he said. But he remembered the pain. 'Or to lose a child,' he added. It would take them about fifteen minutes to get downtown to the mayor's office, where they would have to tell Mrs Sanchez her boy was dead.

He wished it were further away.

So he could work out what to say.

EIGHT

IT WAS OBVIOUS THINGS WERE bad, because Kate asked Liz to meet her in the Sundae Shoppe. This was an old-fashioned ice-cream parlour they normally tried very hard to stay away from. It had been at least three weeks since they had last succumbed to its siren call. When Liz arrived, Kate was in a booth with the remaining half of a banana split for company. Feeling strength was called for in the face of adversity, Liz ordered a simple milkshake. 'Well?'

'He called again.'

'Damn.'

'I don't know what to do.' Kate was near tears.

'Yes you do. Call the phone company. Tell Jack.'

'I can't. If I call the phone company it will be in the public domain, they will come to the office and do things to the phones. Everybody will want to know why.'

'And if you tell Jack?'

'I can't tell Jack. He's all caught up in the Mayhew murder case – you know how he is. I'd only be an annoyance.'

'And you're afraid to tell him.'

'Yes. Things haven't been exactly perfect between us lately.'

'I think you underestimate him,' Liz said, leaning back as the waitress placed the milkshake in front of her, along with a glass of iced water.

'I know you're right. I'm just so ashamed of being so stupid.'

'Well, it was only the one cheque, right?' Silence. 'Kate?'

'Two,' Kate said in a low voice. 'I also advanced him fifty dollars for books.'

'Oh, Kate. You . . .' Liz was momentarily lost for words.

'I think the apt word is idiot,' Kate said. 'But he showed such promise . . .'

'Yes – for fiction, obviously,' Liz snapped. She, like Jack, hadn't liked Michael Deeds either. Too handsome, too arrogant, too ready to accept any favour as his due. Liz hadn't known what had got into Kate that time, even when Kate showed her the boy's work. Liz could see he was talented. But to her that excused nothing.

'I brought in a tape recorder and recorded his call,' Kate said, showing a little spirit.

'To what end?'

'I don't know.' Kate was miserable. 'Evidence?'

'You plan to take him to court?'

Kate sighed. 'Obviously not.' She looked down at the little voice-activated tape recorder beside her on the bench. It was one she had got as an experiment to take notes, but she had been unable to stand the sound of her own voice on it. 'I guess I wanted you to know how awful he sounded. The things he said.'

Liz leaned forward and touched Kate's wrist. 'Kate, I believe you. I know he is a bastard and that you aren't guilty of anything except being naïve and rather stupid.'

'Gee, thanks.'

'Well, sorry, but it's true.' Liz had a practical and organized mind, and did not much care for prevarication. To her the right thing was the straightforward thing, but Kate was her oldest and dearest friend, and she knew how upset she was. 'Did he have anything new to offer?' she asked, sipping her milkshake.

'No. Just the same stuff about how much of a slut I am and how he was going to tell the Dean and that I had to stop poaching students. He's very angry about that. I don't know what he's talking about. It's not as if I go out into the street and drag students into the building and sign them up.'

65

'No, but it obviously bothers him. What about dear little Michael. Did you poach him?'

'Not really. It was his own idea. I just told him he had real writing talent and that . . .'

'That he might be happier as an English major?'

Kate hung her head. 'Yeah.' She looked up again. 'But my creepy caller keeps saying students, plural, not singular.'

'And what was Michael before he transferred?'

'I honestly don't remember. Maths? Physics? Something like that.'

'I think it's time to consult the oracle,' Liz said.

'Who's that?'

'The departmental secretary.' Liz stood up. 'Come on, you don't want the rest of that anyway.'

'I do.'

'Not as much as you want to end this stuff.'

They walked over to New State Hall and took the elevator up to the new English department, which took up all of the top two floors. The departmental office was in a glass block in the centre of the topmost floor and there they found Sandy, PA to the head of department.

Sandy was tall and very thin, with a kind heart but a short fuse, who did not suffer fools gladly. She was, as usual, looking harassed. When Kate said she needed some help, Sandy started to glower, but relented when she saw how worried Kate was.

'I need to know how many students switched their majors to English in the last two terms,' Kate said.

'What for?' Sandy asked.

'It's to settle a bet,' Liz said quickly. 'A know-it-all in the library is giving us a hard time.'

'Can't see it's any of their business,' Sandy said.

'No, well . . . could you do it? Do we have those kind of records in the computer?' Kate asked anxiously.

'I guess so . . . sort of,' Sandy answered slowly. 'Do you need it right away?'

'It would make life a lot more pleasant,' Liz told her.

'Please?' Kate asked.

Sandy grinned. 'You ought to patent that look. Go and have a cup of coffee in the lounge and I'll do what I can. Shoo!'

They went down and availed themselves of the coffee machine, settling back on the black leather and chrome sofa with their feet up on the smoked glass coffee table. The decorator who had 'done' the department was obviously someone who retained an eighties outlook.

About fifteen minutes later Sandy appeared in the doorway with a printout in her hand. 'Here you go,' she said. 'Not as difficult as I thought.'

'Oh, thanks, Sandy, you're a sweetheart,' Kate said, accepting the printout. Liz grabbed for it and began to read.

'What's this all about really?' Sandy asked.

'Guy says you're poaching students,' Liz muttered.

'Oh, one of those,' Sandy said knowingly. Kate and Liz looked at her in surprise. Sandy shrugged. 'We get it all the time from the other departmental secretaries, how we're the biggest single-subject department because we're luring students away, but you know as well as I do we're overloaded as it is.'

'Too true,' Kate agreed. Several of her freshman and sophomore classes were too big for comfort.

'Is that all?' Sandy asked, obviously curious.

'That's all,' Liz assured her.

'Thanks a lot, Sandy,' Kate said again.

Sandy waved and went back down the hall, leaving them to peruse the printout.

'Science,' Liz said. 'You got four from science, two from art, one from history and one from social studies. That's only eight. What the hell is he on about?'

'Michael Deeds was a pre-med student,' Kate said slowly. 'So was Janet Linley – I'd forgotten her. I don't know any of the others. Oh, wait a minute – the one from social studies I had in a class too. He was hopeless, didn't even belong at university.' She sighed. 'So are you saying this damned caller is from the science department because we had four transfers, including Michael?'

'It looks possible,' Liz said.

'But it's an enormous department, with all kinds of subsections, chemistry, biology, physics . . . there must be at least a hundred on the faculty. And mostly men, too.'

'I know, I know.' Liz rolled the printout into a tube and began to tap it on her knee.

'Well . . .'

'I'm thinking, I'm thinking,' Liz said. Her eyes fell on the tape recorder Kate had put on to the low table in front of them. 'I'm thinking.'

Maria Sanchez was a very handsome woman, tall and stately, with glossy black hair caught up in an efficient French pleat. She was dressed with care and style in muted colours. Her desk was set into a corner and was rather larger than some of the others. And neater.

She had known they were coming up, because she had been notified from downstairs, but when she actually saw them her face drained of colour. However respectable the family, the police rarely bring good news. And Tos's face said it all.

'Who?' she asked.

'Ricky,' he replied without thinking and reached out to grasp her arms as she wavered slightly before regaining her balance.

'He is hurt?' she said almost hopefully. 'I didn't see him this morning – he must have come home late last night . . .'

'I'm afraid he's been killed,' Stryker said gently. 'We're so sorry, Mrs Sanchez.'

Her face went blank. 'You'd better come in here,' she said, turning to lead them into a small conference room. Inside, she sat down abruptly on one of the chairs that encircled the central table and waited.

'He was found in an alley off French Street,' Tos said.

'And?' she prompted, when he cleared his throat.

'Somebody hit him with something,' Tos managed finally. 'It was very quick, from behind. He was robbed of his wallet, watch. He was wearing his hospital identity tag. It might have been some addict after his keys.'

'*Madre de Dios*,' she said, crossing herself. 'First Leo, now Ricky.' Her face stayed calm, but tears overflowed. She was obviously a woman of great self-control and Stryker, standing back, thought she seemed both intelligent and efficient. No wonder her desk was larger than the others. 'At least with Leo we knew,' she continued, her voice unsteady but still under control. 'Is it a curse on our family? I am not superstitious, but—' She looked up beseechingly into Tos's face. 'I cannot really take it in, you know? You spoke out there. You speak here. I hear you, but I don't hear you. It is very strange.' She was beginning to come apart as the truth sank in. 'I don't understand,' she said in a half-whisper. Then the shaking began. Suddenly she let out a wail and collapsed sobbing on to the table, her head sunk into her folded arms, her shock and grief completely overwhelming her.

Tos stood helplessly beside her, patting her shoulder, near tears again himself. 'I'm so sorry,' he kept saying. 'So sorry.'

It was the worst part of the job. Normally a woman police officer would have been sent, but they had gone themselves out of respect for Pinsky and his involvement with the family.

Stryker waited patiently until the woman regained some vestige of control. It took a while. He looked out of the window – they were high up in the municipal building and gulls wheeled past, providing movement in the vista of tall and small buildings that made up the downtown area. During the day the many offices were busy, the streets were filled with bustle, but when darkness fell a change occurred. Grantham was trying to rebuild its inner city, but it was taking a long time. Most people still stayed away from downtown after business

69

hours. And it was strange, because it looked so normal in the daylight: clean, modern, in a way even beautiful.

It was only at night that the rats came out.

Mrs Sanchez was getting herself together, but her chest still heaved with deep, uneven breaths that caught in her throat. 'Will I have to identify him?' she asked. She had learned the routine the hard way, when her husband had been killed.

'I'm afraid so. Ned Pinsky gave a preliminary ID,' Stryker said. 'He sends his condolences. He was very fond of your son.'

'Yes, and Ricky liked and respected him,' she said almost formally.

Stryker waited a moment. 'There will have to be an autopsy because . . .'

'I know. I understand,' she said resignedly. 'What do you want me to do?'

'Go home, Mrs Sanchez,' Stryker said gently. 'We'll take you . . .'

'No, I have my car,' she protested. 'I will need my car in the morning to come back to work.'

'I'm sure they'll understand if you take some time—'

'No.' She shook her head. 'There is much to do. I can do it best from here.' Where she could not break down again, where she had to keep her head high. Where she was respected.

'But you must go home now,' Tos said firmly. 'I'll drive you home in your car, Lieutenant Stryker will follow us. We'll get someone to stay with you, to tell your children when they come home from school . . . please, Mrs Sanchez. For their sake.'

'Yes,' she agreed. 'Yes. All right. Thank you.' Slowly, she stood up. She glanced at Stryker, who had pretty much stayed in the background, and then turned back to Tos. 'Ricky had no enemies; people liked him. He worked hard, he had ambition. He was not a bad person.' She reached out and touched the lapel of his jacket. 'You will find out who did this?'

He nodded, his face grim. 'We'll find out.'

Kate and Liz drove to the address the music department secretary had given them. Liz had come up with an idea. It was wacky and strange, and maybe even impossible. But she knew a man who could tell them and perhaps help them, too. Liz felt protective of Kate, as was often the case. Kate was a strong woman, there was no question about it, but she had weak points and Stryker was one of them. If Liz could help Kate straighten this out quietly she would. Only one more person needed to know about it.

She parked and they got out to walk up the drive. It was a pleasant home on a tree-lined street. When they reached out to ring the bell it sounded before they could make contact, making them jump.

'One of David's little gizmos, I guess,' Liz said.

The door was opened by a young, slim girl with dark hair and huge eyes. 'Yes?'

'Hi, I'm Professor Olson and this is Professor Trevorne. We arranged to see Professor Waxman.'

'Of course.' The girl smiled. 'Come on in. I'm Abbi. David is stuck into something at the moment – would you like some coffee?'

'Great,' they said together and followed Abbi into the large kitchen. The kitchen was classic and very lavish – butcher's-block work surfaces, beautiful glass-fronted cabinets and stainless-steel equipment. A well-stocked spice rack showed that somebody loved to cook. Abbi saw they were impressed and laughed. 'Ill-gotten gains,' she explained. 'David bought me a new kitchen with the proceeds of a score he wrote for a documentary about building a hydroelectric dam in South America. My ambition is to earn enough to redecorate his study for him. So far I can only afford to paint the closet.'

'What do you do while your husband makes music?' Kate asked, as Abbi filled the coffee machine and got down some big mugs, including a special one obviously destined for her husband.

'I was a copywriter in a big agency – but now I free-lance. We're hoping to start a family, and with me at the office or flying everywhere to client meetings and so on, it wasn't practical. I like being at home. This place is wired like Cape Kennedy for computers, thanks to David, and it's easy for me to concentrate here. That's my excuse, anyway. Really, I just like being near David.' A large, sonorous 'clang' filled the air and they all flinched. 'Well, most of the time, anyway,' Abbi added with a chuckle.

'Does that sort of thing happen often?' Liz asked. She'd never heard anything quite like it.

Abbi laughed. 'Occasionally. He's working on some-thing oriental at the moment, a score for a travelogue. You should be here when the Tibetan horns start up. It sounds like the plaintive wail of a dying buffalo stuck in the mud.' There was a rush of tinkling bells. Abbi cocked her head at the sound. 'Those aren't so bad . . . as long as he doesn't do them over and over again. It's worse here in the kitchen – let's go back to the living room. He's more or less soundproofed that.'

The living room was not as perfect as the new kitchen, but it was very comfortable. No two items of furniture matched, but they all blended and some of them were obviously classics of their kind. A planter's chair in one corner, a chaise longue, a deep leather chesterfield sofa made the room seem like a gathering of friends. When they were settled, Kate smiled at Abbi. 'You look very contented,' she said. 'Obviously marriage suits you.' Kate didn't meet many married couples these days – Abbi seemed to her an interesting oddity, someone young and settled, as opposed to the students she dealt with day by day who were always suffering from some kind of personal or academic crisis.

'I'm pretty happy,' Abbi admitted. 'Aside from the clangs, bangs, bongs, tinkles, twitters and clatters, David and I get along great.'

'How did you two meet?' asked Kate, always curious about other people's romances.

'I met him when he came into the agency with the score for a particularly weird television ad I'd written . . . it kind of went from there. He's very clever – but mostly I overlook that. He's just a really, really nice person.' She grinned. 'And scxy, too.'

'We need his help on a project,' Liz informed her. 'A pretty weird project.'

'Should suit him just right,' Abbi said. 'And here he is.'

In the doorway loomed a charming bear of a man, wearing a sweater and chinos. David Waxman was tall and well-built, and his smile was devastating. No wonder Abbi fell for him, Kate thought. He had a diffident manner and was obviously a bit shy. Liz, who knew him from committee work at the university, made the introductions.

'They have a weird project,' Abbi told her husband with a grin. 'But they haven't said how weird yet.'

'The weirder the better,' David said. His voice was surprisingly soft for such a big man. 'I could use some distraction.' He turned to Abbi. 'I just can't get it right, somehow. Damn thing keeps eluding me.'

'David's built a new electronic instrument,' Abbi explained. 'And he's trying to compose on it as well.'

'I don't know how I get myself into these things,' David said morosely. He sank into a big leather chair that was obviously his and his alone. 'I get an idea, mention it to someone and the next thing I know I'm up to my ears in details, details. I spend more time on the phone than I do anything else. Now they want me to help market the thing and all I want to do is get on with my music.'

'David has an unfortunate capacity for thinking up ideas that make money,' Abbi explained with a smile. 'Personally, I think it's great, but he lives for art and all the commercial side of it gets in the way.'

'Aye me,' David said in a gentle, self-mocking way. 'How I suffer.'

'And how our bank manager loves him,' Abbi put in. 'Me, I'm just a hack. Both of us spend more time on the phone than anything else.'

'Ah,' said Kate. 'It's the phone we need help on.'

'I'll leave you to it, then.' Abbi stood up and gathered the empty coffee cups, discreetly retreating with them to the kitchen.

Quickly Kate explained the basic problem and Liz's idea that David might be able to help them identify the nasty phone caller by his voice.

'Hmm – interesting,' David mused. He thought for a moment, then jumped to his feet. 'Come on down to the studio.'

'Watch where you step,' Abbi warned with a smile as they passed through the kitchen. 'You could either trip, electrocute yourself, or blow every fuse from here to the Canadian border.'

'It's not that bad,' David protested. 'As long as you stick to the path.'

'It's a pretty narrow path.' Abbi chuckled, closing the door of the dishwasher. 'Meanwhile, Twister and I have to write an ad for a new cat food.'

'Twister?'

'Our cat.' Abbi pointed to a large grey-and-white lump on a rocking chair in the far corner. The cat was wound so tightly into a ball that Kate had thought it was some kind of furry pillow – very avant-garde.

David and Liz stood by patiently while Kate and Abbi exchanged details about their respective cats. Finally the three of them trailed down the stairs to the basement, leaving Abbi to her feline researches.

'Good heavens, I see what she means,' Kate said, as they left the stairs and entered a huge room filled wall to wall and floor to ceiling with . . . things. Kate recognized some conventional musical instruments and the cloth fronts of speakers, but everything else seemed to consist of electronic mysteries. Dials and switches everywhere – it was quite overwhelming. In fact, the only thing really recognizable was the dog who sat watching them from his bed in the corner. His ears were up and he looked curious.

David laughed at their stunned expressions. 'I know, it's kind of complicated at first glance. It's really pretty straightforward – this is a multi-track recorder, this is a forty-eight-track mixing board where we can bring all kinds of things together. This is what we call an ADAT. These are synthesizers – I can do Wave-Table synthesis and Physical Modelling, as well as Additive synthesis. And this is a sampler – that takes bits of sounds and lets me play with them. Over here is a reverb, digital compressor, phaser—'

'Shades of *Star Trek*,' Liz gasped.

David laughed. 'Not that kind of phaser.' He turned to another piece of equipment. 'This is my latest acquisition – an Avalon 737 with tube compression. It has a noise gate to cut out hiss. I've also just got a mackie digital built-in CD burner.' He smiled as Liz's eyes appeared to cross. Kate seemed interested in all of it, if a bit bemused. 'OK, OK – I'll leave out all the computers and microphones,' he said, relenting. 'Let's just say I've got a lot of stuff down here to do with music and sound, OK?'

The dog, having come over and sniffed them carefully, had retreated back to his bed, but was still watching them, hoping they might suddenly produce something to eat.

'How come you have two rooms?' Kate wanted to know and Liz sighed. Kate had always been fascinated by technology – even if she didn't understand it. It came from having an engineer for a father. If she didn't rein her in soon, they'd be here all day.

'That room over there is for input – where instruments are played into microphones.'

'Oh. So you could record people playing things?'

David grinned. 'That's what I do best – except it's usually me playing them. I do not, however, sing. Much to Abbi's relief.'

'Which of these things would you use to help us?' Kate wanted to know, absorbed in looking at the slides and switches and dials.

'Actually, what you need is pretty basic,' David said,

settling down on a rolling stool. 'It's the analysis that will be complicated. But I'll be using a sound spectrograph, which is a sound wave analyser. I use it for analysing sounds and music, but it can be used to analyse speech, too.' He indicated an instrument with a computer monitor. 'Of course, I can't make the kind of analysis that would stand up in court – you need a trained technician for that, I believe – but I could certainly tell one voice from another and see if they match in a gross analysis. If you want any more than that you'll need an expert, which could cost big bucks.'

Liz glanced at Kate. 'We'll be glad to pay for your time and—'

'Hey, I don't like nasty phone callers any more than you do,' David protested. 'I'm happy to help you. I think you're pretty clever to realize you could catch this guy by his voice. But why haven't you gone to the phone company or the police? Isn't this kind of vicious phone calling illegal?'

Kate hesitated, then explained more fully and confessed her worries. He had a very sympathetic face, listened patiently as it all came out. 'None of it's true. We think it's a faculty member. If it is, we don't necessarily want to take him to court – just get him straightened out before he makes more trouble.'

'For the honour of GSU?' David asked, raising an eyebrow. 'That's pretty idealistic.'

'You're a member of the faculty yourself. Surely you've got some loyalty towards the place,' Liz said.

'Sure. They pay for all this,' he answered, gesturing around. 'Well, a lot of it. And all I have to do is teach, which I really enjoy. Even so, the kind of hassle you're talking about can be nerveracking. I'm sorry you're being bothered like this.'

'I know,' Kate agreed. 'He seems to enjoy it so much . . . it's awful. Can you help?'

'I'll sure try,' David said in his soft voice. 'It's pretty simple.'

76

It might have been simple to David Waxman, but it took a lot of explaining for Kate and Liz. Especially when he made clear that they would have to get each suspect to repeat certain words so he could compare them. It would require some kind of script and some words would have to be the same as in the phone call Kate had already recorded using a simple cassette recorder mike held to the receiver. It was the first time Liz had heard the voice and she saw immediately what Kate meant about the irritation factor.

David listened to what they had and scowled. 'Bastard,' he said. 'But the quality isn't really sufficient for what we need. Let me check.' He put the tape into another machine, played it through the computer into the spectrograph and sighed. 'You really need a mike right in the receiver. Let's look at what I've got that will help you.'

They looked and then looked at each other. This was *not* going to be as easy as they had thought. After half an hour, though, they had the equipment and the instructions straight in their minds – and in their notebooks.

'How long do you think it will take?' David asked. 'Getting all the samples, I mean.'

'Well, a few days at least,' Kate said. 'Maybe a week.'

'That suits me fine.' David nodded. 'I have this other thing to finish and it should take me about a week. Then I'll be free to analyse your data. It's not exactly my field, but I think I can do a good job on it. If I get stuck, I know a guy who is really expert – but like I said, we'd have to pay him.'

'That's fine,' Kate said firmly. 'Whatever it takes is fine with me. It's really nice of you to help me out.'

David waved a negligent, well-kept hand. 'Happy to. The Waxman Boys are known for their services to humanity.' When they looked puzzled, he chuckled. 'My brother is a doctor. He's always telling me what I do is selfish, that I should have been a doctor like him and saved people's lives.'

'Well, you might be saving someone's reputation here,' Kate told him. 'Not a bad thing.'

'And no blood,' David said. 'That's what I prefer, believe me.' He reached out and flicked a switch. The result was a cacophony of sound, including (they thought) the dying buffalo horns Abbi had mentioned. 'There.' David mercifully flicked it off after a minute or two. 'What do you think of that?'

'It's very . . . loud,' Liz said, absently rubbing her ear.

'Interesting,' Kate said at the same time.

David grinned. 'Philistines,' he said. 'It's the music of tomorrow.'

'Maybe it will sound better with lyrics,' Liz suggested.

'Words are Abbi's department.' David got up to gather together the equipment they were taking with them. 'Me, I just make the songs that make the world go round.'

'And round and round and round,' said Abbi from the doorway. 'Come up and have some cake before you go. It will soothe your savaged ears.'

NINE

NEILSON WAS LUCKY. HE HIT the ER during a brief lull and was quickly able to find the doctor in charge. He was a man of medium size, light-brown hair, fair-skinned, looking rather rumpled in his green cotton scrubs. He wore small steel-rimmed glasses and a long-suffering expression. He also looked very tired, but his eyes were everywhere, constantly checking on everything in the ER. According to the plastic ID badge clipped to the pocket of his scrubs, his name was Dan Waxman.

'What is it this time?' he asked wearily.

'I beg your pardon?' Neilson was startled.

'Did we forget to fill out some papers, or are we treating someone you want to arrest, or—'

'No, no, nothing like that,' Neilson said quickly. 'I have to tell you that one of your employees has been killed. We found him in his hospital clothes, and—'

'Who?'

'A young orderly named Ricky Sanchez,' Neilson told him.

'Good God,' the doctor said, physically stepping back as if from a blow. 'He worked an extra shift last night . . .' He seemed stunned. 'Where did you find him?'

'In an alley off French Street,' Neilson said. 'He had been struck from behind, several blows to the head, fatal.'

'But he was fine last night,' the doctor protested, then heard himself and had the grace to blush. 'This is terrible. Poor Ricky.' They both moved against the wall as a gurney with someone bleeding heavily and moaning loudly was rushed past them by two ambulance men, chased by a nurse waving a clipboard.

'Ann-Catherine,' Dr Waxman said, grabbing another nurse who was going by. 'Ricky Sanchez has been killed.'

The nurse, who seemed to have some seniority, looked astonished. 'But ... are you serious?' She glanced at Neilson.

'I'm afraid so,' he confirmed.

'That's terrible,' she said. 'That's—'

Another nurse grabbed her arm. 'The patient in Four is bleeding out,' she said.

'Sorry,' Ann-Catherine said and ran after the other nurse.

'You knew Sanchez well?' Neilson asked, after carefully looking both ways before stepping back into the centre of the hallway.

'Oh, sure. Ann-Catherine and I interviewed him for the job. He was recommended by someone over at the university.'

Neilson stared. A connection with GSU. 'Not a Professor Mayhew, by any chance?'

'No.' Waxman frowned. 'Who's that?'

'Oh, nothing.'

Waxman shook his head disbelievingly. 'I just can't take it in. Was it a mugging?'

'Yeah,' Neilson said. 'Wallet and watch gone. Also maybe he had keys, like to your drugs cupboard?'

'No. Nothing like that. Keys to his own locker, maybe, but nothing to do with drugs. He was just an orderly.' Waxman appeared barely able to cope with the obvious. He seemed suddenly aware of that himself and shoved his hands into his pockets. 'Dammit, I deal with this kind of thing every day,' he said apologetically. 'I mean accidents, sudden trauma, things coming at you without warning. So you'd think I could handle it better. But this is so far out of left field – Ricky Sanchez – just so weird.' He shook his head despairingly. There was the wail of a siren outside the double doors and people began shouting. Waxman's attention wavered.

With Pinsky in mind, Neilson asked another question. 'Was there anything special about the boy?'

Waxman grinned. 'He was a human sponge. Wanted to know everything. Always asking, always curious. I thought it was a sign he would be a good doctor. He was in pre-med, you know. And he would have been good, too. It's a damn shame.' Waxman's eyes were on the double doors, on the nurses, running.

'Questions about anything in particular?' Neilson asked – one last throw of the dice for Pinsky.

But Waxman shook his head. 'Not really. He was just a lively kid with a lively mind. Nice kid, too. I liked him a lot. Eager to learn, eager to help. Always eager to help anyone, any time. Look, I have to go.'

'OK, Doc. Thanks.' As Neilson closed his notebook he saw Waxman heading towards the sound of the approaching ambulance.

Well, he'd tried for Pinsky. Nothing ventured . . . and nothing gained. So much for fancy theories. Neilson walked slowly out of the hospital and back to the car. Ricky Sanchez was just another French Street fatality. Whether he was worried about something when he died or whether he was full of the joys of spring really made no difference. When you're dead, you're dead. Another number, another statistic, another ending to another show.

Pinsky drove home slowly, hoping Denise was not back from classes. But as he reached the house he saw her little car already in the drive and so he parked in the street, leaving her an escape route. He had a terrible feeling she would want to flee from him when he told her. Run to her friends, seek comfort, get away from his presence. But she did not.

'I don't understand what you are telling me,' she said, white-faced, sitting in a corner of the dark-green sofa and clutching a pillow to her chest as if it were a teddy bear. 'You're saying that it wasn't just some kind of mugging?'

'I'm afraid that's what the others think. He was robbed, no getting around that,' Pinsky said reluctantly. 'But you know he kept trying to see me, we talked the other night about something that was troubling him . . .'

'And you told him to confront the person he was worried about,' Denise said in a flat voice.

'Yes,' Pinsky whispered. 'I did.' She looked so small and vulnerable against the dark sofa. He felt as if he had struck her, felt her pain, felt his shame.

'And you think he must have done that,' she said, still in that flat voice. 'And that person killed him?'

'I just think it's possible.'

'But that would make some kind of sense, wouldn't it?' she persisted.

'Yes,' he whispered again. 'It would.'

She seemed to suddenly focus on him, her father, and his obvious misery. 'You feel guilty, don't you?' she said. She had always been very perceptive concerning his moods and the moods of others. 'You think it was somehow your fault because you didn't get back to him, didn't follow through?'

Pinsky nodded.

'Well, I don't think you should,' Denise said, although her voice trembled a little. 'Ricky wouldn't tell me, either. He was really funny about it, secretive, mysterious. It was really bothering him, but he wouldn't talk about it, or tell me anything. He was the same with you the other night, wasn't he? Just wanting to know what to do next in some kind of theoretical situation?'

'More or less,' Pinsky admitted. 'I tried to get him to give me some details—'

'But he wouldn't.' She hugged the pillow tighter to her, her knuckles pale as she clutched the piped edge. 'I know. I think he was going a little nuts about this thing, whatever it was. He felt kind of guilty and kind of excited and kind of confused. . . . He did say once that if he was

82

right it was terrible and if he was wrong he was an idiot. But he just didn't know.'

'Do you think it was about something at school or the hospital?'

'I'm not sure. I think the hospital, really, because he was so caught up in things there. Maybe school, though. He had a class with some professor he thought was some kind of weirdo. The guy kept pushing him to work harder, hassling him about his future, seemed to think Ricky could save the world.'

'Name?'

'I can't think of it . . . I'll try to remember.' She eyed him. 'Daddy, maybe it was just a mugging, like Lieutenant Stryker thinks. Maybe Ricky was just unlucky. You know that's a bad area.'

Pinsky rubbed his temples. 'I know it looks that way, but—'

'Just because you feel bad—'

'I can't help it, honey. Something in me says there is more to this than just a mugging. Which isn't nice, I know. I mean—'

'You mean murder. Premeditated murder.'

'I guess I do. It sounds melodramatic, I know. The others think I'm nuts, of course. Because I'm upset. Because I liked Ricky.' He looked at her curiously. 'You don't seem . . . as upset as I thought you would be.'

'No, I don't, do I?' She frowned. 'Maybe it hasn't hit me yet. Like a bit of food that's too big to swallow – it kind of chokes you off.' Her eyes met his and while there was unhappiness there, he also saw deep regret for something more than a life lost. 'Ricky and I hadn't been getting on very well lately,' she said slowly. 'We've been going out a long time, and it . . . was sort of . . . stale. I think we were going to break up soon, Dad. And it didn't really hurt. I've been noticing other guys and I think he's been looking around, too. We go back a long way . . .' Her eyes filled with tears. 'Old friends, we were like some old couple . . .' Her voice caught.

He waited.

'But now he's dead,' she said and that flat voice was back. 'He's dead. And we don't know why.' Tears were running down her face. 'Do you think you can find out why, Daddy?' She was a little girl again, looking for reassurance, no hate, no blame. Pinsky could have wept himself with relief. Such a good girl, so sane, so intelligent, so compassionate. Ricky would have been a fool to give her up. But Ricky had been no fool.

Except about this one thing, this thing that he had been hugging to his chest, fretting about and . . . excited? Denise had said he seemed guilty and excited. What had he learned? What was it that had killed him? Because Pinsky was as certain as he could be that Ricky had gone one step too far, taken one chance too many with someone who had not seemed to him to be dangerous, but who was, in fact, ready to kill. Why?

To keep a secret, obviously. To hide something that Ricky had discovered. He had deduced, or observed, or overheard something so wrong that someone had been prepared to kill to hide it. Had Ricky been the only one to know or guess? Were others now in danger, too? Having killed once, the person responsible might have no compunction about killing again. It had to be something so vital to their lives that taking another life was small in comparison.

Find the ego.

That was his job, that was always his job. But if it was going down as a random street crime, it wouldn't be his job. Or anybody's job, come to that. And that was wrong. It was just wrong.

'Daddy?'

'Yes, honey?'

'When will Mom get home tonight?' Her voice was no longer flat, but was getting smaller and smaller.

'Soon, baby, she'll be home soon,' Pinsky reassured her and went to sit beside her, hug her, rock her until her mommy came home. And while he rocked, he began to think . . . where to start, where to start, where to start? In a little while he would ask Denise about Ricky's friends. But not yet. Not just yet.

First he had to decide how to proceed.

First he had to have a plan.

Neilson did the report on Ricky Sanchez's death, putting it down as a homicide and robbery, adding it to the standing list of street crimes. There would be follow-ups by other detectives, but he knew – as they all knew – that it would probably never be solved. So many, so many. As for Pinsky's conviction that it was deliberate murder – well, Pinsky had been very upset. Maybe if they hadn't been caught up in the Mayhew investigation they could have paid more attention, but he did report the suspicion to the pair of detectives who would be following up. He owed Pinsky that much. And they were good, Jackson and Sloman. They might come up with something.

It wasn't until the next day that the trouble started.

Pinsky came in looking haggard but determined and made straight for Stryker's office. 'I want to be assigned to the Sanchez case,' he said a little more loudly than was necessary.

Stryker considered him. It looked as if Pinsky hadn't slept much since the Sanchez boy had been found the previous morning. 'No way, Ned,' he told him. 'I talked it over with Fineman. Even if we were going to pursue your theory, he wouldn't want you involved. You're too close to the situation.'

'Balls,' said Pinsky uncompromisingly. 'You just want to write it off. I heard it's been given away for follow-up.'

'Jackson and Sloman are good men, and Neilson did tell them about your suspicions. We want to be fair and sensible, Ned, but the balance of probabilities makes it look like a straightforward mugging. It's just a coincidence that the boy was worried about something. People get killed at very inconvenient moments – anything could be going on in their lives, but not necessarily be connected. If it had been a traffic death would you be as worried?'

'Yes,' Pinsky said flatly. 'And so should you be.'

Stryker sighed heavily. 'Let it go, Ned. We need you on the Mayhew investigation. It's complicated, it's high level—'

'And Ricky was just a spic kid,' Pinsky finished bitterly.

Stryker scowled. 'You know better than that,' he said icily. 'I don't work that way and I don't think that way.'

Pinsky knew he had overstepped the mark. He took on a more pleading tone. 'You're dismissing Ricky's death when there are aspects to it that should be investigated.'

'Talk to Jackson and Sloman if you like, but you are to stay on the Mayhew case. We need you there,' Stryker repeated. 'If they come up with anything, we'll think again.'

'They won't bother.'

'I don't agree,' Stryker said.

There was a long silence.

'I have vacation days coming,' Pinsky said abruptly.

Stryker knew instantly what he meant. He sympathized, he even thought there might be something in Pinsky's theory. But the balance of probabilities said otherwise. There was nothing he could do. 'No, Ned. Stay away from it.'

Pinsky glared at him. 'I feel pneumonia coming on,' he growled. 'I feel very, very sick. And that's the truth, as it happens.'

'I wouldn't be a bit surprised,' Stryker agreed, because Pinsky did look bad, off balance and not much good to man or department. And he was afraid that whatever he said or Fineman ordered, Pinsky was not going to let go of this thing. 'You've had a shock, you need to take some time,' he said carefully.

Pinsky looked momentarily surprised.

'But', Stryker continued, 'stay home, Ned. Rest. Relax.'

'Oh, of course I will,' Pinsky said sarcastically.

'I mean it, Ned. Stay away from it.'

'What I do on my own time is my business.'

Stryker considered asking him to leave his badge and gun, but that would be tantamount to suspension and there was no call for it. Ned was upset and he might make a stab at trying to find backing for his suspicions. If hc did there was nothing Stryker could do about it – as long as he didn't know about it, or it didn't get back to Fineman. He respected Pinsky and he privately acknowledged that there might be something in his suspicions, but he just couldn't commit any more departmental time to it. Somehow, when they weren't looking, the bean-counters had got into the Grantham PD. Budget ruled and everything got prioritized. At a less busy time he might have the luxury of looking into the Sanchez case more deeply. As it was, his hands were tied. Fineman had spoken. Maybe if it had happened anywhere else but French Street . . .

'I wish I could do more for you, Ned. But it's on the record as a random mugging. As I say, if Jackson and Sloman—'

'Fuck Jackson and Sloman,' Pinsky said. 'It's Fineman, isn't it?'

'It's policy, Ned. Priorities.'

'It's bullshit and you know it,' Ned snapped. Stryker just looked at him.

'Have a good rest, Ned,' he said quietly. 'Take it easy. Come back when you're ready.'

Pinsky turned towards the door, then turned back. 'I'm ready now. The trouble is you aren't,' he said and went out.

Being a gentleman, he did not slam the door.

But he wanted to.

TEN

'DEAR GOD, THIS PLACE IS beginning to look like wire-tap city,' Liz said, gazing around. It was an exaggeration, but she had a point. 'What is all this going to do to your phone bill? And what is Jack going to say?'

'He doesn't need to know a thing about it,' Kate replied, brushing her hands together with satisfaction as she surveyed her new 'laboratory'. When she had lived in this flat the entire sitting room had been devoid of furniture – just the expanse of deep, long-pile carpet in a lush golden shade and a few big pillows. She had had to furnish it in order to rent it, but had concentrated on junk shop finds and pieces culled from ads in the newspaper personal section. The effect was eclectic and simple. Students can be rough on a place, but as she limited herself to graduate students she knew personally, she felt safer than most that not too much damage would be done. But the carpet – her precious and expensive carpet – showed the inevitable tracks of wear and about that she was sad. Still, nothing lasts for ever – and she made a mental note to employ a professional carpet cleaner before she let the flat again. It was sheer luck that she hadn't installed someone this term. She took a deep breath and ignored the floor.

David Waxman had lent her a number of items; she had purchased the rest on her own credit card. She and Jack might live together, but they still maintained separate bank accounts, along with a common household account, and this was one of the times when she was grateful they had kept it that way. No questions to be asked. The phone bill for the flat was back in her name and came to her directly at the university. She had carefully maintained the flat as a fallback, should she and Stryker ever come undone. While it seemed unlikely, she liked having her own life apart from the one they shared. It made her feel safer somehow. She was still reluctant to commit fully to a man who dealt with violence for a living and could be killed at any moment. Suppose they had children? She loved him very much, but something in her held back, still, from that last commitment. Knowing she was being unfair to Jack didn't help.

'How long do you think it's going to take?' Liz asked, sinking into a chair.

'I don't know. A week?'

'Oh, really? And when do you propose to do your teaching and paperwork? Or do I detect an approaching request on the horizon?'

'Well, you're so close . . . just downstairs. You *could* help,' Kate acknowledged. 'Just a few phone calls would help a lot.'

'Uh-huh. And just how creative do I have to be to carry out this little assignment?' Liz wanted to know. 'Am I to be a person doing a survey, someone selling something, an unknown admirer . . . what?'

'Oh, all of those would be fine,' Kate said enthusiastically. 'David said we had to get at least a minute of each voice. More if possible.'

'Why did I ever suggest this? It's become a farce,' Liz said mournfully, looking around. 'Are you sure you remember how to set all this up?'

'David wrote out the instructions for me,' Kate said, producing several closely written sheets from her backpack. 'If I can read his writing, that is. He said to call him if I have any problems.'

Liz sighed. 'Why I ever introduced you to him I will never know.'

'If I remember rightly, it was something about going about this in a scientific manner, wasn't it?'

'Yes,' Liz agreed glumly, accepting responsibility and standing up to the challenge. 'Well, come on, the sooner we rig all this up the sooner it will be over.'

'No, the sooner we can begin,' Kate said with a gleam in her eye. 'Whoever you are, out there, with the vicious mouth – we're gonna getcha.'

'Heigh-ho Silver,' Liz muttered.

'The difficulty is that orderlies go all over the hospital,' the personnel woman said. 'Are you sure it had something to do with his work here?' This seemed to distress her more than Ricky's death.

'No, not at all,' Pinsky said, sitting back in his chair. He had come without an appointment and made free use of his badge. The only risk was running into Jackson or Sloman, but he didn't think that was very likely. He knew they had already moved the Sanchez case down on their list. As he had expected. 'It was just an idea. We know he had been troubled about something lately.'

'This killing . . . are you saying it was deliberate?'

'He was robbed,' Pinsky admitted.

She looked triumphant. 'Well, then,' she said, as if all had been explained.

Pinsky sighed and pressed on. 'Anybody who watches television knows enough to try to make a murder look like a robbery. It could have been a sudden outburst of temper, spur-of-the-moment kind of thing . . . we're just looking for anything that might be relevant.'

'A hospital this size is like a small city,' the woman said. The sign on her desk read Penelope Witten and she wore no wedding ring. She was about fifty, dressed in a mannish suit but also in a frilly blouse, her hair scraped into a very tight bun that seemed to draw the skin back from her bones. Her mouth was large and she wore bright-red lipstick. Pinsky kept watching her mouth, he couldn't help it. It seemed to have a life of its own, twisting and pursing as she spoke. 'We have many departments, hundreds of employees, incredible amounts of machinery and thousands of patients, all with their own stories, their own backgrounds. He could have found out about a patient, a member of the maintenance staff, administration, nursing . . .'

'And doctors,' Pinsky finished for her.

'Well, yes,' she admitted. 'But doctors are trained to save lives, not take them.'

'A common fallacy,' Pinsky said and was pleased to see her stiffen. 'Doctors are human beings like the rest of us,' he went on. 'They can be venal, vicious, vulnerable – all the normal things that man is heir to. They are not holy men.'

'Of course you're right,' she said, patently believing he wasn't. 'But professional people have standards. They are trained to control their emotions in the face of the pain and suffering they see constantly. It is rare to have a doctor who expresses much of his feelings day to day.'

'All the more reason to have them burst out at an inconvenient moment,' Pinsky said. 'So you can't tell me where the Sanchez boy worked, specifically?'

'He was assigned to the ER, so naturally he spent a great deal of his time there. It is a chaotic place, of course.' And obviously that rankled with her. No order, no control. Disgusting. Her own office was like a nun's cell: plain, orderly, every surface gleaming, nothing out of place. 'But he would be taking patients all over the hospital to various departments. And would be able to *go* all over the hospital without being questioned.' Obviously an unacceptable situation to Miss Witten.

'Ah,' Pinsky said. 'So you could say he was kind of invisible?'

Although it seemed impossible, her features tightened even more. 'I see what you mean, but I assure you if he was ever in an inappropriate situation, he would have been noticed. There are, of course, many drugs available in a hospital. We have thefts all the time, no matter how carefully we try to control and regulate the drugs. We have had to dismiss people before who had helped themselves to something saleable on the street.'

'And you think that's what Ricky Sanchez was doing? Peddling stolen drugs?' Pinsky was amazed at the leap of reasoning. But of course, this woman would far prefer Ricky Sanchez to be guilty than one of her precious staff. That wouldn't reflect on the hospital; that wouldn't intrude on her carefully guarded world of rectitude and public service.

'Well, I have no reason to think that, of course,' Miss Witten back-pedalled. 'But it *has* happened before. And the world of drugs is a violent one, as we have good reason to know in the ER. Victims of all kinds are brought in every day. We are a public hospital, we treat everyone. Anyone.'

But oh, Pinsky thought, *you wish that they were all from a better class of society, millionaires who would endow out of gratitude instead of losers spitting on the floor out of ingratitude.* She was a piece of work, was Miss Witten. And, he had no doubt, a tough cookie good at her job, if not very well liked. 'So you can't tell me any specific duties that Sanchez would have performed?'

'As I said, he could have gone anywhere in the hospital. Patients from the ER have to be taken up to the operating theatres, up to various wards and so on. Also orderlies are sent on errands to collect and deliver blood, drugs, reports et cetera. They are a very valuable part of the staff and we couldn't run the hospital without them,' Miss Witten said with some pride. 'They are vetted very closely. Sanchez was, too.' She indicated the file on the desk in front of her. 'He came with exemplary references, and we found him to be diligent and reliable.'

'All the more reason to think his killing to be unusual,' Pinsky said.

'No. All the more reason to think his killing an unfortunate accident, the kind that happens every day, I'm sorry to say. We treat the victims of street crime in the ER all the time. You could almost say it was normal.' Miss Witten wasn't going to give an inch. 'I still think it likely to be drug-related.'

'There were no drugs found on him,' Pinsky said.

'Because he had probably sold them,' Miss Witten countered. 'We will do all we can to assist you, of course, but I do think you will find that drugs are behind it, as they are behind so much of violent crime these days.'

'An interesting point of view.'

'One born of bitter experience,' Miss Witten said. 'I had a close friend die of a drug habit that got out of hand. She was killed by a dealer to whom she owed more than she could pay. She was made an example. The man still thrives.'

Ah, thought Pinsky. Ah.

Miss Witten stood up. 'I will see you are issued with the proper identification to allow you to go anywhere in the hospital and speak to whom you like. But I must ask you to try not to interfere with the efficient running of the various departments.'

Pinsky stood, too, relieved that his bluff had worked. 'I'll try to be quick and discreet,' he promised. And added to himself, *I'll interfere if I have to, lady. I'm sorry for your loss, but I've got a killer to find. If he's here in your kingdom I'll get him. No matter who he might be.*

Or, he amended, she.

'They've located the husband,' Neilson said, hanging up the phone. 'He was in Indianapolis, on a selling trip.'

Joe Muller looked confused. 'What husband?'

Neilson sighed. 'Professor Mayhew's husband. Remember? The lady professor who got shot in the eye in the bedroom in the early hours of two days ago? The case we're supposed to be on?' He spoke rather bitterly.

He had not taken it well when, the previous day, Stryker had told him that he would be taking on Muller as his partner while Ned was on leave. 'But why?' he'd demanded. 'He's a rookie, this is a big case.'

'Because he needs to get his feet wet,' Stryker had said. 'He can't sit around on his ass reading old cases for ever. He'll be fine, you'll see. And he can learn a lot from you.'

Hah, Neilson had thought. *A little snake oil for the squeaking wheel.*

93

He glowered down at Muller, whose brain seemed to be picking up speed.

'Oh,' said Muller. '*That* husband.'

'Yes, that husband. They're bringing him back to Grantham this afternoon. He's not a happy man. He *says* he didn't kill his wife.'

'What else would you expect him to say? That he did it and he's glad?' Muller asked, not quite innocently.

'Very funny,' Neilson snapped. He missed Pinsky already, felt oddly off balance without him. He hoped he would be back soon. Stryker had said he was taking a few days' leave to rest. Neilson knew better and he had a feeling Stryker knew better, too. Ned was going to follow up on the Sanchez kid himself.

He could get into big trouble if it got back to Fineman. But it was his own time and, as long as he didn't abuse the badge, it should be OK. Neilson smiled wryly to himself as he led Muller out to watch Stryker and Tos interview Professor Mayhew's husband. They would stand in the room beside the one-way mirror and Muller would have his first lesson in interrogation.

Ned was good at interrogation. Ned would abuse the badge and anything else to get at the truth. As far as Ricky Sanchez went, guilt was driving him. While it was, his normal stubbornness was magnified beyond control. He'd find the truth if it was there.

Ned Pinsky. Avenging angel.

Was it justified? Neilson didn't know. What he did know was that it was not a very smart thing to do if Ned wanted to earn his pension. Why couldn't he let things rest?

Because he was Pinsky.

Because he knew he was right.

Even if he was wrong.

Donald Mayhew was indeed small, dark and handsome, exactly as his neighbour, Mrs Koslewski, had described him. He was also angry and upset.

'I left on my trip Sunday evening the way I always do,'

he said, shifting in his seat as if his pants were too tight. 'I wasn't here on Monday. I don't know what happened. They tell me my wife is dead and I'm wanted on suspicion of murder and they don't even respect my grief, just throw me in a cell and then drag me back here. I want to see my wife's body because I don't believe it; there has to be a mistake.' He wound down, finally out of breath. His eyes were bloodshot, his voice trembled.

'There is no mistake, Mr Mayhew. Your wife's body was identified by a work colleague and a neighbour, but of course we would like your corroboration as well,' Stryker said calmly.

'My wife is dead, you say my wife is dead. Isn't that bad enough? I can't believe this is happening to me. Why would I want to kill her? I loved Elise.' Mayhew was extremely rattled, going from not believing his wife was dead to accepting it as a fact even though he hadn't yet seen the body. Obviously the night in an Indianapolis police cell had had its effect – his clothes were wrinkled and he had a day's growth of beard. Oddly enough, this gave him a more macho aspect than his delicate features would otherwise have indicated. His hair was thick and in considerable disarray. He looked like a male model for one of the more expensive aftershaves. He slumped into one of the chairs around the table. There was a silence while they assessed one another.

'Look,' Mayhew said after a minute. He had taken several deep breaths, but his voice was still unsteady and sounded odd in the bare interview room. 'Could you just tell me what happened?'

'You tell us,' Stryker suggested.

'But I wasn't *there*,' Mayhew repeated. 'Jesus, can't you get that through your heads? I was in Dayton all of Monday. I got there Sunday night so I could start fresh in the morning. I always do that.'

'Leave the night before, you mean?' Tos asked.

'Yes, yes. I'd run my usual circuit for several days and then after my last appointment I would drive straight home on the last day, no matter where I was. It's a routine I've always followed.' He shifted in his chair, looked from Stryker to Toscarelli. 'Listen, can I see my wife's body, please?'

'In a while, Mr Mayhew,' Stryker said. 'Let's just go over your movements from Sunday night, all right? In detail.'

Mayhew buried his face in his hands, then ran them through his hair, tumbling it about even further. A cowlick stood up on top and another fell over his forehead. Behind the one-way glass, Neilson marvelled at it – no matter what he did, the guy looked better and better. Except that he was very pale, very agitated and very, very strained. Very fashionable – definitely on for that dissipated European appearance they seemed to feature in all the ads.

'Can I have a cigarette?' Mayhew asked plaintively.

Tos gave him one from a fresh pack he'd bought that morning. He'd abstained for several years – but he always carried them for just such situations. Tos lit Mayhew's cigarette, then left the pack on the table.

'So, you say you left home on Sunday evening,' Stryker prompted. 'What time?'

'After dinner – around seven. I got to Dayton about ten that night, checked into the hotel, went to bed.'

'Alone.'

'Well of course alone. Three hours' driving in the rain and you expect me to party?' Mayhew asked resentfully. 'Maybe you don't remember, Sunday night was a bitch.'

Neilson remembered. He'd got soaked going from bar to club to a girl's apartment. Monday morning had been nice, though. He wished he could remember the girl's last name so he could call her. He'd written her number down on a napkin, but had lost it. Beside him Muller shifted from one foot to the other, straining forward to hear every word.

'What hotel?' Stryker asked.

Mayhew sighed. 'The Belvedere. I always stay there.'

'So they know you?'

'Yes, they do.'

'How often do you stay there?'

'About once a month or so. I have regular circuits.' He rattled off the names. 'On this one I start in Dayton and work south and west.'

'And what do you sell?' They already knew, of course, having got his travel details from his employer.

'If it's in a doctor's office, I sell it. From paper clips to computers,' Mayhew said. 'Furniture, too. The works. We have a big catalogue, lots of small clients and a few big ones. Mostly it's stationery, that kind of thing, stuff that runs out. But when they want new chairs or examination tables or single-replacement computers, we want them to think of us first. That's why it's important to keep up the contacts. The personal touch. A lot of firms don't bother with that any more, but we do. It pays off.'

Especially if the doctors' office managers are women, Neilson thought. Mayhew had it going both ways – he was handsome and he was small – they either wanted to bed him or mother him, or both. What had some girl told him once? She liked small men because they tried harder. Neilson, of average height and build, came nowhere in comparison. He was not inclined to like Donald Mayhew. Any more than he was inclined to like Muller, who was also small and rather pretty. Muller stood quietly beside him and Neilson gave him a glance before returning his gaze to the interrogation room. Muller was expressionless, making Neilson wonder whether he was awake in there or not.

'So you got up and ate breakfast, and then what?' Stryker persisted.

'I saw customers all morning and a couple after lunch, then it was back on the road again,' Mayhew replied.

'A list would be good,' Stryker said. 'A list of the people you saw would be very helpful.' He pushed a pad and pencil towards Mayhew. 'Write them down and the times you saw them.'

Mayhew suddenly went even paler. 'You're not going to contact them, are you? How's that going to look? I mean, I've built up a relationship with these people, and then you go asking questions because my wife is dead—'

'Because your wife was murdered,' Stryker corrected.

'Oh, God,' said Mayhew and rumpled his hair again.

An hour later they took him to the morgue to identify his wife's body. Fortunately the ruined eye socket was on the far side, away from the viewing window, so the damage wasn't visible. Even so, he moaned at the sight of the body, nearly gave way, but managed to whisper that yes, that was Elise.

'You've got to find out who did this!' he demanded when he'd got his breath back in the ante-room, sitting with his head low between his knees. 'You have to.' His voice sounded odd coming from below them.

'Then you'll have to help us, Mr Mayhew,' Stryker said. 'For instance, I believe Professor Mayhew was in the habit of having students visit your home. Is that right?'

'Yes, she did. She believed in individual tuition for really promising graduate students. She wasn't that far off being a graduate student herself and remembered how some professor had helped her then. She said it was payback time.'

It was an unfortunate choice of words.

'Do you know the names of these students?' Stryker asked.

'Not all of them, offhand. I know one is named Jerry, and another is Lois . . . but there were others. There'll be a list at the office. They all seemed to be nice kids. Oh, except Jerry, who was kind of . . .' He trailed off.

'Kind of what?' Stryker prompted.

'Kind of pushy, edgy . . . she said he was a genius and I guess that was supposed to excuse his bad manners. I didn't much like him, but he was probably OK. Lois was kind of quiet, mousy, but Elise really liked her; said she was a lateral thinker, showed real promise. It didn't show to me, but I didn't know a damn thing about Elise's work so I'm no judge. You'll have to talk to them, I guess. You'll see what I mean.'

'Anybody else used to come to the house?' Tos asked.

'What do you mean?' Mayhew seemed puzzled.

'Other instructors, professors, that kind of thing. Colleagues? Or friends? Did your wife have any special friends?'

Mayhew sat back and frowned. 'What do you mean by "special" friends, exactly?'

'Oh, long-time girlfriends she might have lunch with, confide in, that sort of thing,' Tos explained.

'Oh. I don't know. Maybe. I'm sorry, my mind is kind of everywhere at the moment, I don't know if I'm coming or going. I didn't sleep much last night and now, seeing her . . . it's really true and I still can't believe it. I really can't.'

And the handsome little man began to cry.

ELEVEN

PINSKY HAD TO START SOMEWHERE, so he went to the radiography department which was just down the hall from personnel. He wasn't crazy about hospitals, but it all had to be done. At least there was no blood on X-rays. No disgusting fluids on an MRI. No bleeding wounds, no screaming – well, hardly any: a broken leg can smart a bit, he conceded – but no real visible misery. It was all technical. He liked technical. It had sharp edges and clear lines.

'Can I help you?' asked the girl on the reception desk. She was about thirty, with a trendy hairdo and even features, but wore far too much make-up. Her voice was metallic and quite unpleasant. 'Do you have a pink slip?'

He suppressed the remark he could have made about never wearing anything but black. He produced his warrant card and shield. 'I'd like to talk to the person in charge, please,' he said.

'She's very busy.' The receptionist was both unimpressed by his credentials and annoyed that he had no pink slip or any other important and necessary piece of paper that she could stamp, file, clip, pierce or otherwise deal with. 'You'll have to wait.'

'Fine.'

'I'll tell her you want to talk to her.'

'Fine.'

'You can sit over there,' she said, waving towards some rather uncomfortable-looking chrome and plastic chairs lined up against the wall.

'Fine,' Pinsky repeated. He had no illusions that this gorgon, for all her youth and good looks, was going to facilitate his interview with any speed whatsoever. Which was fine, as he had said. It would give him a chance to observe her. And the others. Because while he sat there, orderlies came and orderlies lingered and orderlies left, some with patients, some with papers, some with no visible means of support. Just hanging around, looking and listening.

Just as Ricky might have done.

Next Pinsky tried a medical ward. That meant nurses, lots and lots of nurses. Coming, as he did, from a household that included three women (his wife, his daughter and his mother who lived in a granny flat attached to the house), he felt comfortable with nurses who were mostly women after all. But trying to catch one and to make her stand still and talk to him was like trying to catch butter-flies with a torn net. The white-uniformed creatures squeaked past him on rubber soles, hurrying here, hurrying there, all with the intent expressions of someone on a life-or-death mission, even if it was only with a bedpan.

He finally caught one who, for a brief moment, looked unoccupied. He introduced himself and asked about Ricky Sanchez.

'I'm afraid I don't know anyone of that name. Is he a patient?'

'No, he was an orderly.'

'Oh.'

'He was killed yesterday – you might have noticed it in the papers this morning.'

'I'm about to come off night duty. I don't read news-papers. You say he was killed?' She was a heavy-set woman with greying hair cut short and piercing blue eyes.

'That's right. And we're trying to trace his recent move-ments in the hospital.'

The woman snorted. 'Good luck. They're everywhere,

101

those orderlies, unless you need one. Then – they disappear.'

Pinsky produced a picture of Ricky, supplied by Denise. It was a good likeness of the boy, it showed him to advantage. But the nurse shook her head. 'Listen, they all look alike, orderlies. They come, they go . . . some work only for a while, others you do get to know a little . . . but if he worked mostly in the ER like you say, we wouldn't have seen much of him here. Sorry.'

And that was the story with most of the other nurses, too. It was daunting. Until he came across Agnes Morton.

'Oh, Ricky. Sure, I know him. You say he's dead?' She seemed very shocked. She was a woman in her late forties, still fairly attractive, blonde, a little scattered in her manner.

'Yes, he was murdered.'

'Oh, dear God,' she said, horrified. 'He was a nice kid. I got to know him because he helped me with the computer – I just couldn't get the hang of it and he spent about an hour with me once until it made sense. It was real nice of him, don't you think?'

'Don't they teach you about the computers in nursing school?'

'Back then they taught us about nursing,' Agnes said. 'The new young nurses are clued up, but us older ones, we're expected to just *know*.' She grimaced, wrinkling up the freckles on her nose. 'I only came back to nursing a year ago. I guess I'm just kind of slow on the uptake. I have a lot of trouble with all the new equipment, too. I get there, but it takes me longer than the others. I think I was meant to be born in a different century or something.' She grinned. 'You know, past lives and all that.'

'But you knew Ricky Sanchez,' Pinsky persisted.

'Yeah, like I said. He was real nice to me.' She sighed. 'It's sad he got killed. Was he shot?' She seemed to take a professional interest in the method used.

'No, hit on the head with something,' Pinsky said a little impatiently. Her question seemed a bit ghoulish to him. 'At least, that's how it looks. We're waiting for the PM.'

'Sometimes they find other stuff,' Agnes told him sagely. 'Like in Agatha Christie . . . some slow-acting poison or like that. Drugs, maybe. His hair wasn't falling out, was it?'

'What?'

'Oh, it was in one of her mysteries, how nobody knew why someone was dying but it was thallium poisoning. See, there was this nurse who noticed . . .'

'His hair was fine,' Pinsky said hurriedly. She was one of the most difficult kind of witnesses to interview, the kind who read lots of murder mysteries, and were full of half-baked theories and convinced of their own expertise in detection. They took longer to deal with than all the others put together. At least this one seemed to favour Agatha Christie. The traditionalists weren't too bad as they tended to be fairly simplistic in their outlook and favoured motive over opportunity or method. It was the ones who read the current forensic best-sellers who were the worst. They 'knew' all the latest jargon, the equipment, the tests, everything. It was daunting – a lot of them knew more than he did about it. 'His skull was shattered,' he said. 'Pretty straightfor-ward.'

'Oh.' She seemed a bit disappointed, but she also seemed to genuinely regret Ricky's death, which helped him like her a little better. He was working on autopilot at the moment, trying to forget Ricky as the boy he knew and to think of him as 'the victim'. It helped, gave him a little distance. But he was still full of guilt inside, and grief, and anger. It didn't help his work, he knew, but he couldn't help it. The best he could do was to keep trying to suppress it, at least while he was working.

'Do you know if he was particularly friendly with any of the other nurses?' Pinsky enquired, before she could start asking about the weapon and vouchsafing more theories.

'I don't know. I met him when he brought up a case from the ER when I was practically in tears with this computer, and he noticed and came over. That was all.'

That sounded like Ricky, Pinsky thought. He wouldn't have liked to see a woman in tears. Not if he could help. 'He was good with the computer, was he?' he asked.

'Oh, an absolute whizz,' she said. 'And he explained it really well. I felt ever so much better about it after that. It didn't scare me any more, see? He made me realize how it was just a machine, and my slave, really. It did what I told it to do; it didn't do anything it hadn't been told to do. It was just like a parrot, sort of. Of course, if someone put in the wrong things to do, it would mess up . . .'

Pinsky knew very little about computers. He could just about manage to use the one at work, but mostly he left it to the support staff and secretaries. 'Have you ever seen Ricky anywhere else in the hospital?' he asked.

She seemed confused. 'I don't go anywhere else in the hospital,' she said. 'Except the cafeteria and occasionally X-ray. I have seen him in the cafeteria sometimes, if I was on a late duty. He worked late afternoons and evenings, I think. He was going to school, he told me. He was pre-med.' From her expression this seemed to confer some kind of special status on Ricky Sanchez. 'Doctor-in-becoming.

'Did you notice if he always ate with the same people?' Pinsky asked. 'Or what?'

'Mostly he ate with a book on the side,' she said. 'I mean, I didn't see him all that often down there, but it was always with a book. Oh, no – once I saw him with some girl from the pathology lab, a phlebotomist.'

'A what?' Pinsky was completely thrown by this weird word.

'A phlebotomist – a blood taker,' Agnes explained. 'They come up and take blood from the patients for testing. You know, they have these little trays . . .'

'I see,' said Pinsky, feeling a little unsteady. He hated needles and these people used needles . . .

'But I don't know her name,' Agnes said kindly. 'I'm sorry.'

'Well, you've been a help,' Pinsky said without much conviction. 'Thanks very much.'

'I'll try and find out her name for you,' Agnes offered. 'One of the other nurses might know – at least her first name, anyway. I never noticed.'

'We appreciate any information you can give us,' Pinsky said formally, wanting to go someplace where there was a chair and maybe even coffee. The problem was huge. It was all beginning to get to him.

Phlebotomist?

Jeesh.

Pinsky located the chief resident of the ER in the staff lounge, where he was dozing on a couch, an empty coffee mug held loosely in his hand and resting on his stomach. It was fortunate he had emptied it before falling asleep, Pinsky thought.

'Dr Waxman?'

Waxman sat up as if he'd been hit with a cattle prod. 'I'm here, what is it?' He looked up at Pinsky, then re-adjusted his wire-rimmed glasses which had moved a little off-centre. 'You're not supposed to be in here. Staff only. You'll have to—'

Pinsky held up his ID and flashed the gold badge. 'I'd like to talk to you about Ricky Sanchez,' he said.

'What?'

'About Ricky Sanchez. He was an orderly here and he was—'

'Oh, right, right,' Waxman said, rubbing his temples. 'Sorry. Yes, Ricky. What about him?' He swung his legs down and sat up. Pinsky pulled over a chair from the table in the centre.

'My name is Ned Pinsky. I answered the call on his murder. I'm also a friend of the family. Ricky was badly

105

worried about something over the past week or so and before he died he called me about it. I think he found out something that got him killed.'

'Whoa, wait a minute,' Waxman said, putting up a hand. He squinted at Pinsky through his glasses, as if they weren't helping him to focus. 'The officer who came the other day didn't say anything about this. Are you saying Ricky wasn't mugged?'

'I am,' Pinsky said firmly. 'He phoned me and said he knew something that might destroy a career.'

'A medical career?'

'He didn't specify,' Pinsky admitted.

'I need more coffee,' Waxman said, getting up with a grunt. 'Want some?'

'Yes, thanks.'

When they were both supplied with liquid stimulant, Waxman eyed Pinsky carefully. 'I want to get this straight. Ricky called you and said he knew something that could ruin somebody's career, you think it was somebody here in the hospital and that Ricky was killed to shut him up?'

Pinsky raised his eyebrows. The guy was sharp. 'That's exactly what I think.'

'And that's what the Police Department thinks?'

'Well . . .'

'Aha,' said Waxman with a grin. 'You're on your own.'

'You're fast,' Pinsky said.

Waxman laughed and shook his head. 'Not really. I watch a lot of TV and read a lot of crime novels. It's my way of relaxing. Normally, if this were official, there would be two of you, right? To act as one another's witness and so on?'

Pinsky smiled ruefully. 'Right.'

'And you would be asking for all kinds of statements.'

'Right again.'

'Hmm.' Waxman leaned back against what remained of the torn upholstery. 'You could get in trouble for this.'

'Damn, you must read a lot,' Pinsky said, not without irony.

'Oh, I'm a real whizz,' Waxman said. 'Actually, if you want the truth, you've got guilty conscience written all over you. You say Ricky called you, but you didn't say you did anything about it.'

Pinsky sighed. 'I didn't,' he admitted. 'I got caught up in something else and I forgot. I expected him to call me back when he knew more details.'

'Bummer,' Waxman said with real sympathy in his voice. 'But what makes you so sure? I mean, people get attacked every day – believe me, I know. We fix up the victims and the crooks – equal time, equal bandages. Ricky could have just been unlucky. The officer who was here yesterday seemed to think that was the case. Just in the wrong place at the wrong time. We get an awful lot of patients from French Street violence.'

'Yes, but why?' Pinsky asked. 'Why was he down on French Street? It's not the kind of place anybody sensible would go at night unless he was a drunk or a drug addict . . . and Ricky was neither.'

'He could have been a drug addict,' Waxman said reluctantly. 'It happens in hospitals . . . the stuff can be got, used, covered up. We try to be as careful as we can, but . . .'

Pinsky shook his head. 'No way. He was working hard, he was getting good grades, he was dating my daughter – all straight.'

'Dating your daughter?' Waxman's eyes widened. 'It gets worse.'

'Yeah,' Pinsky concurred. 'It gets worse.' He gave Waxman some of Ricky's background.

'I must say, I'm surprised your superiors don't listen to what you have to say,' Waxman admitted.

'Oh, they listened. But I was told to lay off because I am emotionally involved and they dropped it on other detectives. My partners are following up a bigger case . . . they have to prioritize.'

'Tell me about it,' Waxman agreed. 'That's the name of the game here too, especially when we get a rush on.'

He considered Pinsky and part of the ceiling, and his coffee mug and his own shoes. 'How can I help you?' he finally asked.

'This is the pathology department,' Dr Waxman said, opening a door and leading Pinsky into a small ante-room. They had been to odontology, oncology, the diabetes clinic, audiology, cardiology. The place had departments Pinsky had never heard of or imagined existed.

In every department Waxman had introduced him and explained why it was important that everyone they spoke to gave their full concentration to the problem. Pinsky was so grateful to him he was nearly in tears inside. Never once did Waxman indicate it was other than an official inquiry.

They went through another door into a very large laboratory with several people at work on various pieces of apparatus. Pinsky recognized a microscope, but that was about the extent of it. It was very quiet in the room, despite all the people in it. 'This is where blood tests and tissue samples are analysed, sometimes against the clock. Say a surgeon will send down a bit of a tumour to be examined while he has a patient open on the table. He'll want to know the status of the tissue before he proceeds, and he won't want to keep the patient anaesthetized any longer than absolutely necessary. So someone has to be prepared to work fast. There are also several research projects going on here, more long-term work, under both government and private grants. This is also where our post-mortem exams are done.' He gestured. 'Through there. Want to see?'

'Not particularly,' Pinsky said. 'When you've seen one post-mortem . . . you know.'

'Oh, I know very well,' Waxman said, amused. 'I passed out twice during my first one. Got dragged out, came back, got dragged out again. Humiliating. But we adjust.'

'Why would Ricky come here?'

'He might have brought blood samples for cross-matching or tissue for testing. He might have wheeled down a dead patient. He might have brought in or taken out reports that someone needed urgently,' Waxman answered. 'All kinds of reasons. This is a big department.' He led Pinsky over to one of the long tables. 'This is the research section. Barney, do you have a minute?'

A small man put down what he was working on and came across. 'Waxman, what the hell are you doing here?' he asked cheerfully. He had an elfin face and ears that stuck out, but his eyes were both compassionate and alert. A thick fuzz of bright-red hair covered his skull, kept short but not controlled. 'Slack time in the ER?'

'Never,' Dr Waxman said. 'This is Detective Sergeant Pinsky.' He turned to Ned. 'Barney Schoenfeld is the head of the big heads around here.'

'Big heads?' Pinsky asked.

'The researchers.' Barney smiled. 'We, of course, call them geniuses, but everybody else has their own rude words. It's because we rarely communicate with the lower orders. It's tough in the ivory tower, but we occasionally come out for coffee.'

'Glad to meet you,' Pinsky said, liking the little man immediately.

'Sergeant Pinsky is investigating Ricky Sanchez's death,' Waxman explained.

'I heard about it. That was a damn shame,' Barney said. 'He was a nice kid.'

'You knew him?' Pinsky asked.

Barney laughed. 'We all knew him. Nosiest kid I ever met. Nice to see, really – he was always collecting information. He was really into pathology, he said. Wanted to go into forensic pathology, or maybe paleopathology—'

'He's dazzling us with footwork.' Waxman grinned. 'Every day that went by, Ricky wanted to do something different. He was very open to suggestion and kept falling in love with different specialities.'

'Yeah,' Barney agreed. 'But it was kind of flattering, too.'

'Which is how he got to know so many people in the hospital,' Waxman said. 'There's nothing like an audience for whatever it is that you do – he made each one he talked to feel like the world's greatest expert.'

'That's for sure,' Barney confirmed. 'Take Forster, over there. Or Duggan. They were crazy about him.' He lowered his voice. 'He was like a pet and everyone tolerated him. But even Sherwin – he even would irritate Sherwin sometimes with all his questions, would you believe, and Sherwin has the patience of a saint. Come and meet them.'

They followed Schoenfeld over to the far corner where a tall, gaunt man was peering into a microscope and making notes – it looked like he was counting, for the notes were all figures.

'Ivan, this is Sergeant Pinsky of the police. Waxman you know.'

Sherwin looked up. 'Sorry, I'm busy,' he said, but he smiled.

'You're always busy,' Barney agreed amiably. 'But do you remember a kid named Ricky Sanchez, always used to come in here?'

'And ask questions,' Sherwin said, his hands straying to the notepad and pencil. They kept moving as he talked, the pencil revolving in his long, thin fingers. 'Very nosy kid.'

'Well, that nosy kid is dead,' Pinsky said abruptly.

Dr Sherwin couldn't have been more than forty-five, judging by his hands, which were neat and well-kept. But he was obviously caught up in his work and his eyes kept going back to his microscope. 'Oh, dear,' he said. He didn't seem particularly interested. 'Too bad.'

'Do you remember anything unusual about him?' Pinsky asked. 'Anything he was particularly nosy about?'

'He wanted to know everything. He'd stop me in the hall, even, to ask some question or other. Not so much lately, though. Which was a relief, to be honest. I'm not good at handling interruptions.' Like this one, he seemed to imply.

'So you don't know what he was interested in, say, last week?' Waxman asked.

'No idea at all. Sorry,' Sherwin said. 'Can I get back to work now? My specimen is drying out.'

'Sorry,' Pinsky echoed and they moved away.

'Sorry about that,' Schoenfeld said. 'He's a nice enough guy, but he's never been what you call sociable. Brilliant in his way. Trouble is, he pushes too hard. Only sees his own point of view. He got turned down for a big grant last month for just that reason. He wanted to go too far, too fast. It happens . . . we get caught up in our subject and think it is the only one worth pursuing.'

'Sometimes we're right,' said an attractive brunette as they came up beside her area. But her smile softened her statement.

'This is Felicity Duggan. She and her partner over there – Jan Forster – are working on the neuropathology of Alzheimer's and Parkinson's.' A blonde woman further down the bench waved vaguely as she pored over what looked like skull scans against a light box on the wall. 'This is Sergeant Pinsky, Felicity. He's working on the homicide of Ricky Sanchez.'

Dr Duggan's eyes filled with tears, but she kept them from overflowing. 'He was a lovely boy,' she said. 'Always so interested in everything we were doing. Encouraging, too. I liked it when he asked questions . . .' She smiled at Pinsky. 'We all like to talk about our work. If someone shows the least interest we're off and running.'

'Speak for yourself,' came a hoarse and amused voice from the other end of the bench. 'I'd rather do it than talk about it,' added Jan Forster, unclipping the sheets of acetate from the light box and switching it off. 'You'd talk to him for hours and we'd get behind . . .'

Felicity blushed. 'He was a handsome boy and . . . well, I had a soft spot for him, I admit it. He was so enthusiastic. He reminded me of when I started out.'

'Before you became old and raddled and cynical,' commented Dr Forster, putting down her negatives and coming up to them.

'True.' Felicity laughed. Then she frowned again. 'It was terrible, what happened to Ricky. Working late hours . . . I suppose none of us is safe on the streets any more.'

'He wasn't just mugged,' Pinsky said.

She looked surprised, as did her partner. They exchanged a glance. 'But I thought—'

'It was personal. It was murder.' Pinsky used the word like a club – it was often effective. Mostly because he believed it so intensely himself.

'Good God,' Dr Forster said. 'Are you serious?'

'I'm afraid so,' Pinsky said. 'I think whoever attacked him meant to kill him.'

'But why?' Dr Duggan asked.

'Probably to stop him asking questions,' Pinsky told her.

'Oh, no.' Felicity Duggan shook her head. 'Surely not. Maybe it was over a girl, or . . .'

'We're looking into all the possibilities,' Pinsky said quickly. 'Whatever the reason for his death was, we'll find it.'

'Oh, I hope so,' Felicity said and her partner nodded agreement. 'If there's anything we can do . . .'

'We'll let you know.'

As they walked away, Pinsky looked at Schoenfeld. 'Are they any good at what they do?'

'Why do you ask?' Schoenfeld seemed startled.

'Well, they're so . . . ordinary. And attractive.'

'Chauvinist,' Waxman accused. 'They happen to be two of the best researchers we have – right, Barney?'

'Right,' Schoenfeld agreed. He led them to another bench. A very small, very old man was crouched over a very large ring-binder. 'Here's another example of deceptive beauty.' He grinned. 'Dr Leo Wesjici. He's just a kid, of course, but we have high hopes for him.'

'You jest, you terrible man,' said Dr Wesjici. 'It is true I am only twenty-eight, but I work hard. It takes its toll.'

'Dr Wesjici is working on diabetes research,' Schoenfeld explained.

'Really? I know someone who has diabetes,' Pinsky said, thinking of Sheriff Matt Gabriel in Blackwater Bay.

'You probably know more than one,' Dr Wesjici said. 'There are literally millions undiagnosed, leading to other things – kidney failure, heart problems . . . it is a bad thing. A sneaky thing.'

'Did you know Ricky Sanchez?' Pinsky asked.

'The Question Master?' Dr Wesjici chuckled. 'That's what I called him. A very intelligent boy. He made one or two remarks that were very insightful. He was only pre-med, but a very, very smart boy. He read way beyond his assignments. We lost a good one there.'

'Did he ever seem worried to you?' asked Pinsky. 'Interested in anything specific lately?'

The old man thought for a moment. 'He had a lot of questions about bones. Whether diabetes would show up in the bones, leave its mark as it were.'

'Would it?' asked Waxman.

Wesjici shrugged. 'It was an interesting question. It got me thinking . . .'

'You never stop thinking,' Schoenfeld said affectionately. He glanced at the others. 'He doesn't work here any more, you know. Officially retired years ago. He just drops in every single day to use the library. Nobody pays him, he just keeps on going.'

Dr Wesjici shrugged. 'Money I got, time I don't. Nice meeting you, Sergeant Pinsky. If you want to know about diabetes, I'm your man.'

'I'll bear that in mind.' Pinsky smiled. As they walked away he spoke in a low voice to the other two. 'He comes in unpaid? He's that serious?'

'We're all pretty serious here,' Barney said. 'So many diseases, so many possibilities . . . so many failures. And only so many grants to go round, hey, Waxman? I hear

113

you got turned down for one a while back.'

'So I did,' Waxman agreed. 'But I have a line on another source, so it's just a matter of plugging away.'

'Research depends on money, it's as simple as that,' Barney explained, gesturing around. 'This is a city hospital. We all have our regular work to do and it comes first. But our own research is funded by outside money as the hospital never has any to spare. It supplies the facilities, which are costly enough, because of the prestige our research gains for it. But there's never enough room, never enough of anything. Gets you down.'

'Amen,' Waxman echoed.

'You mean you do other work in addition to your hospital work?'

'Sure. You don't think we're in this for what they pay us, do you?' Barney said. 'Hospital doctors do not get big money. Our only hope of rising in the world is to discover something – a cure, a treatment – we could patent and sell. Meanwhile we do the blood counts, the tissue analysis, the post-mortems – all of it. When we can snatch a moment for our own work, we do.'

Waxman cleared his throat. 'Barney is working on leprosy. You're not going to get rich on a leprosy cure, Barney.' He turned to Pinsky. 'Ask him why.'

'Why?' Pinsky dutifully asked.

'Because it's a rotten disease that still strikes the poorest people in the poorest parts of the world and somebody has to do something,' Barney said in a suddenly urgent voice. 'There's no glamour in it and, God knows, no money, but if you ever saw . . . ever knew . . .'

'Barney was in the Peace Corps,' Dan Waxman said. 'He saw a lot of leprosy. It marked him, if you'll pardon the pun.'

Barney flushed. 'Don't kid around, Waxman.'

'I'm not,' Dan said with respect. 'I just wanted Sergeant Pinsky to know that money isn't always the goal, OK, Barney? Some people still do stuff because they care. Like you, like Leo Wesjici.'

114

'Tell that to some of the others,' Barney muttered. 'They've all got dollar signs in their eyes.'

'Not Sherwin,' Waxman said.

'No, maybe not. Hard to tell with him. His brother died of AIDS and I guess that was enough. But the big money in research today is in AIDS, unfortunately.'

'Unfortunately?' Pinsky asked, surprised.

'It's a terrible disease, I'll grant you,' Barney said. 'But its incidence is still small compared with heart, cancer, stroke, Alzheimer's . . . they all need that kind of funding if we're going to get anywhere with them. But no – it's all red ribbons and AIDS that the stars and the politicians get excited about. Makes you sick . . . ha ha.'

'Forster and Duggan are working on Alzheimer's,' Waxman explained. 'Murphy over there is working on colonic cancer.' He looked around. 'Where's Fitz?'

'Out sick,' Schoenfeld said. 'He phoned in and said he was dying, by which we assume he has a slight cold. Fitz is a hypochondriac,' he explained to Pinsky. 'All pathologists are a little hypochondriacal. It goes with the territory.'

'We have a pretty good record here for research, considering we are a city hospital,' Waxman continued. 'Mostly due to Barney, here, who gets the grants and does the donkey work for everyone else. You do good, Barney.'

'Yeah. But mostly I do blood counts.' Barney grinned, trying to get out from under Waxman's serious praise. 'What we could really use in here is more technicians.'

'I'll bring it up at the next medical board,' Waxman promised.

'Like hell,' Barney said. 'You've got your own corner to fight. ER is like a bottomless pit for funding.'

'Amen,' Waxman said. 'Do you mind if we look around?'

'Be my guest.' Barney waved a gracious arm. 'We have nothing to hide.'

Waxman took Pinsky around the department, as he had in others, introducing him to staff. From there they went to three further departments, before heading back to the ER and some more coffee in the staff lounge. Pinsky was very grateful to Waxman for giving him so much of his obviously valuable time.

Waxman shrugged. 'My shift was over anyway. I'm not on until tomorrow night now. And I liked Ricky, you know. I liked him a lot.'

'This is getting more and more difficult,' Pinsky said, settling down at the battered table that took up most of the centre of the shabby room. The furniture was a collection of cast-offs from waiting rooms around the building that had gone past being seen in public. There were two couches, the table in the middle with no two chairs alike and built-in cabinets all around the edge of the room, most of them with broken doors. Assorted medical equipment was shoved willy-nilly into nooks and crannies, storage space apparently being at a premium everywhere. Pinsky looked at Dr Waxman over the edge of his coffee mug, while Waxman slumped on one of the couches. 'Ricky seems to have gone everywhere and might have seen anything. Would he have known what he saw or heard?'

Waxman sighed, his own coffee mug riding up and down where it rested on his abdomen. 'In Ricky's case, probably. That's the trouble, isn't it? The boy was too smart for his own good. In this department alone he could have noticed a lazy intern who was fudging results, although I can't think who that would be, frankly, they all bust their butts out there. He could have noticed samples being mixed up or mislabelled, or somebody stealing drugs, or something a rushed examination missed, or he could have overheard something a patient said—'

'Enough, enough.' Pinsky held up a defensive hand. He suddenly felt overwhelmed. He had thought it would be easy, but he was already in over his head. Investigating the hospital was like investigating an entire small town. And if he saw something wrong he would have no idea

116

what he was looking at. It was hopeless. 'To find out what Ricky found out – if he found out anything at all – I'd have to be as smart as he was. To know as much about medicine as he did . . . it's impossible.'

'I see what you mean.' Waxman nodded. 'I don't know what to suggest.'

'I don't suppose you'd help me out, would you?' Pinsky asked.

'Me?' Waxman looked astonished and sat up a little.

'Yes. I know you're busy—'

'You haven't seen the half of it,' Waxman said. 'You ought to be in the ER when things are really going . . .'

'I have,' said Pinsky ruefully. 'Been shot, knifed and beaten up – not all at once, mind you. I've seen how this place resembles the monkey house at the zoo sometimes. The point is, I'm out of my depth here.'

'What you're saying is you want me to go around the hospital doing a private investigation?' Waxman asked, a half-smile on his face. 'A medical private eye?' The idea seemed to appeal to him.

'Yes,' Pinsky confirmed. 'Of course, there is always the possibility that *you* killed him, in which case . . .'

'Thanks a lot,' Waxman said wryly.

'In which case you would do your best to cover up the reason,' Pinsky continued inexorably. He didn't believe it for a minute. As he instinctively knew Ricky had been murdered deliberately, so he judged Dr Dan Waxman to be worthy of trust.

'So if I found something I would be a hero, but if I didn't seem to find anything I'd be a suspect?' Waxman finished his coffee and stood up to get a refill. He lifted his mug in a silent question.

Pinsky shook his head. 'I guess you would.' He moved his mug around the table, matching it to the various rings left behind by coffee drinkers before him. 'Sounds bad, doesn't it?'

'Sure as hell does.' Waxman tilted his head and looked at Pinsky quizzically. 'The trouble is, I don't have all that much opportunity to roam and ask questions. And I know these people personally, most of them.'

'Which is an advantage. Do you like all of them?'

'No, of course not. Which might affect my judgement.'

'It was just a thought,' Pinsky said reluctantly. 'Sorry – it's asking too much.'

'On the other hand, someone killed Ricky, so something is obviously wrong. I can't condone that, can I?'

'I don't know. Can you? I know there are a lot of grey areas in medicine, especially where ethics are concerned. The value of the one as against the value of hundreds and stuff like that.'

'Oh, yeah,' Waxman said. 'I know all about that, believe me. I've had to sew up many a criminal, knowing what he'd done to the victim in the next cubicle. What he might do again once he was back on the street. It's not easy. We just have to leave moral questions to others, get on with the job and try not to think about it at night. I've had to treat cop killers, rapists, paedophiles, you name it. My only business is preserving life, Sergeant, no matter whose it is.'

'So if you found a doctor who was . . . I don't know . . . killing patients through incompetence, say, would you report him?'

'To my peers, yes. To you, probably not,' Waxman admitted. 'Not right away, anyhow. There are procedures for that one.'

'But that might be exactly the kind of thing Ricky noticed?'

Waxman nodded. 'It could be something like that.'

'And would he have known who to turn to about it?'

Waxman sighed. 'Probably not. And so he would have spoken to the person directly and . . .' He pondered the point. 'I see why it's bothering you. I don't think that would be enough to kill for, though, you know. You can argue back about apparent incompetence, make a case for Ricky being untrained . . .'

'So it would be something more?'

'I think so.'

'And if so, something worth blowing the whistle on?'

'Yes.' Waxman walked away a few steps, hit his hand gently against the table edge, walked back. 'I'll look around. I'll see if I can see what Ricky saw.'

'Thank you,' Pinsky said gratefully. 'But be careful.'

'Danger is my middle name.'

'How reassuring for your patients.'

TWELVE

'WELL, THAT'S A WRONG ONE,' Kate said, hanging up the phone and stopping the recording. 'Turns out P. Fancher is a woman. Our friendly monster is definitely male.'

'Some women have deep voices,' Liz pointed out.

'Not that one. She chirped at me.'

'Who's next?'

'Um . . .' Kate ran her finger down the list. 'Fitt, Oscar.'

'You want me to take this one?'

'No, thanks. I'll do it. I might recognize the voice right off.'

'You'll be lucky.'

Kate was dialling. Her face assumed a serious expression, much to Liz's amusement. Kate acted with her whole self, which was why she was not much good at prevarication. So far, however, she was doing OK. 'Professor Fitt? Good morning. This is Mrs Dowling in the bursar's office.'

'That's a new one,' muttered Liz.

'How are you today? That's good. We're trying to assess class loads this year – how many classes are you teaching this semester? Yes, I know we should have a record, but the paperwork hasn't come through yet. Yes. Yes. Well, that seems reasonable to me, does it seem so to you? Uh-huh. And are any of them giving you trouble? Any difficult students? Fine. So you're quite happy? I'm so glad. Thank you very much. Goodbye.'

'Let's see now, you were just from the bursar's office, you have been doing a survey on student unrest, you've tried selling insurance – that was a bust – and you've been

120

an old student trying to get a recommendation. What's next?'

'Well, I can't use the same excuse for all of them, can I?' Kate protested. 'Word would get around – "Have you heard from that woman . . . Have you been bothered by . . ." and so on. They do talk to one another.'

'Not your guy, I'd bet,' Liz countered. 'I bet he's a loner, crouched over his telephone, spewing his poison.'

'What a picture,' Kate said.

'Class load is a good idea, though,' Liz continued. 'I mean, he must have plenty of time on his hands, you should pardon the expression. Maybe he's a research fellow rather than a teacher.'

'Interesting point.' Kate stood up and stretched. 'Want some coffee?'

'Always,' said Liz, also standing. 'Let me get it. You try one more.'

'Oh, heck,' Kate complained, sitting down again. 'I thought I might get a break.'

'You will – after one more,' Liz directed as she headed towards the kitchen. She had seen that the initial novelty of this approach had been wearing a little thinner with every call. Kate was a great enthusiast and a great starter, but a bad finisher. She needed encouragement to persevere.

After a minute, as she filled the coffee maker, Liz could hear Kate's voice from the front room. 'Professor Gumbaugh? Good morning, I'm lucky to catch you in. How are you today? Oh, this is Mary Toogood, I'm a stringer for the *BMJ* here in Grantham. Yes, the *British Medical Journal*, that's right. We do like to keep up with foreign news, too. Could you tell me what you're currently researching? Oh, really? That's very topical, isn't it? No, of course I wouldn't expect to know details, just the general gist of what you're looking into . . . it's for a survey, you see. No names, of course. What size classes do you have? Do you work with individual students? Does that leave you much time for your own work?'

Liz grinned and began to search the cupboards for some cookies. Kate needed to keep up her strength.

Until they checked out Mayhew's movements for Sunday and Monday, Stryker had no official reason to hold him and he was released with instructions to stay in the city. He asked about his car and Tos said that they would arrange for its return from Indianapolis. Meanwhile he could use his wife's car. They drove him home and took him in. The master bedroom was still taped off and sealed, but he said he would sleep in the guest room. He seemed too exhausted to do much else. They left him to it, watched him carrying his suitcase into the guest room as if he were only a visitor as in all the hotels he frequented on his selling trips.

'So,' Tos said. 'Not as straightforward as we thought, is it? I believe him. Do you? Do you think he killed his wife?'

Stryker shook his head. 'I don't know. I don't think so, but it's possible. He could have driven back here instead of going south, shot her, then continued south during the night. Depends on what time he checked into the hotel. Or he could have checked in, then driven back from Dayton, shot her, and returned to the hotel by the morning and come down for breakfast as usual. Those big hotels don't notice much and if he took his key with him he'd have no reason to speak to reception, would he? It's possible. Maybe Indianapolis can get a mileage reading for us and we can work backwards . . . if we can find out what it was when he started.'

'We're going to have to check it all out,' Tos said, starting up the car. 'It's going to be a long haul.'

Stryker agreed. 'We'll have to interview all her grad students, her colleagues . . .'

'Old girlfriends or boyfriends,' Tos added. 'Routine, all of it, and all of it necessary. Someone argued with Elise Mayhew and shot her. If it wasn't her husband, who the hell was it?'

'Santa Claus,' Stryker suggested.

'Too early,' Tos said. 'He's still building toys up north. Try again.'

'The Easter Bunny.'

'Recharging his batteries.'

'Oh, shit,' Stryker said. 'We can't cover all this by ourselves. We'll have to give more of it to Neilson and Muller.'

'What do you make of Muller?' Tos asked, curious.

Stryker shrugged. 'He listens, which is a very good start. I don't know how he'll hit it off with Neilson, who is a bit of a firework himself. Ned used to keep him under control. Now Neilson has to be top dog. I'm hoping it will steady him to have a rookie to look after.'

'Interesting,' Tos said neutrally.

Stryker glanced over at him. 'You don't approve?'

'Hell, you're the boss, Jack. Muller looks good enough to me. Maybe more than good enough. You sure Neilson will stay on top of him? Maybe it will be the other way round. Muller is a quiet one. You have to watch the quiet ones.'

Stryker smiled. 'I know.' He frowned. 'Don't really know what to make of him yet. Sometimes I get the impression he knows a lot more than he lets on.' He shrugged. 'Meanwhile, we just have to go on a step at a time, one foot in front of the other. For all the easy ones we wrap up in hours there have to be some stinkers in the pack and this Mayhew case is one of them. We'll walk the walk, we'll talk the talk. We'll get there in the end.'

'By which time we'll be old and broken,' Tos said.

'Hell, no. That's just how we start out.'

Pinsky was dejected about his experience at the hospital. So he decided to approach it from a different angle and went down to French Street to see if he could get any information. He had no luck there, either. They spotted he was a cop straight off, or worse, some kind of social

123

worker. Either way they gave him nothing at all. He decided to go to Mike Rivera.

Mike had worked French Street off and on for years. His undercover identity was so good the story went that he dropped back there now and again on his own time just to maintain it. Nobody on French Street questioned that he disappeared for months at a time. They all did it, chasing the warm weather, maybe trying to dry out in a detox programme, perhaps stuck in jail or hospital. But Mike kept his hand in and his ears in, too. He had picked up a lot of stuff on French Street, aside from the dirt and the lice. But when Pinsky enquired he found he was on vacation. He was also told Mike had moved recently and no longer lived in the fairly decent rooming house that had been his home for the past two years.

To Pinsky's amazement, Rivera now had a condo in one of the flashy new buildings downtown, overlooking the river. It had a balcony and that was where Rivera had been sitting when Pinsky arrived. He got Ned a beer to match his own and led him back out on to the balcony.

'How the hell did you rate this?' Pinsky asked, sitting down on one of the chairs placed either side of a fancy wrought-iron table. Far below, the river glittered like a silver snake and one of the big container ships moved slowly along towards the bridge.

'I inherited it,' Mike said. 'Out of the blue. My grand-mother owned it, rented it out. I didn't know about it, none of us did until she died. We always wondered where she got her money from, because she lived pretty comfort-ably. We still have no idea when she got this place. But she willed it to me, to make up for . . . well, the divorce and everything, I guess. She always had a soft spot for me. The others got cash – they're all settled with fami-lies – but I got this and no mortgage, either. Pretty nice, hey?'

'The taxes must be high,' Pinsky observed.

'Worth every penny,' Mike said. 'I think it's why I haven't been so eager to go down on the street for the

124

past six months. I find the river so interesting – always something going by.'

The afternoon was warmer than it had been recently and the view was everything Mike said it was. Pinsky sighed. 'Lucky bastard.'

'Yeah.' Mike grinned. 'I know. But I'm worth it,' he said in imitation of the cosmetic ad.

Yes, you are, Pinsky thought. For Mike had had a rough time over the past few years, losing a child, then a wife. Sometimes things balance up. Quietly, carefully, he outlined his problem.

'What was the kid doing on French Street?' Mike asked immediately.

'That's part of the problem,' Pinsky explained. 'I don't know if he had some reason for being there, or if he was just unlucky. Of course, nobody will talk to me. I need someone like you – hell, I need *you* – to go down there and find out what's going on, if anything.'

Mike scowled. 'It's been a while.'

There was a moment of silence.

'Are you doing OK, Mike?' Pinsky asked. He sensed a change in Rivera, a sadness, a reluctance.

Rivera shrugged. 'Doing better since I got this place.' He chuckled. 'That old grandma of mine was a doozy. Do you know she was worth over three million when they totted it all up? Played the market, apparently. Bought property, stuff like that. But she must have known the end was nigh, as they say, because she sold up a lot of stuff a few months before she died, put it all in the bank. Just kept this place for me – like she knew I needed a home. And I did. It's changed me, having a place like this. I don't know how much longer I can go down on the street like I used to. Guess I'm getting old.'

'How long until retirement?' Pinsky asked.

Rivera shrugged. 'Could take it in five, could go on another ten. Up to me, really. My captain said he wants me to stay, but I don't know. It's not the same any more for me. I can't get into it like I did.' By 'it' he meant his alternative street persona. 'Here, come and see this.'

He got up and Ned followed him into one of the bedrooms – the place had three. This one had no furniture but contained only two black plastic refuse sacks. Rivera opened one and a sudden smell of decay and dirt rose into the freshness of the room, defiling it. 'Would you like to live here and then change into these clothes?' Rivera asked, pulling out a selection of filthy sweaters, trousers etc.

'Listen, I never understood how you could do it before. I get the point.'

'Yeah,' Mike said, twisting the bag closed again. 'So I think I'm taking my pay under false pretences, you know? Because I sure as hell am not as good in records as I am on the street, but I'm not so good on the street these days, either. I don't know what the hell to do.'

'Would you go down there for me?' Pinsky asked.

Mike gently kicked the black plastic bag again. 'I used to enjoy this. Hard to believe.'

Looking around, Pinsky agreed. The nicest thing that had ever happened to Mike Rivera was also one of the worst things that happened to him in terms of his usefulness to the department. Moving from a soulless room in a boarding house to the street was no great leap, but from this – a jump too far. Pinsky shivered slightly from the thought of climbing into the clothes in one of the black bags. Clothes in which Mike would not be alone for long, as the lice and their assorted friends returned.

But maybe it was just the cool breeze from the open balcony door. Outside a boat hooted twice and, from far below, traffic rumbled on the streets. Mike had climbed pretty high up from the gutter.

'I know it's a lot to ask,' Pinsky said softly. 'I seem to be pulling in a lot of favours over this, but I let the kid down, Mike. I should have listened, taken five minutes for crying out loud . . .'

Rivera looked at him, understanding in his eyes. 'I'll try.'

THIRTEEN

JERRY HAUCK SEEMED TO KNOW he was a genius and made every attempt to live up to the role as Professor Elise Mayhew's star student. His hair was wild and wiry, his glasses were tiny and wire-framed, his clothes were clean but ill-matched and wrinkled, he was unshaven and he had a pencil behind his ear. An Einstein wannabe, no mistake. He viewed Stryker and Tos with a heavy scowl. 'This is bad,' he said. 'She was brilliant, just brilliant and he goes and shoots her. Jesus wept, what a waste.'

'Who shoots her?'

'Her old man, obviously. He was real jealous, always snarfing around when we were there, giving us the beady eye, making us feel like shit for taking up her time.'

'You think he was jealous of you?'

'Not me personally. All of us. Me, Lois, Chan and Galumph.'

'Galumph?'

'Oh, that's what we call him. His name is actually Morrie Garrison, but he's a big bastard and kind of galumphs around. It was Lois who started that. She's kind of . . . weird. Really intense, but sort of silly, too. She likes nicknames. That's the only one that really stuck. She tried me with Jez, but I wasn't having it. No dignity, you know? A person needs their personal dignity.'

Stryker sighed. How true. 'Were you often at Professor Mayhew's house?'

'A couple times a month, not all of us at the same time except sometimes when she wanted a discussion group.

Mostly she dealt with us one or two at a time, so as to give our work proper attention. She was real generous with her time and that was tough because she was real pressed with her own book deadline. We're only MA candidates. She had some real fresh insights into urban tribal units.'

'Urban tribal units?'

'That's my thesis subject. Gangs. The homeless. Bridge clubs. You know.'

'I don't, actually, but I'll take your word for it,' Stryker said. 'So her husband was jealous of the time she gave you.'

'Well, he shouldn't have been, it was part of her job, after all. I mean, she gave more than she needed to, I'll grant that, but even so, he was a pain in the ass. The girls liked him, though. Pretty boy.'

'You only mentioned one girl, Lois.'

'Chan, she's a girl. Chan Mei Mei. She opted for Chan before Lois could get a look in with Mei Mei and maybe change it to Mimi, just for the hell of it. You know, "Your tiny hand is frozen"?'

'*La Bohème*,' Tos said. Stryker gave him an odd look – but, of course, Tos was Italian. Opera was in his blood.

'Yeah. Anyway, what do you want to know?' Jerry leaned back in his chair and regarded them over the top of his glasses. They were in the library, where they'd tracked him down to one of the research carrels. He had been deep in taking notes from a large tome full of pictures of teeth. They didn't look like human teeth.

'Did Professor Mayhew ever mention any trouble she was having with any students? Any friends? Anybody?'

'You mean, "did she have any enemies"? That's the way it goes, isn't it?'

'More or less.'

Jerry shook his head. 'No. She never talked about personal stuff, just what we were working on. She was all business, no games. Lately she did seem kind of . . . frazzled, but we figured that was because of the book.

We haven't seen so much of her lately.'

'When was the last time you saw her?'

'Last Saturday, I think it was. Or Sunday. Oh, yeah, Sunday definitely. Because he was there, her husband, and he came back from doing the shopping. He did the shopping. He did a lot of the stuff around the house because she was working on her manuscript and with us and stuff, and teaching, of course. He made his own schedule. He's some kind of travelling salesman, I think. He was packing to go away that night, and kept coming in to ask where his socks were and stuff like that. He didn't need to ask, if you ask me, but he did, just to interrupt.'

'So you saw her on Sunday. Just you, or were there others there, too?'

'All of us. It was the first time we had all been there in weeks. All together, I mean. We were deconstructing Chan's thesis, helping her get it tighter, sharper. Like that. Chan was being brave about it, but it was hard for her. Elise had to give her a cuddle halfway through.'

'Was Professor Mayhew an affectionate person?'

Jerry grinned. 'Oh yeah – she was a toucher. A shoulder patter. In a motherly kind of way, even though she wasn't that much older. She was a really nice person. You felt she really cared if you were doing good or bad, you know?' His face went a little loose and he cleared his throat. 'I don't know who we'll get now. Maybe Winchester himself. That'll make a change. Him and his damned hula-hula shirts.'

'Were any of you particularly close to Professor Mayhew?' Tos asked.

'She liked me,' Hauck said. He said it in a flat voice, not bragging, just stating a fact. 'Because I'm difficult. She said she was a difficult student, too.'

'You don't seem difficult to me,' Stryker observed.

'You're not competition,' Jerry said. 'And you're not in my field. I want to help you because I care about what happened to Professor Mayhew, so I'm being very, very nice. Is that so strange?'

'Not at all. Can you tell us where you were on Sunday between midnight and six a.m.?'

'Asleep. Alone. At home. I live with my parents,' Jerry said simply. 'Some relatives had been over for the day and when I got back I went out with my cousins for a few drinks. Came back home about nine. Then studied until . . . well, until midnight, I guess it must have been. Then went to bed.' He peered at them. 'Was that when . . . when she was killed?'

'Yes, according to the best estimate we can make. Neighbours heard arguing and then the shot and then a car driving away.'

'I don't drive,' Jerry said. 'I never learned. I'm not very well co-ordinated, made a mess of it in driving class, didn't go on with it. Bus is good enough for me at the moment. I might give it another try after I get this Master's. In case I have to move someplace else to teach or whatever. Gotta drive in this country, right? Everybody does. Makes me feel out of it, but mostly I get lifts from friends or take the bus.'

'So you don't own a car?'

He gave a bark of laughter. 'Are you kidding? The price of books in my field being what it is? I'm lucky to still live at home, or I couldn't take my MA. Or my Ph.D., which I fully intend to do, especially now.'

'Why especially now?'

'Because of her,' he said simply. 'She said I should and now she's dead. Well, I have a kind of obligation, right? I should go for it, like in her memory, sort of. Seems only right. Besides, I want to. And my parents want me to. And so I will. And *then* I'll learn to drive. OK?' He seemed to be getting worked up gradually and his voice was getting louder. Was this what Donald Mayhew meant about his being 'difficult'?

'Nice,' Tos said. 'In her memory. Nice thought.'

Jerry subsided. 'Yeah. Right.'

'Anything else you can think of that might help?'

Jerry shook his head. 'Are you going to talk to the others?'

'Yes, of course.'

'Maybe they can help. I'm not very observant of people I know, only strangers. She was a good woman, a good teacher, a nice person, that's all I know. She knew that it was hard to do this work, hard to do it really well. And it has to be done really well, because it's a crowded field and a very competitive one, no matter what anyone says. Every discovery is important. It's like poking around with our eyes taped up, so few clues, so little to go on.'

'Amen,' said Stryker. 'I hear you.'

Ned Pinsky drew up in front of the Sanchez house and turned off the engine. The house was a nice ranch-style set in a good amount of ground. It was only a few blocks away from his own home. The front lawn showed patches of mud, summer wear and tear. And some leaves were beginning to fall, studding the green with red and yellow.

He had rung ahead and knew Mrs Sanchez was at home. Obviously her original idea of going in to work had been overtaken by her grief. And, no doubt, the details of arranging Ricky's funeral. To say nothing of comforting Ricky's brother and sister, and seeking comfort from them.

Even the strongest of us will buckle under sufficient pain, he thought, and she was a very strong woman. Which is why he was shocked when she opened the door. Gone was the elegant lady he'd known before. This was a broken woman, lost in the folds of a loose housecoat, her once shining hair twisted up in an attempt at a chignon that was already coming apart. Her eyes were sunken and without make-up she showed her true age.

'Hello, Ned,' she said and stepped back to let him in.

'Maria,' Ned said in a soft voice. 'I'm so sorry.'

She shrugged as she closed the outer door. 'Yes.' She sighed. 'So am I. But there is nothing to do. It is done, it is over, Ricky is gone.' She moved towards the living room. 'Sit,' she said. 'I have made some coffee.'

He wished she hadn't. He wished he could just do what

he'd come to do and get out again, but he knew he would have to sit down and talk, admit his failure, ask her forgiveness. There was no way out of it.

The living room showed signs of misery, too: newspapers scattered on the floor, ashtrays overflowing and unemptied, a stack of photo scrapbooks tilting as if to slide, the curtains half drawn and then abandoned, giving the windows a weary look. Maria Sanchez had always been houseproud. Maybe one day she would be again.

Maria came in with a tray, mugs of coffee, a pitcher of milk, a sugar bowl, a plate of cookies. Something in her was hanging on to the amenities.

Ned sank back on the sofa and watched as she laid the tray on the cocktail table, then backed off, taking her own mug, coffee black, and with a minute gesture indicated he should help himself. She sat in a large armchair beside the cold fireplace and sipped her drink. For an instant he caught the scent of brandy and then it was gone. Adding milk but no sugar to his own mug, he sat up straight. 'About Ricky—' he began.

'You have found his killer?' she asked, but not eagerly. It would make no difference to her if they had – Ricky was dead and her grief had taken her beyond revenge.

'No, not yet,' Ned admitted. 'I . . . Ricky wanted to talk to me earlier in the week . . .'

'Did he?' She closed her eyes. 'What about?'

'I don't know,' Ned said. 'That is . . . something was troubling him and he wanted advice. But he wouldn't tell me exactly what it was, because he wanted to be sure before he did anything that might hurt someone else.'

Maria nodded. Another long, thin strand of her dark hair escaped from the pins and drifted down beside her cheek. 'That was Ricky,' she said. She opened her eyes. 'He gave no indication?'

'Not really. Just that he thought someone was doing something "wrong" – possibly but not necessarily illegal – and how he should go about dealing with it.'

'What did you tell him?'

This was the hard part. 'I said he should be sure of his facts, and that perhaps he should talk to the person concerned.'

'Is that what got him killed?' she asked, her voice hardening a little.

'I don't know,' Ned said miserably. 'He said the person wasn't dangerous, that he was all talk . . .'

'But now Ricky is dead.'

Ned sighed. 'Yes.'

She closed her eyes again and when she spoke they remained closed. 'That was his biggest fault . . . doing things his own way. No matter what, doing things his own way.' She paused, still with her eyes closed. 'He misjudged this person.' Her eyes opened suddenly, piercing him. 'You misjudged this person.'

'I knew nothing about the man. Not even if he was in the hospital where Ricky worked or at the university – nothing,' Ned said, knowing he sounded defensive. 'But if he is responsible for Ricky's death, we will find him. He will be punished.'

She shrugged again. 'We are all being punished.'

Ned frowned. 'By his death, you mean.'

'No. For our neglect.'

'But I—'

She raised a graceful hand. 'No, you misunderstand. When my husband died I turned to Ricky. He was a strong boy and he felt the weight of his responsibility. I could have stopped work then. I should have. The three of them needed a stable home, a responsible parent always available as they grew up. But I kept working to ease the loneliness, let Ricky take the weight of making sure the younger two were looked after in those ways. Yes, I made sure they were fed and clothed . . . but I wasn't there for them—' She almost smiled. 'Isn't that the phrase, "there for them"? Most importantly, I wasn't there for Ricky. I assumed he was fine, could handle it all. But he was just a boy. Still just a boy. With a boy's ego, a boy's conviction that he was invincible, a boy's love of adventure.'

'He reached out to me,' Ned whispered. 'I wasn't there for him either.'

'No,' she said and, while it was obvious she agreed with him, her voice held no accusation. 'They are so hard to judge, these ones of eighteen, nineteen, twenty. They see so much, know so much, and yet underneath they are . . . still so vulnerable. We forget that. We forget they are still children because they walk like men and talk like men, but they are boys. Just boys.'

'I could have done more.'

'Yes and so could I. But we didn't – and now the opportunity is gone.' She drank more of her coffee and whatever else was in that mug. 'But I have two more and you have Denise, and we can do more for them. I have decided, Ned, to take early retirement. I will be here for them. You will be there for Denise. That much we can do.'

'You're a very forgiving woman, Maria,' Ned said humbly.

'Not to myself,' she said. 'Not to myself.'

They sat there in silence for a moment, then Maria stood up. 'When you phoned you said you wanted to see Ricky's room.'

Startled out of his reverie, Ned nodded and stood up. 'If I may, please. There could be something there . . . I should have come sooner, but there is another case . . .'

'The lady professor?' She gestured towards the newspapers. 'I read about it. I think Ricky knew her.'

Ned's eyes widened. 'Really?'

'I think so. Her name was familiar somehow.' She turned, putting her empty mug on a nearby small table, and went out into the hall. 'His room is down this way.'

Ricky Sanchez had not been an ordinary boy. Ned had known that, but it was verified when he saw his room. There were no posters of pop groups or sports heroes. There were books – literally hundreds of books on tall shelves that reached the ceiling. There was a narrow bed, tightly made. There was a desk with a computer and neatly stacked notebooks. There was a comfortable chair with a reading lamp beside it, a footstool and, now for ever lonely, a cat curled up in the comfortable chair.

'You've cleaned the room,' Pinsky said, disappointed.

'Not at all,' Maria said. 'I have not been in here at all.' She turned suddenly. 'I cannot be in there now,' came her voice as she retreated quickly down the hall.

Ned went over and stroked the cat. Tiger-striped and plump, it looked up expectantly, then sank back down. Wrong loving hand.

'Sorry,' Ned whispered.

He went to the desk, pulled out the chair and began to go through the notebooks, the drawers and, eventually, the computer. 'Tell me, Ricky,' he whispered. 'Tell me who it was.'

'Well, that's the last of them,' Kate said, putting down the phone and switching off the recording equipment. She stretched and rubbed her temples. 'Went more quickly than I thought, thank God.'

'Did you recognize any of the voices?' Liz asked.

'Not really. A couple were . . . close, but didn't sound exactly right. So either we're on the wrong track, or the guy has been disguising his voice when he talks to me.'

Liz looked at the recording equipment, the malevolent little red and green eyes, the dials, the switches. 'Well, he won't be able to disguise it from these little monsters – assuming you caught up with the right one. What if there are no matches?'

'I'll be really disappointed,' Kate said. 'Because then we only have the rest of the world to consider.'

'Well, you can start with the rest of the faculty, other departments and so on,' Liz pointed out. 'You don't have to take on the whole world just yet.' She got up and went to the window to look out on the street. The long line of trees shed shadows and leaves on the cars below, which were parked like colourful beetles along the kerbs. She was very worried about Kate.

As if reading her friend's thoughts, Kate spoke reflectively. 'You know, in a way I wish I'd never started all this. I've been neglecting my class work. The kids are getting away with murder – I haven't assigned a paper in almost two weeks. And then there's Jack.'

Liz turned to look at her. 'What about Jack? Have you finally told him?'

Kate shook her head. 'No. To be honest, I've been avoiding him, which hasn't been difficult as he's caught up in this case of his. And when we do see one another I seem to have developed a terrific ability to turn the simplest statement into an argument. I know I'm behaving irrationally, but I can't seem to help myself. I know he's confused, poor guy.' She straightened up. 'But he's on edge, too. Something more is bothering him than the death of that professor.' She gave a harsh laugh. 'We're quite a pair at the moment.'

'This whole thing is not very healthy, Kate. You have a gleam in your eye I haven't seen there before.'

'I want this man on the phone dealt with,' Kate said with a vicious edge to her voice. 'He's very sick, he should be put away.'

'But you do realize that by not dealing with it directly you may be contributing to his sickness, don't you?' Liz asked.

'The damage is done. Having got myself into this mess, it is up to me to get myself out of it,' Kate insisted.

'Just so long as you remember that cornered animals fight harder and have nothing to lose,' Liz said worriedly.

'He's out there, Liz. He's driving me nuts. He's ruining my relationship with Jack.'

'I think you're doing a lot of that all by yourself,' Liz said.

Kate ignored that. 'He needs to be reached and stopped before phoning me isn't enough. He's enjoying what he's doing to me. In fact, I think that's become his whole *raison d'être.* But eventually he'll tire of my gasps, and anger and pleading. Eventually he'll act. And then—'

'I think you need a drink and a plate of something fattening,' Liz said in a practical voice, as she saw Kate drifting off into a worried reverie, her hands working convulsively. 'Too much theory, not enough action. Come on . . . Rico's. We definitely need Rico's and his best calories.'

'OK.' Kate seemed to awake to the present and looked around at the stacks of tape cassettes, each labelled with the name of the person recorded. 'But we have to get all this to David Waxman so he can start analysing it.'

'Later on will be fine. When you've had a little ravioli.'

Kate laughed. 'You sound like Tos.'

Liz seemed pleased. 'Do I? Good. Tos is very sane.'

'And I am not?'

'And you are not,' Liz agreed. 'And what's more, I'm beginning to worry about myself. I think we need to go into another line of business. I hear there's good money in digging swimming pools.'

Lois McKittrick was, as Jerry Hauck had said, a mouse: small, bird-boned and big-eyed, her hair hanging round her face in straight strands under an equally straight fringe. She seemed, behind her large glasses, to be peering out at the world very cautiously. 'I don't know what to say,' she said in a surprisingly deep voice for someone her size. But there was a wheeze there, too. Her breathing was a little laboured. She seemed very nervous. They had caught her between classes in New State Hall. 'I saw her on Sunday, she seemed just the same as always.'

'How do you mean?' Stryker asked. 'The same as always.'

'Well, nice. She was wonderful to us; she listened to all of us, she was interested in us, she cared about us. So if we got upset – and Chan got upset – she would be upset, too. On Sunday, though, I think she was more worried about her own thesis than Chan's, but anyway, she gave Chan a hug. We were supposed to discuss my paper, then, but she said there wasn't time and she was tired. So I didn't get a hug. But I wasn't upset,' she said rather defensively.

'Weren't you?' Tos seemed interested.

'No. I don't let myself get upset because it sets off my asthma and I can't breathe. I have to be *very* careful. That Jerry Hauck insists on smoking when he knows how it affects me and she told him to stop it on Sunday.' The big eyes blinked behind straight, stiff lashes. The other students flowed around them in the wide hallway, and lockers banged open and shut. She flinched at a particularly loud one near them. It seemed to worry her. Everything seemed to worry her.

'Did she show favouritism towards anyone?'

'She was very nice to Chan, but then Chan was making a fuss.'

'Do you mind telling us where you were on Sunday night?' Stryker asked.

'What? When?'

'Sunday night,' Stryker repeated patiently. 'The whole evening and night.' Suddenly the hall was dead quiet, as the doors to the various rooms closed and classes within began. They were left alone in the middle of the hall, with only a few students in the distance, walking away. The abrupt silence was eerie and for a moment their voices were over-loud.

'Oh. Of course. I went to a movie. It started about eight, I think. I went with a friend, Nan Prescott. Then I went back to her place for a coffee and I think I got home about eleven or maybe a bit later. Then I went to bed.'

'Do you live alone?'

'No, I share a house with three other girls, but they were all away for the weekend and I don't know if they were in when I got home or not. I just went straight to bed. We each have our own rooms, share the kitchen and so on. The usual thing.' She looked up the hall, down at her feet, anywhere but at them.

'Can you give us Miss Prescott's number or address? Will she verify this?'

'Well, yes, of course she will. Why wouldn't she?' she asked, her voice sliding towards shrill. The bony little hands were white-knuckled, as she clutched her books to her chest. She looked around as if seeking support.

'And can you think of anything else that might help us to find the person who killed Professor Mayhew?'

'But . . . didn't her husband kill her?'

'We don't know who killed her.'

'Oh, I thought . . .' Her voice trailed off.

'What did you think?'

'I thought Jerry said it was her husband who killed her.'

'You've talked to Mr Hauck?'

'Well, sure. When we heard we all got together in the library on Monday afternoon.'

Stryker and Tos exchanged a glance. Hauck hadn't mentioned this little gathering.

'Why?' Stryker asked.

'*Why?*' She seemed surprised he should ask. 'Well, to decide what we should do. I mean, we wanted to go to her funeral, whenever it was, and to send flowers from all of us. And we were worried about getting a new faculty sponsor . . . but mostly we just wanted to be together. You know. Like a family should be.'

'You think of yourselves as a family?'

She seemed embarrassed, now, and gave a bizarre little giggle, half laugh, half sob. 'Well, we are, in a way. Elise's family. Well, weren't we?'

'I don't know,' Stryker said. 'I was never a grad student, I don't know how these things work. I thought she tutored you individually.'

'Yes, but also together in seminars. We were . . . special to her. Not like her regular students. She worked closely with us. Very closely.' She drew a long, wavering breath. 'And now she's gone and we don't have anybody.' The eyes behind the glasses were suddenly larger, magnified by tears that didn't fall.

'But you'll be assigned another faculty tutor, surely?'

'Oh yes. But it won't be the same. Not the same at all.' She glanced at her watch, blinking fast. 'I'm late for my next class. Is that all?'

'Yes, for the moment. Thank you.' Stryker and Tos watched her walk away, a small figure in the wide hall, a little stiff-legged.

'What do you make of her?' Stryker asked.

Tos shrugged. 'I see what Jerry Hauck meant. Intense and a little silly with it. Hard to imagine her studying something as heavy as anthropology, though. She seems more the type for poetry or art.'

'Yes,' Stryker agreed. 'Still, from what I understand, it isn't all digging up bones in the desert. Mayhew herself wasn't the type for fieldwork, Winchester said. Maybe little Lois modelled herself on her mentor – all paper research.' In the distance the outer door banged shut and in a moment they could see Lois McKittrick running across the Mall towards the library.

'They have classes in the library?' Tos asked, surprised.

'Oh yeah, sometimes,' Stryker said. 'Space is valuable in a university. They have seminar rooms over there.'

Tos sighed. 'This is like visiting a foreign country any time we have to come here. These people . . . they're all strangers. Not like the perps we usually deal with.'

'But you know Liz,' Stryker said, as they began to walk towards the front of the building, their footsteps echoing in the empty hallway. 'You know Kate. She's not a stranger.'

'Oh, well, Kate is different,' Tos said expansively.

'Don't kid yourself.' Stryker grinned. 'To us they're regular people, but down here, they're laws unto themselves.'

FOURTEEN

DR DAN WAXMAN WAS NOT enjoying the life of a private detective. For one thing, he had little time to spare from the ER, so it was a hit-and-miss operation. He knew there could be many other reasons why Ricky had been killed – something to do with the university, a love rival, even a straightforward mugging, which was apparently the official version. Pinsky would have to deal with anything else. He had been impressed with Pinsky and had felt great sympathy for his obvious guilt. To be honest, if it hadn't been for Pinsky he would not have thought further about Ricky's death, other than to mourn his loss. But the hospital was his beat and he was doing his best, because he was beginning to feel guilty too. Not specifically about Ricky, but about all the people who died and were ignored because there was no time, no money, no inclination to question their deaths other than attributing them to the obvious.

He felt guilty about snooping on his colleagues. But the lure of adventure was strong and, as he was secretly addicted to detective fiction, he pressed on with the search. Mostly he was appalled at the clear evidence of sloppy practice and careless management he encountered. He knew an overstretched and underfunded city hospital was not in a position to maintain standards of perfection, but some of the things he saw were upsetting. Particularly the loneliness of the isolated patient. In the ER he patched them up and sent them on to the various departments above, or patched them up and released

141

them. There were so many that it was next to impossible to follow up most of the cases. But he wished there were time, because if he did his best, he expected his colleagues to do the same. Some did not. There was also a shortage of doctors, nurses and ancillary staff.

What he had *not* found was outright wrongdoing. Most of what he saw was the result of poor funding, overwork and bad housekeeping. The only place he worried about – and he could not say why – was pathology. There were a number of research fellows in there doing things they played close to their chests. He found he was unable to summon up the ingenuous appearance of innocent enquiry to find out what they were researching. They viewed any questions with suspicion, fearing someone else might steal their results and publish first. It was the only really closed door he'd found and for that reason it piqued his interest. Other surgeons and physicians in other departments had their pet research projects, but they were quite open about them – soliciting information of all kinds to help them discover everything from a cure for the common cold to a new kind of suture technique.

When he met his brother for lunch, he mentioned what he was doing – or trying to do – over a meal in their favourite small family-run Mexican restaurant. 'So now, in addition to diagnosing broken legs and measles, I'm a private investigator.'

'You and me both,' David said.

'What – don't tell me somebody stole your metronome?'

'No, no . . . a woman at the university is being harassed by phone. Blackmailed, really. She's gathering samples and I'm going to be comparing voices electronically. We figure to nail the guy.'

'You can do that?' Dan asked, intrigued.

'Sure . . . it's not really very complicated,' David told him.

'This is getting creepy,' Dan said. 'What is it about the Waxman Boys?'

'Our unique qualities are being recognized, that's all,' David said, grinning. 'It's a small world.'

'I believe someone already said that,' Dan observed. He considered for a moment, leaning back as the waitress took away their salad plates and put their main courses down before them. The aroma of hot spices percolated upwards, making his mouth water. 'Maybe this assignment of mine is a cover-up,' Dan mused. 'Maybe Sergeant Pinsky thinks *I* killed Ricky and he wants to see if I come up with anything or not.'

'Come on,' David said. 'You're getting paranoid. Have you come up with anything?'

'Not really. Not yet.' Dan cut into his enchiladas. 'The trouble is Ricky was all over the place, always asking questions. That's why the guys in pathology make me wonder. They are pretty paranoid themselves about their work. Especially the genome stuff. Murphy acts like he's developing germ warfare for some unnamed country – and he could be, he's a mercenary type. Even Ivan Sherwin, normally a sweetheart – you'd think he was on the verge of a cure for AIDS. When they see me coming, they actually cover up their notes. Even Forster and Duggan – and I've dated both of them – give me the cold shoulder.'

'Maybe because you've dated both of them,' David suggested with a grin.

Dan shook his head. 'No. They're all a little nuts down there next to the morgue. Oncology is serious, paediatrics is jolly, psych is actually quite normal, considering. But path—' He hummed the theme from *Twilight Zone*. 'If it makes me curious, it probably made Ricky curious. But that's as far as I've got.'

'So one of them killed this Ricky kid in order to be the first to publish his findings? He thought Ricky would steal his research?'

'No, that doesn't make sense. Ricky was just a pre-med student. He was very smart and pretty advanced, but he wouldn't have known half of what he was seeing. If that.'

'Well, maybe it isn't medical,' David suggested thought-fully. 'Maybe it's to do with administration, budget, something like that. Maybe he found something that showed someone was stealing money from the hospital funds.'

'How the hell would he do that?' Dan asked, amazed. Something like that would never have occurred to him.

David shrugged. 'I don't know. But you see only the medical side. A hospital is run by managers and accountants – plenty of bureaucrats, plenty of opportunities for siphoning off money . . . you should think about it.'

Dan looked reflective. 'Barney does all the admin for path grants as well as running the department itself. And he places the orders for equipment, supplies, that sort of thing.'

'And is he the type to have sticky fingers?'

'I don't know. It wouldn't be the first thing I thought about him, but I suppose it's possible. Maybe I should tell Pinsky about Barney. They could investigate that – the police have people who specialize in financial crime, don't they?'

'I think so,' David said, pushing away his empty plate after spooning up the last drop of sour cream.

Dan eyed him. 'How come you come up with stuff like this all the time? You're supposed to be a musician, head in the clouds, listening to the music of the spheres or whatever the hell it is you listen to.'

'Whatever I do seems to turn into business for someone or other,' David said. 'The Internet site, the personal computer idea . . . whether I want to or not, I get to find out about all kinds of financial and commercial crap. People just take ideas and run . . . and then I get all the flak.'

'Some flak,' Dan said, with slight envy. 'Money, you mean.'

'Well, yes. And I don't care about money any more than you do . . . but it keeps coming in.'

'I should be so lucky,' Dan mourned. 'You know what I earn.'

'Invent a new surgical instrument,' David suggested. 'There's money in that, isn't there?'

'It isn't enough I have to run the ER and play amateur detective, you want me to start being an inventor already?' Dan asked plaintively.

'Only if you want to make money,' David answered.

'I'll think about it.'

'Good,' David said approvingly. 'And when you do, I know just the guys to market it.'

Dan eyed him. 'You *have* gone over to the dark side, haven't you?'

'Only on Wednesdays,' David explained. 'I only think commercially on Wednesdays. Otherwise I'd go nuts. And today is Wednesday.'

Dan glanced at his watch. 'Which means I'm due in the ER in twenty minutes.'

'It also means I get stuck with the bill – again,' David grumbled good-naturedly.

'I am but a poor struggling hospital doctor still burdened by academic debt,' Dan said. 'My head is awhirl with possibilities, problems and patients. You, on the other hand, are a Wednesday Man when it comes to finance. Pay the bill.'

David laughed. 'OK . . . but tell you what. If I do find out who this phone caller is, you have to get him some psychiatric help or something.'

'I'll think about that too.' Dan waved and dashed out of the door. David sat at the table a bit longer, musing about the coincidence. It seemed as if – whether they wanted to or not – the Waxman Boys were getting tangled up in murder and wrongdoing. It was interesting. Very interesting. Despite himself he realized he was enjoying his contact with crime. Which was wrong. Wasn't it?

'It's just a coincidence,' Stryker said. Neilson had handed him Ricky's class schedule, which Pinsky had left for him at the desk downstairs along with a note asking him to show it to Stryker and argue his case for him. He said he

145

didn't trust himself not to kick Stryker or Fineman in the ass.

'Biology, physiology, chemistry, German, English, physics and this anthropology course with Professor Mayhew. It's pretty tenuous – it's a big university. That Ricky might be taking a class from a murdered professor is unusual—'

'Especially when he was murdered himself,' Neilson pointed out.

'Yeees,' Stryker said slowly. 'I know – it bothers me too. Maybe we should keep it in the back of our minds as we go along. Have you talked to Ned recently?'

'He's never home.'

Stryker stared at the papers on his desk. 'And we know why.'

'What if Fineman finds out about what he's doing?' Neilson asked.

'Well, we'll just have to make sure he doesn't find out. Ned obviously needs to work out his guilt somehow. If running around and bothering people is going to do it, fair enough. He's pretty safe – unless somebody complains.'

'Oh shit – I never thought of that,' Neilson said.

'Look, our focus is still Professor Mayhew,' Stryker reminded him. 'Not Ricky Sanchez and not Ned Pinsky. I know he's your partner, but our primary problem is the Mayhew homicide. Is that clear?'

'Yeah,' Neilson said in a low voice. 'But if he calls me . . .'

'You can't control who calls you,' Stryker told him. 'Straight choice – hang up or listen.'

'I guess so.' Neilson smiled.

Stryker was not happy. He was being pulled in two directions and he was a little angry at Pinsky for putting him in that situation. There was some merit in Pinsky's theory and he had admitted that to himself from the beginning. He respected Ned and Ned's instincts. But the captain had spoken and the Sanchez case had been left aside – more or less. It would be looked at, of course – detectives in the squad working on other things would be aware of its unsolved nature, would be alert for connections. But that was the best they could do. There were so many street homicides, mostly to do with drugs, and so many on French Street.

Sometimes Stryker wished he were back in uniform, where things were black and white, and decisions and problems like this belonged to someone above him. Someone who would probably handle them better than he did. Someone who knew what he was doing.

He never really felt that kind of steady confidence. Just that he was going along in the half-dark with a weak flashlight, dealing with things as they came into view, not knowing what was best and expecting to be exposed as a failure at any minute. How do you reconcile sensitive and tough? he asked himself. You don't.

You just do the best you can.

And then there was Kate, pulling him in yet another direction. She had suddenly become a stranger, short-tempered, fretful. He had thought it was just PMT and ignored it, but when he considered it he realized it had been going on for longer than that. He didn't keep track of her menstrual cycle, but he was sure it was more than that.

The previous night he'd asked her, not for the first time, if anything was wrong. She said things were going badly in one of her classes. Maybe he should give her a ring. He glanced at his watch. He knew her class schedule for this term. She would be in her office about now.

But there was no reply.

He frowned.

That was odd.

FIFTEEN

CHAN MEI MEI WAS A beautiful Chinese girl, but very serious. She, too, wore big glasses, like Lois McKittrick, but on her they seemed rather glamorous, doing little to hide her delicate features or flawless complexion. She wore the usual student costume of loose sweatshirt and jeans, as if to deny her femininity, but her shapely figure was difficult to disguise. If anything, she was a little on the plump side and it occurred to Neilson that she gave fat a good name.

Neilson and Muller talked to her in her home, which was not the best thing they could have done. Her parents were very suspicious of them and hovered in the background, ready to spring if they tried anything 'funny' with their precious girl. The room they were in was obviously the main living room of the family, and it was an exceptionally tasteful combination of Western and Eastern furnishings, with a cream background and many accents of red and gold. There was a large glass-fronted cabinet containing a number of jade figurines and also a very large television set in one corner. The furniture was dark wood, but beautifully upholstered in rich brocade, upright but surprisingly comfortable. They were offered tea, but refused with thanks.

'This is terrible,' Chan Mei Mei said. 'She was a good woman and an excellent teacher. We were all very shocked. I thought Lois was going to have an asthma attack right there in the library, she was so upset. Her breathing was terrible and she was shaking.'

148

'Everyone has only good things to say about Professor Mayhew,' Muller commented. 'Is that really how she was?'

Chan Mei Mei nodded. 'Truly, really,' she said. 'If you had asked me to name people who might be murdered, she would never have occurred to me. Other professors, yes ... there are a few who are extremely unpopular. Freidman and Torrance in biology, Schaeffer in philosophy, Jenkins in English and maybe also Bloxby in English. Nobody in art, funnily enough.' She caught their expressions. 'This is my field of interest,' she explained. 'The interaction of teachers and students. The exercise of power and coercion, sexual harassment, intimidation ... and so on. It was very amusing to Professor Mayhew, who kept teasing me that there was no such thing. But of course there is.'

'By the students or the teachers?' Neilson asked.

She gave him an appreciative glance. 'A very good point and something I am covering in my thesis.'

'I understand the others gave you a rough time about your thesis on Sunday,' Neilson said.

She sighed heavily. 'Because the subject is so close to them. Some felt I was too biased, others that I was not harsh enough. And I have some trouble with logic.' She smiled suddenly and the effect was disconcerting. Clearly, in her case brains and beauty were combined, but she seemed to have an unfair advantage over the rest of humanity. Neilson was quite overcome.

Her parents, standing in the doorway, stirred slightly.

He cleared his throat and consulted his notebook. 'Was Professor Mayhew behaving normally at that session?'

'You mean was she in a good humour?' Chan Mei Mei asked. 'Yes, she was, although she was a little distracted she still tried to be supportive. I got several hugs in the course of the afternoon. She seemed just fine, but towards the end she said she had a headache and we broke earlier than we had expected. She had been working so very hard, you see. On her book.'

'I understand her husband was present.'

149

'He was in and out, as always when he was at home,' Chan Mei Mei said dismissively. 'He was an annoyance, but she didn't seem to mind. It's obvious he was jealous of the time she spent with us. He always seemed to me to be an angry little man, resentful of her brains and position. But that is just a personal opinion you understand. I did not particularly like him.'

'Miss McKittrick seemed to think he was attractive.'

Chan Mei Mei shrugged. 'Lois is . . . vulnerable to appearances. She is an odd girl. But her work is first-class, so we overlook her silliness. I think she is a very insecure girl. Poor Garrison can barely stand to be in the same room with her, but then he is not exactly a sensitive man. She makes him nervous, the way a mouse makes an elephant nervous.'

'And Jerry Hauck? What about him?' Muller asked. He and Neilson had been brought up to speed about the interviews so far. He was very excited to be working on such a complicated case so early in his assignment to the department. He knew Neilson wasn't happy about working with him and he understood that. Everybody seemed to be worried about Ned Pinsky but nobody said anything aloud. It was very weird.

Chan Mei Mei flushed, bringing a dusky rose to her cheekbones. 'Jerry Hauck is an animal,' she said. 'He is very smart and he thinks that gives him permission to destroy everyone else. But it does not.'

'He was rough on you on Sunday?'

'Very,' was the short reply.

'And what was his relationship with Professor Mayhew?'

'She thought he was wonderful,' Chan Mei Mei said thoughtfully. 'I have yet to discover why. His manners are atrocious, he doesn't have good personal hygiene, he is aggressive . . .'

'But she liked him?'

'Yes.'

'Do you think there was a sexual attraction there?' Neilson wanted to know.

Again, her parents stirred and glanced at one another in dismay, but Chan Mei Mei was unfazed by the question. 'I suppose it is possible,' she said slowly. 'But I think it was more of an intellectual attraction. He really has a first-class mind,' she finished wistfully. 'It seems so unfair that . . .'

'That what?'

'That it is contained in such a third-class human being,' she said briskly. 'Is there anything else?'

'You say that Professor Mayhew was not bothered by her husband's constant intrusions.'

'No, she wasn't. I think she was sometimes impatient with him – perhaps because he was not her intellectual equal. It was hard to tell . . . she didn't call him "darling" or anything like that, but there was obvious affection there. She was an affectionate woman.'

'We were told she was "a toucher, a hugger".'

Chan Mei Mei smiled. 'Yes, she was. After all, she was not so much older than we were – maybe only six or seven years. It felt like a family.'

'Apparently Lois McKittrick said the same thing.'

Chan Mei Mei gave a delicate snort. 'She would. She also talks about bunnies and pussycats and bow-wows.'

'You're not serious.'

She giggled. 'No, but she is nearly as bad. She puts on a tiny voice, uses a simpering manner.'

'She makes you nervous too?'

'No, she makes me sick,' Chan Mei Mei said. 'She plays the "girly-girly" card in relationships. I think that is despicable. People should be straight with one another. Man and woman should be equal. The whole "geisha" thing with some women infuriates me. Why should we pander to men? They are no better than we are.'

Her father looked furious at that, but her mother managed to hide a small smile behind her hand.

'Is there anything else you can tell us about Professor Mayhew? Did she ever mention any special friends? Was there any gossip in the university about her private life?'

'No,' Chan Mei Mei said with an air of surprise. 'Do you know, there wasn't. Students are great gossips and so are faculty . . . but I never heard anything about Professor Mayhew, good or bad. That's odd, isn't it? I mean, you'd think there would be *something*, even that she was a tough marker or biased in favour of physical anthro, or something. But there wasn't. I think I would have heard if there was. Truly.' Her expression was earnest. Neilson decided he was in love. Again.

'Just as a matter of form, can you tell us where you were on Sunday night and Monday morning?' Neilson enquired.

'Do you mean my alibi?' Chan Mei Mei asked with a small giggle. She raised a hand in a graceful gesture. 'I was at home with my parents, of course. We had a little dinner party, and when our guests departed I went to bed and slept the night through. I slept quite late and only learned about Professor Mayhew's death when Jerry called me the next morning.'

'And do you have any idea who might have killed Professor Mayhew?'

'None at all. I wish I did, I would like to help.'

They thanked her and left – much to her parents' obvious relief. Chan Mei Mei seemed unfazed by their visit. Indeed, she was probably unfazed about most things, Neilson thought. Beauty and brains were a formidable barrier against the world. He thought he would like to know her better, but the father also seemed a rather formidable barrier to that idea. He sighed heavily. So many beautiful women, so little time.

Muller had heard about Neilson. Some of it good, some of it very worrying. Especially Neilson's habit of falling in love at the least convenient times during an investigation. Therefore, knowing exactly what was in his new partner's mind, he gave him an indulgent glance. 'You aren't Chinese,' he said.

'I know that.'

'But a man can dream?'

'Ah, so,' agreed Neilson. 'Ah, so.'

Morrie Garrison was the last of Professor Mayhew's graduate students to be interviewed and he was a complete contrast to the other three: both huge and muscular, his hair was short, he didn't wear glasses and when they found him he was training with the wrestling squad in the university gymnasium. The GSU gym was ancient and shabby, and the boys twisting and tumbling on the various mats were young and sweaty. The sound of thudding and grunting filled the air, along with the odd crashes and cracks that resound within any large enclosed space. Thin light came through the high, dirty windows and dust motes danced among the beams. Neilson and Muller settled on the bottom rank of the bleachers and waited.

Sweaty and a little dazed with being repeatedly slammed on the mat, Garrison finally sat down beside them and wiped his face with the towel round his neck. 'What can I do for you guys?' he wanted to know. His face was red with his recent exertions and his voice was gravelly. He resembled a wet bear, but his smile was gentle.

They showed him their warrant cards and he ducked his head a little mockingly. 'I didn't do it – whatever it is,' he said.

'We're investigating the murder of Professor Mayhew,' Neilson said.

His face changed immediately. 'Oh, sorry – I didn't think. I was only joking. Bad habit of mine.'

'We understand you were at her home last Sunday with her other graduate students,' Neilson continued.

'Yeah, I was there.' He wiped his face again with the towel. 'They were all attacking poor Chan. It was ugly.'

'Ugly?'

Garrison shrugged. 'It seemed all right to me, what she was saying. Kind of interesting, but not my field. I'm the only one of Professor Mayhew's graduate students who's doing physical anthropology for my Master's. The others are cultural or material.'

153

'What's the difference?' Neilson asked.

'Um, well . . . cultural is about how people act towards one another, what kind of rules they live by, morals, ethics, that kind of thing. That's Chan. Also Jerry, who is into tribes.'

'Yes, he told us that.'

'Right. Well, material is artefacts – the things that civilizations produce that show how they lived. Pots, fabrics, scrolls . . . more like archaeology, really. But it works with modern groups, too, like totems and baskets and weapons . . . all stuff like that. Me, I am a bone man.'

'Sorry?'

'A gravedigger. I study bones and the stories they tell. That was Professor Mayhew's speciality, too. I mean, she taught all kinds of anthropology to undergraduates, obviously, but bones were her thing. She was writing a book – a really great book – it was going to be called "Diseases of the Dead".'

'How can the dead have diseases?' Muller wondered.

'Had, not have,' Garrison said. He leaned forward, his big hands expressively mobile. 'You can see by looking at bones whether they suffered from rickets, say, or had healed fractures or arthritis – that kind of thing. Also nutrition – Harris lines in the bones show famine, periods of no growth, which we can equate with historical facts. TB, anaemia, leprosy – all those show up in the bones. We also can get height, weight, reach, cranial capacity, deformities and cause of death, either neonate or . . .'

'Whoa,' said Neilson. 'There's only one death we're interested in here.'

'Yeah, of course. Sorry.' Garrison sighed. 'I don't like to think about it. About her, I mean. Being dead, I mean. She was going to do great stuff, really interesting work . . . she was actually arranging for me to go on a dig in Ohio – an early Quaker pioneer settlement. We think the colony was overcome by plague or something viral, but it could have been simple starvation due to a meagre harvest, and the cemetery . . .' He stopped. 'Sorry, off again. I don't suppose I'll go, now. Unless someone else can get me in.'

'How did Professor Mayhew seem on Sunday?'

'Seem?'

'Happy? Sad? Worried?'

'No, just ... the way she's always been lately. Not all there. Nice and kind and interested and supportive – but she was thinking about the book. In the back of her mind, all the time, thinking about the book. She told me it was nearly done. I was going to do reference checking for her. There's nobody else on the faculty who specializes in forensic anthropology now. Nobody else who gets excited about bones in the way she did. I suppose you think that's crazy?'

'Everybody to their own thing,' Muller said.

'Of course, it might have been the phone call that distracted her,' Garrison said musingly. 'Before that she was pretty OK, but after ...' Garrison's breathing was back to normal and he was beginning to relax.

'What phone call?' Neilson asked.

'Oh, she got a phone call about four o'clock.' His voice was somewhat muffled as he wiped down his face and head with a towel.

'Nobody else mentioned a phone call.'

'No, I don't suppose they did. They were all too busy arguing with one another. I was watching Elise.'

'Tell us about the phone call,' Muller suggested.

'It kind of made her angry – she listened for a minute or two, then slammed the phone down and swore. She didn't usually swear, but she said something about a "damn bastard". Somebody made her mad, but she didn't explain. Just got back to Chan's thesis. But I could tell there was something kind of niggling at her. She looked tired, suddenly, and said she had a headache a little while later, so we broke up the session.' All at once his eyes filled with tears. 'She was so great. It kind of upset me to see her looking like that. And now ... we're gonna miss her like crazy, you know. It really hurts not to have her there to go to, to talk to. I could kill . . .' He paused, looked down at the towel he was wringing like someone's neck, then shook himself and gave a half-choked laugh. 'Bad choice of words.'

'You seem angrier than the others,' Neilson observed.

'Do I?' Garrison considered that. 'Probably testosterone,' he said. 'I'm still hyped from my workout.'

'Would that show in your bones when you were dead?' Muller asked out of left field.

Garrison smiled. 'Yeah, it would. Well, muscle development would; they could tell I was a big guy who worked out. No rickets, though.' The tears were still there, but stayed unshed. 'She used to say we were dealing with ghosts . . . the whispers that the bones gave out, telling us about who they had been and how they had lived. And died. She was shot, wasn't she?'

'Yes,' Neilson said. 'In the head.'

Garrison nodded. 'Where it would hurt our memory most – in her brain. Her brain was what made her different. Her brain and her heart.'

'They're what make us all different,' said Neilson.

'I guess,' Garrison said, standing up. 'I'm getting morbid and I'm getting cold. Anything else I can tell you guys?'

'Where were you on Sunday night and Monday morning?' Muller asked.

'I left with the rest of the wrestling team for a meet in Atlanta. We flew out about eight o'clock. Is that when she was killed? Sunday night?'

'Yes.' Neilson looked up at him. 'So you didn't meet with the other grad students in the library on Monday afternoon?'

'Did they? No, I didn't get back until Tuesday. That's when I heard about the professor. I called the others right away, and they told me what they had decided, about flowers and going to the funeral and stuff like that. It was fine with me, all of what they decided. Anything else?'

156

'What did you think of Professor Mayhew's husband?' Neilson asked.

Garrison grinned. 'The mouse that roars? He was OK. Just jealous, that's all. Kind of a pain in the ass, but OK. Why? Do you think he did it?' His face darkened as he realized what they were implying. 'Do you?'

'He was out of town, like you were.'

'You sure?'

'We're checking on it,' Neilson said.

'Good. Good. Because if it was him . . .'

'Yes?'

Garrison stood there, flexing his muscles as he clenched and unclenched his hands. Then he slowly let go. 'Oh, hell . . . the point is, it's done. I hope you find who did it, but it doesn't matter to me. Not now. She's gone . . . end of story.'

'Don't you think the murderer should be caught?'

Garrison drew a deep breath and exhaled strongly enough to fell several trees. 'Sure, of course. But it won't change anything, will it?'

'We like to think it makes a difference,' Muller said.

'Do you?' Garrison looked down at them, considering. 'Yeah, I can see where you would. It's your job, right?'

'Sometimes it's more than a job,' Neilson said, thinking about Ned Pinsky. 'Sometimes it's personal.'

'Thanks for your time, Mr Garrison,' Muller contributed. 'Is your coach around? Just to confirm your trip to Atlanta?'

'Sure. Come on – his office is over here.'

Muller started after Garrison, then looked back. Neilson was still sitting on the bench, staring into space.

'Coming?' Muller asked.

Neilson looked up. 'Coming,' he said and slowly stood to follow.

SIXTEEN

'THERE!' SAID KATE, PLUNKING DOWN the many tapes she and the others had recorded. David Waxman eyed them with no little trepidation. His dog, Milo, sniffed them with interest, then went to lie down in his bed in the corner, thoroughly disgusted that they were not edible. The cat, lying along the top of the sofa, continued to gaze out of the window. What humans got up to was too perplexing to bother turning to look.

'I hope I can do it justice,' David said cautiously. 'This is a new thing for me.'

'The best you can do will be just great,' Kate assured him. 'I'm already fed up with the whole thing and just want to nail this guy. If he realized how angry I am with him, he might just stop because I can be very mean when I want to be.'

David looked at her and grinned. Kate Trevorne not very big and although her curly hair was full of electricity she was definitely not a frightening person. He found it difficult to believe in her protestations of malice. Liz Olson, on the other hand, could have been intimidating under the right circumstances, but her mild expression made him question her efficacy as a threat.

'And', Kate went on, 'Liz could give him The Look.'

'The Look?' David asked, puzzled.

'Show him,' Kate ordered.

Liz gave him The Look. He felt something give way inside him and had a sudden urge to confess all the sins of his childhood.

158

'I have seen her knock an entire lecture hall into stunned silence with The Look,' Kate said. 'She is my secret weapon.'

'Jeesh,' David said to Liz in some admiration. 'How do you do that?'

'It's a gift.' Liz grinned. 'I think it has to do with the size of my pupils in relation to my eyeballs. I can lift my eyelids very high . . .' She shrugged. 'It just happens.'

David looked from the tall figure of Liz to the small but feisty figure of Kate. Then he looked at the stack of tapes. 'Why do I suddenly feel sorry for this guy?' he enquired.

'Aha!' said Kate.

Pinsky had the list of Ricky Sanchez's classes and teachers, taken from his computer. He had started working through them, one by one. Because he knew Stryker and the others might also be on campus dealing with the Mayhew homicide, he had to move around furtively. It was almost funny, he thought to himself. Ned Pinsky, the Sneaky Detective.

But his troll of the teachers revealed the general consensus that Ricky was a bright, hard-working student and showed great promise for medicine, which had been his chosen profession. It wasn't all that helpful that everybody had loved Ricky. He almost wished he could find someone who disliked him, just for contrast.

Professor Greer said Ricky's chemistry was sound. Professor Jolyon said his grounding in physics was good, but his maths was a little weak. He had suggested extra tutoring and thought Ricky had been considering it. Mr Roberts, who taught him English literature, said he had no difficulty in communicating verbally, but his written work was inconsistent. Still, he was a trier, Roberts said. He was willing to rewrite and improve his work. Dr Conelly said he was an outstanding student of physiology, showed remarkable promise and was particularly interested in bones for some reason.

Professor Torrance was most enthusiastic and very

saddened. 'A remarkable student,' he said. He was a small man, very wrinkled for his age, with thinning hair and a large mole on his left cheek. He had a habit of cracking his knuckles that made Pinsky want to slap his hands away. 'His death is a disaster. He would have made an excellent physician, although he was more interested in pathology lately. We talked often about his ambitions and he was wavering. He had a lively curiosity – everything interested him. He was spreading himself too thinly. I would like to think I helped steer him back in the right direction.'

'In what way?'

Torrance scowled. 'It is getting more and more difficult to keep science students, you know. They give up when the work gets too hard. Science is rather unbending, you see. Departments like art and English are easier to please. Children today do not want to work, they want everything handed to them on a platter. It is most discouraging.'

'But Ricky was different?' Pinsky asked.

'Oh yes. As I said. A natural.' Crack went the knuckles and Pinsky winced. The knuckle-cracking seemed to be an unconscious habit. Torrance was gazing into the middle distance as he continued, 'Many of them would be fine if they were willing to work. But they are lazy. And I will *not* lower my standards, no matter what the Chairman says.' Torrance was rather fierce, like a small dog facing his own reflection in a mirror and snarling at it. He seemed full of suppressed energy. 'Other students were jealous, I believe. He had some bullying.'

'Bullying?' Pinsky asked, suddenly alert.

Torrance shrugged. 'You know the kind of thing, teasing him about his high marks, chiding him for working so hard and making the rest of them look bad.'

'Anyone in particular you can remember?'

'One. A boy who was completely out of his depth in science. A physical education major – on a football scholarship – they are required to take a certain number of science courses. What was his name?' He wrinkled his forehead in thought. Pinsky had found him in a small lecture hall and had waited for his class to leave before talking to him. 'Fred,' Torrance said, after a while. 'That was it, Fred Boynton. I believe his nickname was Boomer or something like that. He used to give Ricky a very hard time, as I recall. You might want to talk to him. He's rather a strange boy.' He sighed. 'He failed my class, and I got rather an earful from him and from the coach. It's so difficult with these footballers and basketball players and so on. The school wants them, because the alumni love winners, you see. And when our teams win, which is rarely, they give money. We are always needing money, Sergeant. Sad fact of life. And all we want to do is educate their minds. If they have them.' Torrance gave a dry cackle and had another go at his knobbly fingers. 'If they have them.'

'Well, thank you, Professor Torrance,' Pinsky said. The knuckle-cracking was getting on his nerves. 'Do you know where I might find . . .' He consulted his notebook. 'A Professor Bulstrode?'

Torrance looked at his watch. 'I imagine you will find him in the nearest bar,' he said nastily. 'Bulstrode is on his way out.'

Pinsky actually located Professor Bulstrode in his office and he did not seem on his way out at all. Rather firmly fixed in his chair, in fact, for he was a very fat man with a very red face. The office seemed to be the scene of a recent tornado, but Pinsky was willing to bet Bulstrode knew exactly where everything was and could put his hand on it instantly. Actually, it was very like his own office at home and he felt quite comfortable in the cluttered surroundings. The fat man gestured him to a chair and regarded him benignly. 'Who've you been talking to?' he wanted to know, as Pinsky moved some books on to the floor and sat down.

Pinsky told him and he chuckled. 'Greer is sound, Jolyon is a little dotty, I don't know Roberts and I imagine

Torrance told you I was a drunk,' he said genially. 'He is convinced of it ever since I went a little over the top at the Christmas party.'

'I'm interested in a student called Ricky Sanchez,' Pinsky said.

Bulstrode nodded. 'I thought that might be it. I read about his murder in the papers. Terrible thing. He was a nice boy, I enjoyed teaching him. How can I help you?'

'Were you aware of any difficulty he might have been having in school? Any problems with teachers or students?'

Bulstrode considered. 'Bright kids always have trouble. Fact of life. You're either top of the class or one of the boys . . . you have to make a choice. Ricky chose top of the class. He was full of questions and full of answers, too. Some others resented that. I don't know what the current term of derision is for bright students, but he heard it often, I'm sure. Outside class he didn't seem to have many friends. I believe he had a steady girlfriend, so no trouble in that direction.'

'We understood that there was one particular boy, a Fred Boynton, who gave him trouble.'

'Oh, Fred.' Bulstrode grinned. 'He did seem to have it in for Ricky, now that you mention it. Nothing serious, you understand. Just a lot of teasing, a bit of pushing about, that sort of thing.' He leaned forward earnestly. 'They are still children, you know. I don't care whether they are old enough to borrow money or vote or whatever . . . they are still children when they come here. Full of hormones, full of conflicts, oversensitive, vulnerable. We hit them broadside with facts, facts, facts, and expect them to receive and absorb them with no trouble. It's a lot to ask of a child.'

'Professor Torrance said you lose a lot of science students to other departments.'

'That's true, that's true. Especially to English, which is seen as an easy route. Or art – well, they're all crazy in the art department, that's a given. A lot of latitude allowed and so on. Students come full of their parents' desires for them to become doctors or lawyers or scientists and many just aren't up to it. There's a tremendous drop-out rate in the first year. Even Ricky was wavering. More interested in the dead than the living.' Bulstrode gave a small grunt. 'I can think of a dozen students I would rather have lost than Ricky. Does that sound cruel?' He answered himself. 'I suppose it does. I just mean . . . it's a bigger loss when a naturally gifted student washes out or dies. They do die, you know. Not murdered, but they do die now and then. And it always seems to be the good ones, the promising ones. Perhaps it has to do with stress. Must look into that.' Bulstrode's eyes went to the clock on the far wall of his office. 'Well, if there's nothing else, I have a luncheon appointment . . .'

'Thank you, Professor. If there's anything else we need to know I'll get back to you.'

'Fine, fine.' Bulstrode heaved himself out of his chair and followed Pinsky out, locking his office door behind him. They shared the elevator down to the ground floor, then Bulstrode left him. When Pinsky reached his car he saw him going into a nearby bar.

That was all Ricky's teachers except Professor Mayhew. And he couldn't talk to her.

An hour later he was in a small coffee shop sitting across from his new partner in detection. 'Well?' Pinsky asked eagerly. 'Did you learn anything new about Ricky?'

Dr Dan Waxman sighed. 'Yes and no. Some of the nurses didn't like him because he got in the way all the time, being nosy, stuff like that. He was a good kid, willing to work, but if there was nothing for him to do he was underfoot all the time. Then suddenly, nobody could find him anywhere when he was needed. Turned out he was spending a lot of time lately in the pathology department, talking about bones.'

'Bones?'

'That's what they said. He was nuts on bones. Not

new bones – old bones. Dead bones. He said they told stories.'

'Mayhew,' Pinsky said suddenly. 'He was taking a class in physical anthropology from Mayhew. That's bones.'

'Really?' Dan was too weary to ask who 'Mayhew' was. Obviously some professor or other. 'Well, that's what they said.'

'Anything else?'

Dan considered. 'One thing. Ann-Catherine, my chief nurse, said that one day he was watching her take some blood for typing and cross-matching, and he said something to the effect that anybody in a white coat could do that and nobody would notice. Usually phlebotomists do that, but we rarely have time to call up to pathology for one.'

'Pathology,' Pinsky said with some satisfaction.

'He – Ricky – said that if you put on a white coat and had the blood work-up tray and everything, you could just walk into a patient's room and take blood. Patients accepted that anyone in a white coat was official and just stuck out their arms and looked the other way.'

'So?'

'So, well, it bothered him, apparently.'

'Bothered him how?'

'I don't know, dammit.' Dan felt as frustrated as the man sitting opposite him in the diner booth. 'Ann-Catherine said he just announced this, as if it were some big discovery. She told him he was crazy, that everybody wore name tags and all it took was one patient to object, and anyway, who would want to take blood from people? What good would it do them? It's not as if they were taking a pint – just a vacutainer full, enough to test. Maybe four, five ounces at best. Not enough to satisfy a bat.' He raised his hand. 'And don't start talking to me about vampires. That's what she said. Maybe Ricky suspected vampires were walking around the hospital drawing blood from folks for snacks.'

'Ricky wasn't like that.'

'No, well . . . that's what she said, as a joke. I don't put too much on it myself. She loves horror movies and so on, and has a great imagination.'

'But it was a funny thing for Ricky to say.'

Dan nodded. 'Yeah, it was. Make of it what you will.'

'What about special friends on the staff?'

'Nobody special. Ricky was liked, Ned, but he was just a bit pushy. A bit cocky. That doesn't go down well with everyone, you know.'

'Pushy? Cocky?'

'They all said he was a nice kid, but nobody claimed him as a friend.'

'Yes, he was a nice kid,' Pinsky agreed. 'Now he's a dead kid.' He leaned forward. 'Was that all? Just the pushy, the cocky and the question about taking blood?'

'And the bones.'

'Oh yeah – the bones. See, he had a course with this professor who was murdered . . .'

'Another murder?'

'Yeah, and—'

'There's a connection with Ricky?' Dan suddenly felt a little frisson of discomfort. Maybe this was getting a little too serious. 'Two murders?'

'It wasn't like he was a special student or anything. It was only an introductory course,' Pinsky said. 'He would have been one of hundreds.'

'Even so . . . it's a connection,' Dan pointed out uneasily.

'Yes, it is. But Mayhew is dead and we can't talk to her.'

They sat in silence for a while, staring at the table and moving the condiments around. Then Dan spoke. 'My brother said something about looking for the money.'

Pinsky frowned. 'What?'

'That maybe it was nothing to do with medicine and everything to do with money. Don't you have people in the department who can look into fraud and so on?'

'Sure.'

'Well, could some of them check into that possibility?'

165

Dan asked. Pinsky just looked at him. 'Oh,' Dan said, 'I forgot. You're on your own.'

Pinsky ducked his head. 'Somebody would have to make an official complaint.'

'Not me,' Dan said quickly. 'I don't mind going around making an idiot of myself asking questions, but—'

'But you don't want to get involved,' Pinsky stated wryly.

'Hell, I'm already "involved".' Dan thumped the table with the mustard container. 'I just wouldn't know how to go about making an "official complaint" to the police.'

'Does it have to be the police?' Pinsky asked. 'Don't you have people who handle finance at the hospital?'

'Well, yes . . .' Dan considered for a moment, then began to smile. 'I know one Rottweiler you could stir up. She works in personnel and if there's one thing she's afraid of it's scandal.'

'I've met the lady,' Pinsky told him. 'I'll have a quiet word with her.'

'Sort of like pushing a stick into a hornet's nest to see what flies out?'

'Welcome to police work.'

SEVENTEEN

BOOMER BOYNTON TOOK A HARD tackle from behind and went down, but came up smiling. Pinsky, standing on the sidelines, watched and winced as the practice session continued. The sky was blue but the wind was cold, and he had taken to walking up and down and slapping his arms to keep warm.

At the end of the practice session Boomer came over to where Pinsky waited. 'I hear you want to talk to me.'

'Yes.'

'Well, I gotta shower. I stink. Come on.'

Obediently, he followed him down the tunnel to the locker room which was redolent with testosterone and sweat both old and new. There was a great deal of loud banter and slamming of metal locker doors, and he waited patiently until Boomer had satisfied himself that his shower was complete. The kid was enormous – nearly as tall as Tos but much, much wider across the shoulders and chest.

'Whad'ya want to know?' Boomer asked, as he pulled a sweatshirt over his head. 'My high school record – I was a full-back and—'

'I'm here to talk about Ricky Sanchez,' Pinsky interrupted. 'I'm a cop.' He showed his shield.

Boomer looked around to see if anyone noticed and lowered his voice to a small roar. 'I thought you was a reporter,' he said, his eyebrows drawing together into a monobrow as he frowned.

'No,' Pinsky said patiently. 'I want to talk about Ricky Sanchez.'

'That punk.' Boomer was dismissive. 'I'm not surprised somebody beat his damn brains out.'

'You didn't like Ricky Sanchez?'

'Little nerdy know-it-all,' Boomer growled. 'No, I didn't like him, but I didn't kill him, if that's what you want to know. Thought about it a few times, though.'

'I've talked to a lot of people and they all liked Ricky Sanchez,' Pinsky said innocently.

'Yeah? Well, that's them and this is me. He was a show-off and an egghead. A real nerd. Always answering questions before anyone else, always talking. Some of the rest of us, we would have liked a chance to answer now and then, you know? And the girls . . . the girls were crazy for him, can you believe it? He was short, he was scrawny, but they thought he was great.' Boomer was singing the song of the large man who thinks size is everything. He seemed baffled that someone like Ricky Sanchez would be attractive to women, when all through high school it had been the football players who got the girls. College seemed to be different and apparently it genuinely puzzled him. 'I mean,' he went on, 'I could understand it if it was the brainy girls, but it was all of them, practically. Especially that Denise. She could have had anyone, but she chose him. Crazy.'

Ah, thought Pinsky. *Another one who'd fallen into Denise's rainbow web.* He was torn between being proud of having a beautiful daughter and wanting to punch Boomer out for speaking about her like that. 'Did Ricky have other enemies?'

'Enemies?'

'Did other people dislike him? Anybody you can think of?'

'No, no.' Boomer was suddenly uneasy. 'Hey, listen, I wasn't his *enemy*, I just didn't like him. Like, there's a difference, you know?'

Pinsky nodded. And waited.

Boomer continued, 'If you think I had anything to do with killing the guy . . .'

'No, I don't think that,' Pinsky told him. 'Although it would help to know where you were on Tuesday afternoon.'

'Where I always am – here, at practice.' Boomer raised his voice: 'Do I miss, guys? Do I miss?'

'No.' 'No.' 'No,' came a chorus of answers. Obviously the conversation was being monitored. It occurred to Pinsky, abruptly, that Boomer's team-mates were being protective and he wondered why. He suddenly felt intimidated on his own. He wasn't a midget himself, but he felt dwarfed in this room of giants.

'So I was here,' Boomer said flatly. 'And I didn't like Ricky Sanchez, but I am not glad he's dead because he was a young guy and young guys shouldn't get killed before they can do anything with themselves, you know? He might have straightened out eventually.'

'How do you mean, straightened out?' Pinsky asked.

'Well, learned to keep his mouth shut. He bragged and he was a smart-ass. Nosy, too. I asked him back once, why do you want to ask so many questions? And he said how else would he find out stuff? I mean, nosy or what? Who needs to know everything about everything, anyway? Jeeze.' He leaned forward confidentially, casting a large shadow. 'He knew a lot of stuff about a lot of people, you know. He could have been blackmailing somebody. What do you think of that?' He straightened up with a look of triumph, having produced a genuine theory out of his own brain.

'It doesn't seem to fit with what we know about him,' Pinsky said cautiously.

'Yeah, but that's the clever part. Maybe he had like two personalities, one a nice guy who was just interested in everything and the other the one who used the stuff he found out.' He lowered his voice. 'He wore good clothes, drove a nice car, stuff like that. I don't think he has a rich father, that's for sure.'

'He didn't have a father at all,' Pinsky said. 'His father was killed a few years ago.'

'Oh.' Boomer was a bit taken aback by that. 'Well, that's tough. But maybe he left big insurance?'

'Maybe he did,' Pinsky agreed.

'Otherwise, where did Ricky Smart-ass get his money?'

'He worked,' Pinsky pointed out.

'Oh, yeah?' Boomer was surprised. 'When did he have time to work?'

'The same time you have for football practice. Nice talking to you, Boomer.'

'Yeah, it was,' Boomer agreed and walked away.

'I think I might have a match for you,' David Waxman told Kate. He'd rung her at home after getting no reply at her flat. 'Well, actually, I have two possibles and a probable.'

'Who?'

'I think it would be better if you came over and had a listen yourself. To be really sure, I'd like a friend of mine to have a look, too, if that's all right with you.'

'OK. Can't give me a hint?'

'Better you should hear for yourself. I'd hate to accuse anyone on my own.' There was a pause. 'Liz said the other day that your partner is a cop.'

'Yes, that's right.'

'Is his name Pinsky?'

Kate was surprised. 'No. Stryker. How do you know Ned Pinsky?'

David chuckled. 'My brother is an ER doctor at the hospital and he's apparently helping this Sergeant Pinsky out in the investigation over there. I guess it would have been too much of a coincidence.'

'Oh, I know Ned,' Kate said. 'He works with my . . . with Jack. But I thought they were investigating the murder of a Professor Mayhew. Nothing to do with a hospital.'

'I suppose he thinks homicide is more important than vicious phone calls or he'd be tracking your guy down himself.'

There was a moment of silence at the other end, then he heard Kate clear her throat. 'Actually, he doesn't know.' She went on with a rush, 'I didn't want to bother him with it when he's on a big case, you see. There are only so many cops and so many hours in the day.' Kate sounded defensive. 'This problem may seem big to me, but it wouldn't be much to him. He works too hard as it is. But he hasn't said anything about any Sanchez case lately. He's definitely working on the murder of Professor Mayhew. Did you know her?'

'Vaguely. The music department sometimes gets tapped by anthropology about musical instruments, chants, that kind of thing. Wasn't she small and blonde, kind of intense?'

'I don't know, I never met her,' Kate said. 'English doesn't get consulted much by anthropology. And I don't think she was ever on any of the interdepartmental committees I've been on.'

'It's funny how departments are so insular; a shame, really. Humanities tries to bring music, art and literature together with history. I think we should do more of that.'

'I agree.' Kate was pleasantly surprised at his willing-ness to interact and relieved to leave behind the subject of Jack. 'Although I don't think you have much free time, what with people coming to you for voice comparisons and so on. To say nothing of your composition.'

'I enjoyed doing it,' David said. 'I got some interesting vibes and noises from the voices when I took them apart. Could be used musically, as a matter of fact. I was thinking of going to the drama department and recording some of their voices. They're trained to be flexible – there could be a lot of material there.'

'You mean you'd use voices in musical composition – lyrics and so on?'

'No, no . . . just the noises in the voices. Whole different thing. When you come over for the tapes I'll show you what I mean.'

'OK. When would be convenient?'

'I'll check with Abbi. Come for dinner, you and Liz. Abbi will call you to say when.' David hung up and frowned. Dan hadn't mentioned a cop named Stryker – just this Pinsky. He shrugged. Well, it wasn't his problem. There were always plenty of murders to go round.

He would stick to voices.

EIGHTEEN

AS DAN WAS GOING TO the cafeteria, Barney Schoenfeld caught up with him. 'Hi, Barney,' he said.

Barney did not deliver his usual smile. 'Thanks a lot, Waxman,' he said in a snide voice.

Dan looked at him in surprise. 'For what?'

'For sicking finance on to me.' Barney was very angry and his voice shook a little.

'I did what?'

'You had some theory about financial fraud in my department?'

'Oh . . .' Dan faltered. That had been quick. 'My brother did, actually,' he said defensively and knew it was a coward's comment. 'I only mentioned it to someone as a possibility. Nothing to do with you personally, Barney. He meant anywhere in the hospital.'

'Well, in my department it's all to do with me,' Barney said grumpily. 'I handle the budget allocations, I do all the work on the grant forms so the others can be free to do the lab work. If I were you, I'd watch out for Fitz.'

'Fitz?'

'Yes. Because the guys from the financial department took all my paperwork for review, he's not going to get his grant application in on time. It was a close-run thing as it was, but we thought it would be OK, and then the accountants swarmed in and began messing things up.' Barney took a tray and began to slide it along the runners in front of the steamy food display. 'Fitz was pretty upset about losing the chance for the grant – it was a big one.

173

He is a big guy, remember, with a short temper. And he mentioned your name in conjunction with broken bones.'

'Fitz would be too afraid of breaking a toe to attack anyone,' Dan said cautiously. 'I think.'

Barney sighed. 'You're probably right, but I just want you to know I don't much appreciate what is going on in my department at the moment. I can't get any work done – any paperwork, anyway. What they don't mess up or take away – who knows? It's ridiculous.'

'I'm really sorry,' Dan said. 'I'm sure they must be looking at other departments too, you know.'

'I know, I know . . .' Barney was cooling down. Anger was not natural to him and he was obviously a little embarrassed, now, to have come on so strong. 'It's just – path seems to get it in the neck all the time.'

'It's where the bodies are,' Dan reminded him. Barney chuckled reluctantly. Dan leaned over and picked out a thick piece of chocolate cake, which he placed on Barney's tray. 'Peace?'

Barney sighed. 'Just watch out for Fitz, that's all I say,' he mumbled.

There was a companionable silence as they looked for and settled down at a table. When Dan spoke, his voice echoed a little from the bottom of his coffee mug. 'Done any interesting autopsies lately?'

'What's that, a conversational ploy, like have I read any good books lately?' Barney asked, almost amused.

'No, a little more than that. Have you noticed anything odd coming through? Any rarities? Anything unexplained? Any patterns? Anything?'

Barney considered. 'I had a guy the other day, he was full of diamonds.'

Dan sat up quickly. 'Diamonds?'

'Yeah. A mule, a smuggler. They got him through Customs, then somebody decided they couldn't wait for him to pass them in the natural way – or maybe he made a break for it. Anyway, they offed him. They were trying to cut him open when they were spotted. He was a goner.

When I opened him up, there were the stones. About a million bucks' worth, the cops said. Naturally they were standing over me the whole time, otherwise I might have palmed a few. In fact . . .' He lowered his voice. 'I did. Well, only one really nice one. Gonna have it put in a ring for my wife. Finders keepers, hey?'

'You're a bad man, Barney.'

'Oh, come on, it's the only larceny I ever committed.' Barney finished his coffee. 'Only one I admit to, anyway.' He laughed. 'It was better than doing an AIDS autopsy, though. We have had a slew of those lately and they scare the hell out of me. I think some of them are developing immunity to the drug cocktail or something. They seem to be doing OK, then whammo. It looks bad on our records.'

'Not much we can do about it, Barney. We can talk our heads off, but after those first few years, people stopped worrying so much about safe sex and got careless again. And the druggies share needles all the time. Then they all look at you with those big eyes in their white faces and you feel so damn guilty because you want to scream at them "your fault, your fault, stupid, stupid, stupid", but . . . what good would it do?' He started to shrug, then thought better of it. 'They'd probably sue me for harassment anyway.'

'If they lived long enough to collect, poor bastards.' Barney stood up. 'Well, thanks for the coffee. But remember what I said about Fitz. And he might not be the only one you've pissed off lately.'

'I'll do my best,' Dan said vaguely. He was lost in thought. Visions of diamonds danced in his head.

'I don't know what you mean,' Donald Mayhew said. 'What phone calls?'

'Apparently on the Sunday afternoon your wife got an annoying phone call,' Stryker said. 'It seemed to upset her.'

'I wouldn't . . .' Mayhew paused. He'd said he'd taken

a short leave of absence from his job and was staying in the house trying to come to terms with his wife's death. He looked bad, though, unshaven and gaunt. Grief was making him even smaller. He was more or less dwarfed by the large recliner in which he was huddling.

After a minute he spoke again. 'You know, you're right. I remember now, Elise once said something about nasty phone calls. Mostly on the weekend – that's right. Some man called her and . . . was extremely unpleasant. It made her angry, though, not upset. I mean, not frightened or anything. Elise was a strong woman.'

'Did she know who was making the phone calls?'

'I don't know. I think she might have, because once she said she was going to call him back and tell him off, threaten to report him to the police. But she never said to me who it was. I assumed it was a student. Do you know who it was?'

Tos and Stryker exchanged glances. 'No. We hoped you might know.'

'Sorry,' Mayhew said. He lit another cigarette, although he had just stamped out one that still lay in the ashtray, a thin spiral of smoke rising from it. His hands were shaky. He gestured around, as if to disguise it. 'I'm going to have to sell this place. It was Elise's income that paid for it – she made a lot more than I do. And I don't want to . . . I mean, she's still here . . .' His eyes filled with tears. 'It's hard. When I left that Sunday night, we had argued. She wanted me to be home more and I said what was the point when she didn't pay any attention to me when I was here, and . . . it was all so stupid. I knew she had to finish that book. I knew she cared about her damned students. I hated sharing her with everyone . . . I still do. But . . .'

'You didn't have a chance to say goodbye,' said Stryker with understanding.

'Yes, that's right,' Mayhew agreed with some surprise, looking at Stryker. 'No chance to say goodbye.'

They spent a little more time with him, but nothing came of it.

Out in the car, Tos was unimpressed. 'I still think he might have done it,' he muttered.

Stryker was surprised. 'But the other day it was me who suspected him. Not now.'

'You're a sucker for a crier,' Tos said. 'All those signs, the tears, the not shaving, the not eating – guilt. It all points to guilt, if you ask me.'

'And the phone call?'

Tos was quiet for a moment, then spoke thoughtfully. 'Suppose Elise Mayhew did know who it was. Suppose she called him back after the kids had left and confronted him, threatened to go to the police.'

'And he came round and shot her?'

'It's possible,' Tos said. 'It's really possible, you know?'

Stryker was concentrating on getting on to the freeway, but conceded the point. 'We'd better get hold of the Mayhews' phone bill – there could be a record of her calls that Sunday night. We might be able to nail him. Could it be that easy?'

'Never has been before, but maybe we'll get lucky.'

Stryker snorted. 'It would be the first time this year.'

Dr Dan Waxman had been rushed off his feet for the past eight hours. A fire in a downtown warehouse, followed by two road traffic accidents and assorted patients ranging from a guy with a splinter in his eye to a woman with a sick baby, had kept him constantly on the hop.

Weary and fed up, he opened the door to the outside world and found it was not ready to receive him. At least, not with any graciousness. It was raining and the wind was strong, buffeting him as he left the hospital and started towards the parking building. Pulling up the hood of his anorak, half blinding himself in the process, he stumbled across the pavement and into the relative calm of the parking building. But when he got to where he had parked, he let out a groan of misery. All four tyres of his car were flat. Not just flat but slashed beyond repair. He started to curse when out of the corner of his eye he saw a movement. As he turned, something came at him and he took a hard blow to the head. It didn't feel like a fist – more like an iron bar. His hood softened it a bit, but he felt his eyes crossing and a great sonorous organ began to play chords in his brain. It hurt like hell. *So this is what it feels like to be mugged*, he thought as he went down. The rest was a blur – another blow to the head, a kicking from one or possibly forty-five people, then blackness.

He came to in his own ER. Even before he opened his eyes he knew the sounds, the smell. *Full circle*, he thought and drifted away again. But someone was calling him. *Leave me alone*, he thought. *I want to sleep*. But the voice was insistent. When he forced his eyes open there was a great glare, which hurt too. His head ached and he hurt all over, in fact. It had been much easier to stay asleep.

'Come on, Dan . . . wake up . . . stay with us,' said the voice. He opened his eyes more cautiously and, though blurred, he recognized the face of the neurological resident. What was his name again? Arthur? Charles? Rumpelstiltskin?

His medical training reasserted itself. 'How long have I been out?' he mumbled. His mouth felt stiff on one side.

'About twenty minutes at a guess. We don't know how long you lay there before one of the nurses came by. You're a mess.'

'So I've frequently been told,' he said and closed his eyes again. 'Go away.'

'No. Come on . . . wake up.'

He was being shaken gently.

'That hurts,' he complained.

'Yes, you took a good kicking and you have concussion, but there's no skull fracture. No other broken bones.'

'Well, hooray for me,' Dan muttered. 'If there are no bones broken, then sleep is an excellent idea.'

'Not until you're fully awake – the police are here and want to talk to you.'

'Then will you give me some Demerol and let me sleep?' he bargained.

'Probably. Come on – sit up.'

They managed to get him more upright on the examination table. He peered around blearily and spotted a patient in even more distress than he was. 'Man over there needs help,' he said, trying to lift one arm to gesture. That hurt too. He hurt every possible where and he was definitely not going to be brave about it. 'Ouch.'

'You are off duty, Doctor,' came a voice from his other side. Gingerly he turned his head and saw it was Ann-Catherine, his chief and favourite nurse. Her expression was sympathetic but her eyes said she meant business. 'We'll handle the patients, you get yourself together.'

'Why can't I just rest here for a while?' he asked and heard a definite whine in his voice. *Come on, Waxman,* somebody inside him said. *Set a good example. Piss off,* said someone else inside him. A fight ensued. Eventually he swung his legs over the side and braced himself upright.

'Good for you,' said Ann-Catherine. 'The guy you asked me to call is here.'

'Did I ask you to call someone?'

'In between groans, yes.' Ann-Catherine grinned. 'You were very insistent. You had his number on your mobile.' She stepped back and through the curtains.

A moment later they parted again and Pinsky came through. 'Good God,' he said.

'Is it spectacular?' Dan asked hopefully. 'That's the only consoling thing, to look really, really bad. The rest is just boring.'

'Did you see who . . .'

'No. I think there were about nine of them.'

Pinsky looked disconcerted. 'Really?'

'Hell, no. Just trying to impress you. One guy, maybe two. Most probably one with a big stick and big feet.' He shifted slightly and let out an involuntary groan.

'Haven't they given you something for the pain?' Pinsky asked, wincing in sympathy.

'Not until they are sure my head is clear. Could be a haematoma in there. Or several small men with axes. Something unpleasant, anyway.'

'You weren't robbed,' Pinsky said quietly. 'It was personal. I saw your car.'

'Shit.'

'Do you owe anybody money? Slept with anyone's wife lately?'

'Neither.' Dan took a deep breath and diagnosed a cracked rib.

Pinsky sighed. 'Then it must be you've upset someone by snooping around for me. I'm sorry.'

Dan tried to wave a hand negligently, but it brought tears to his eyes. 'You know,' he began conversationally, 'I've treated hundreds of guys who've been mugged, beat up, whatever. I think I'm going to be more sympathetic in future. This is not my finest moment.' He blinked a few times, then looked at Pinsky warily. 'You really think I've hit a nerve someplace?'

'It looks like it. Hard on you, but it does tell us how seriously whoever it is takes it. At least he didn't kill you.'

'He tried.'

'No – once he got you down he could have finished you off, the way he did Ricky,' Pinsky pointed out. 'He didn't. This was a warning.'

'I would have accepted a printed notice, even a phone call. I'm not a hero. I'd have backed off right away.'

'And you're backing off now?'

'Hell, no.' Dan concentrated hard to keep the room from spinning. 'Now I'm pissed off.'

'Maybe I should let you rest,' Pinsky said, concerned at Waxman's pallor, which was heightened by the contrast with the bruises.

'No, thanks. I want to tell you.' It took him a minute or two to gather his mind, which felt like it was running out of his ears. 'I think you should talk to a guy in

180

pathology called Fitz. He was angry about the money thing. It might have been him.' He spoke confidentially and deliberately, as if very, very drunk.

'And why him?'

'Money,' Waxman repeated. 'Remember I told you my brother thought maybe there could be something like that going on – some kind of skimming perhaps. Embezzlement – that kind of thing. I don't see how, but then I'm no accountant.'

'Oh hell,' Pinsky muttered. 'And I had a word with the ice maiden in personnel yesterday. Maybe that's what hit a nerve.'

'A bit soon, I'd have thought.'

'OK, but listen.' Pinsky had another idea. 'I was talking to my daughter and she told me something Ricky said. Something like "You can see something every day and yet never really see it at all." What kind of thing would he see every day?'

'Now you're asking something,' Waxman said. 'There are routines in every department . . . ours are mostly to do with supplies, because otherwise we are anything but routine. We never know what's coming through the door.'

'But you do have procedures you perform, things that are common to every patient? Tests and so on?'

'Oh, sure . . . depending on the seriousness of the case, of course. Regular tests, blood, urine, respiration, pulse, blood pressure . . . Is that the kind of thing you mean?'

'I think it must be,' Pinsky said slowly. 'He wouldn't have been able to see money skimming every day, would he? I think it must be something you do down here. Something you do every day. Something so ordinary it's done automatically.'

'You mean without thinking?'

'Without thinking.'

Waxman was perturbed. 'You mean it isn't pathology? It's right here in the ER?'

Pinsky shrugged. 'You tell me.'

'I intend to,' Dan said. 'As soon as they give me a new head.'

Just then, Pinsky's cellphone went off. He answered, listened, spoke. 'I'll meet you there in ten minutes.' He cut off. Dan raised an eyebrow – not without difficulty. 'Might be a lead,' Pinsky explained. 'I'll check out this Fitz guy, but I think it might be a red herring.'

'Then maybe you should check out the cafeteria,' Dan said and abruptly went to sleep.

Mike Rivera was waiting outside a Starbucks. He looked a real mess, filthy and defeated. It wasn't just the clothes and the dirt, it was something in his eyes. 'I can't do this any more,' were his first words. His voice was thin and desperate, and he kept brushing at his clothes, now here, now there.

'Take it easy, Mike,' Pinsky said gently. 'You don't have to do anything you don't want to do.'

'It used to be a game, you know? I felt like an actor performing a role in a big movie . . . now I feel . . .' His voice trailed off and he shook his head. 'I've lost it,' he said. 'It's all gone.'

'Come in and have a coffee,' Pinsky suggested.

'They won't let me in there,' Mike protested.

'They can't stop you. Come on.'

The Starbucks staff seemed a little flustered at serving Mike, but they did it with dignity. As the shop was not far from French Street, they were probably accustomed to some less than savoury customers. Pinsky made a promise to himself to patronize the chain more often. 'Now, what was the big hurry?' he asked when Mike had downed two doughnuts and half his coffee.

'I talked to a witness,' Mike answered. 'Somebody who saw the killing. I'm not saying he's reliable or would have much punch in court, but he saw it. He's scared as hell of cops because he's been put into Beaumarchais twice already.' Beaumarchais was the hospital where the psychiatric cases were sent who were considered a threat to the community. 'He doesn't want to go back.'

'He doesn't sound much of a help.' Pinsky was disappointed.

'No, but he said this. He said "two white coats". He said "one white coat hit the other white coat and then ran away". He's real clear on that because he has this thing about white coats from Beaumarchais, of course, but he's definite. He was in the alley opposite and saw the whole thing. He says they argued and then – bam!'

'He said white *coat*? For sure?' Pinsky asked. 'Not white uniform?'

'White coat. Definitely.'

'Waxman wears those green scrubs most of the time,' Pinsky mused, 'but some of the other doctors wear white coats. In fact, most of them do. That makes it definitely the hospital, as if I didn't think that already,' Pinsky said, feeling better. 'This guy say anything else?' He was grateful to Mike for turning up the witness, but irritated by the fact that he hadn't been turned up earlier by the officers interrogating French Street inhabitants the day of the murder. Still, it was a floating population and most of them would have melted away when the police appeared. And, of course, they were all blind, deaf and dumb when it came to telling tales on their fellow wanderers.

'Said it was a man.' Mike shrugged, releasing some less desirable fragrances from his clothing. 'But maybe it was a woman with short hair. I wouldn't say this guy's eyes are real good.'

'But he saw the white coats.'

'Yeah. He did.'

'And he heard their voices. Men's voices.'

'Oh, yeah. Men's voices, yeah.' Mike scratched himself. 'I gotta go home and get clean,' he said plaintively. 'I can't stand this.'

'OK. You done good.' Pinsky started to pat Mike's arm, then thought better of it. 'You want anything else to eat?'

'No, I'm fine, thanks. I wish I could have got more for you.' Mike seemed ashamed of his failure. 'I don't know what it is, I can't talk to these guys now; I see them differently than I did before. I don't know what's happened to me.'

'You're older, wiser and richer,' Pinsky said with a shrug. 'It happens. It's a young man's game, undercover. You aren't a kid any more.'

'I feel like I let you down. And those guys on French Street, I let them down, too. Nobody will talk for them now.'

'Teach somebody,' Pinsky said abruptly.

'What?'

'Look around, find a good strong candidate on the force, teach him all you know. Pass it on, Mike. That's what you can do. Pass on what you learned down there. Social workers too, if you can pin one down to listen.'

Mike had brightened a little. 'You think?'

'Why not? Then nothing is wasted.'

Mike looked at him for a long time. 'Thanks.'

'Thank *you*,' Pinsky said with a tiny, formal bow. 'Now go home and take a bath. You are putting me off my coffee.'

Mike laughed and something came back into his eyes: relief and a kind of pride. 'I wasn't so bad, was I?'

'You were fine,' Pinsky assured him. 'You were the best.'

'You're not a detective, dammit, you're a doctor,' David Waxman said as he helped his injured and groaning brother to his car. 'And you're coming home to stay with us. Abbi is a good nurse.'

'I only need rest,' Dan said.

'And watching. Watching for at least twenty-four hours,' David reminded him as he unlocked the door and removed a parking ticket from under the windshield wiper. 'You were out for a long time, your Dr Mickleman was pretty concerned.'

'Mickleman is a worrywart,' Dan muttered.

'I would have thought that was a good quality in a neurologist.' David opened the car door and eased Dan into the passenger seat.

'Yeah. Just what everybody needs – a neurotic neurologist,' Dan mumbled. He really did want to go to sleep very badly.

David opened his door and got in behind the wheel. 'Maybe you should have stayed in like they wanted you to. I don't know about this discharging yourself. That nurse of yours was very worried.'

'David, I know what to look for.'

'In your normal state of mind, you do,' David said, starting the engine. He knew Dan was a very good doctor, but a good doctor with a massive lump on the head is not quite the same thing. He said so.

Dan managed a grin. 'It is pretty impressive, isn't it?'

'You sound proud of it.'

'Well, now that the worst is over I am. Kind of like battle wounds. I was there, I survived. Ouch.' He had tried to adjust his position as the car lurched forward and succeeded only in banging the hand he was using to give a mock salute into his bruised forehead.

'And your cop friend thinks it was because you were snooping around? Not just a random mugging or a disgruntled ex-patient?'

'I wasn't snooping, exactly. I was familiarizing myself with the functioning of the hospital as a whole. Preparatory to my going into hospital administration.'

'Was that your cover?' David asked in amazement. 'Did anyone believe you?'

'Not the ones who know how much I hate paperwork,' Dan confessed. 'But most of them accepted it. It was perfectly reasonable.'

'But you said you spent most of your time in pathology,' David prompted, negotiating a difficult intersection. 'How come?'

'Well, first of all, that's where the bodies are. I don't know. Something or somebody up there felt odd. They're very intense in that department. Barney was kind of edgy, too. He said I was getting underfoot.'

'Were you?'

'Sure.'

'Enough to worry someone?'

Dan gestured towards his head and face. 'Obviously.'

'So now you can back off, let this Pinsky get on with it, yeah?'

'Well . . . until I go back to work,' Dan said. 'I'm really kind of pissed off about this beating. I never had a single chance to hit back.'

'To hit back and bust a hand?' David pointed out. As a musician he was very aware of his hands and the importance of protecting them.

'You don't think about that at the time.' Dan sighed. 'This was a very instructive experience for me. It will make me a better doctor, a better person.' He was drifting off again.

'Oh, great,' David said in exasperation. 'What are you going to try next, childbirth?'

NINETEEN

'THIS DOESN'T MAKE SENSE,' NEILSON said, staring at the phone records they had obtained from the phone company. They stated clearly that two phone calls were made from Professor Mayhew's telephone on the night in question. 'The first one, at seven o nine, was made to a Professor Albert Torrance. The second was to a number that turns out to be the Suicide Hotline. At eleven thirty-seven, that one was.'

The detectives stared at one another.

'It couldn't have been suicide,' Stryker said after a minute. 'There were no prints on the gun – you can't shoot yourself in the head and then wipe the gun, for God's sake!'

Neilson shrugged. 'There it is, in black and white.' He held out the sheet of paper. 'She called the Suicide Hotline. Or somebody did.'

'We'll have to go down to the university and have a word with this Professor Torrance,' Tos suggested.

'You want Muller and me to go to the Suicide Hotline?' Neilson asked.

'They won't tell you anything,' Tos said. 'Their work is confidential.'

'They might make an exception – if they know anything. People who call up don't usually give more than their first names. If that. They aren't interested in names. Just helping people.'

'It won't cost anything to ask,' Muller said. As he

listened to them he kept rubbing his short hair back from his brow, smoothing it, like velvet.

Stryker shrugged. 'Go ahead. Good luck, but don't hold your breath waiting for a revelation.'

Stryker and Tos drove back yet again to the university and eventually found Professor Torrance in one of the biology labs. The place was empty of students, but there was a drip of liquid from somewhere, as steady as a clock, and a gentle gurgling like a slowly emptying cistern. Their footsteps echoed on the tiled walls and floor. Tos was groaning quietly to himself – there were 'things' in glass bottles and the smell . . . his stomach gave a lurch and he swallowed hard.

'Again?' the professor asked, looking up from where he was preparing a specimen of what looked like a peeled frog . . . or something.

'I beg your pardon?' asked Stryker, putting away his warrant card and badge holder.

'Well, first the other policeman, now you,' Torrance complained. 'I have work to do, you know. I can't keep stopping.'

'Other policeman?' asked Tos.

'Yes. Pilgrim or Spasky or something.'

Stryker and Tos exchanged glances. Pinsky?

'What did he want to know?' Tos asked impulsively, trying not to look at what the man was doing.

'About one of my students. A boy who was killed.' Torrance grimaced. 'A great loss.'

'We're here on another matter this time, Professor,' Stryker said. He, too, found the man's fiddling with scalpel and pins unnerving, for Torrance continued to work as he spoke, staring down at the unfortunate specimen spread out on a board before him. 'Did you know a Professor Mayhew?'

Torrance looked up briefly. 'Yes, of course I did. Terrible thing, her being killed.' He gave a brief cackle. 'Seems to be an epidemic.'

'She telephoned you earlier that night – Sunday.'

'Did she?' He seemed bemused. 'Oh yes . . . she did. I remember now.'

'What was it about?'

'Nothing important. We serve together on the inter-departmental ethics committee. Served, I should say. And she had a question about something . . . what was it, now?' He tilted his head and closed his eyes. 'Oh yes . . . something to do with an entertainment, I think. Some gathering or other. Wanted to know if I was attending or not. I was not. And that was it – very brief.'

The phone call in question had been of two minutes' duration.

'And she mentioned nothing else?'

Torrance made a sudden slash with the scalpel, laying open an extremity of his dead specimen. Tos flinched, Stryker looked away. 'Nothing else that I can recall,' Torrance said, shoving in some pins to hold the specimen open.

'How did Professor Mayhew sound?' Tos asked.

Torrance looked up at that. 'Sound? Sound? What do you mean, sound?'

'Did she seem happy, sad, worried, angry, afraid—'

'Good Lord, no. Just . . . businesslike. As usual. She was a very businesslike person, you know. Very efficient.' He straightened up and reached for a towel to wipe his hands, which he did, thoroughly. Then he took off the glasses he was wearing and exchanged them for a pair he extracted from the pocket of his white lab coat. 'I'm sorry I can't be of more help, gentlemen, but really – I hardly know what to say about it. She rang, we spoke briefly and that was it. Nothing more was said about it.'

'About what?'

Torrance coughed. 'About attending the entertainment. What else would it have been?' He stared at one, then the other, still turning the discarded pair of spectacles in his knobbly hands.

'Well, sorry to have bothered you, Professor Torrance,'

Stryker said. 'I guess it was just a coincidence that she happened to phone you on the night she died.'

'My goodness . . . put like that it sounds very sinister, doesn't it?' Torrance managed a short cackle of nervous laughter. He began to crack his knuckles absent-mindedly. 'Does it mean I was the last person to speak to her?'

'Not unless you killed her,' Stryker said mildly.

Torrance reared back. 'Killed her? Me? Good Lord, no. Why would I want to do that?'

'Why does anyone kill anyone?' Tos asked innocently. He very much wanted to talk to Stryker outside.

But Stryker spoke first. 'Can you tell me where you were on the night she rang – after she rang, I mean?'

'At home, of course. Alone. My wife died some years ago and I have only the dogs for company now. She bred poodles, you see. The last two are still with me. Alexander and Janus. Marvellous company, dogs. A little work, of course, but worth every effort.'

'And on the following night?'

'Monday night?' Torrance seemed suspicious. 'Why Monday night?'

'Just answer the question,' Tos said.

'Well, for goodness sake – Monday night would have been the same. I lead a very quiet life outside the university, gentlemen. I'm afraid I can supply no alibi for you, if one is required.'

'Do you keep house yourself?' Stryker asked.

'No, of course not. I have a woman who comes in three times a week, in the mornings when I am here at the university. We never see one another, communicate by notes. She is very satisfactory, but I never see her. I can't even remember what she looks like, come to think of it. Isn't that strange?'

'Sort of,' Tos said. 'What's her name?'

'Agnes. Agnes . . . um . . . Johnson. Yes, that's it, Agnes Johnson. Why on earth would you want to know that?'

'We're just nosy,' Stryker informed him. 'Always good to hear about a good, reliable cleaning lady.'

'Indeed?' Torrance seemed totally at sea now. 'But what has this to do with Professor Mayhew?'

'Nothing,' Stryker admitted. 'Thank you for talking to us, Professor. We may have to call on you again.' They turned to leave.

'But what for?' came Torrance's querulous voice after them. 'Why are you harassing me like this?'

They left without answering.

'Hey,' Tos said. 'Pinsky was here. Do you think there's some connection?'

'I don't know,' Stryker said. Could it be? He stopped walking abruptly. 'Let's get some deep background on Professor Torrance. And a list of *his* phone calls for the past few months. Both home and university calls, if you can get them. I certainly don't believe in this "entertainment" he said Mayhew called him about. Whoever heard of an ethics committee that gives dances?'

The Suicide Hotline office was not very inspiring, considering the work they did. Small and crowded, with desks that contained only notebooks and a telephone, it looked an uncomfortable place to hear the world's woes. The walls were a dingy tan, there were fingermarks all over the door jambs, and one window was cracked and sealed over with brown tape. It wasn't going to be easy, Neilson thought. Muller was no Pinsky, but he was proving to be fairly reliable and eager for experience. Neilson was adjusting to him, slowly. And Muller was . . . coming along. Slowly.

Looking around, Neilson spoke low. 'You'd think, working in a place like this, they'd be calling each other after a while.'

But there was a little kitchen that looked much used and a few comfortable chairs for relaxing away from the desks. There were two people there when they arrived, a man and a woman. The woman was talking quietly into a phone, the man was making coffee. Seeing them, he automatically added two mugs to the two already in front of him.

'Can I help you?' He was long-haired, bearded,

191

sandalled, sweet-expressioned, like a Renaissance portrait of Christ. He wore two sweaters over a rather ragged shirt and corduroy trousers. *Perfect*, Neilson thought. *Just perfect. I could have described him before I even got here.*

They showed their badges and before they could speak he shook his head. 'It's all confidential. You people know that.' His voice was firm and strong. And a little impatient.

'We can always hope,' Neilson said. 'And this is about a homicide, not a suicide.'

'Ah.' The man nodded as he poured hot water over the instant coffee powder he'd added to the mugs. 'Sunday night?'

Neilson and Muller stared at one another.

'You know about it?' Neilson finally asked.

The man stopped pouring, put down the kettle and opened a small fridge to extract a carton of milk. He sniffed it cautiously, then added it to the mugs after gesturing to them with it to ask, silently, whether they took milk in their coffee. They both nodded and he poured. He pushed two mugs towards them, added sugar to the other two and picked them up. 'Help yourselves to sugar,' he said, and carried the mugs out into the other room, setting one down beside the woman who was still talking quietly into the phone and taking his own over to the comfortable chairs. He settled into one and waited for Neilson and Muller to join him. He seemed ready to talk. Neilson and Muller didn't speak – afraid to interrupt what felt like manna from heaven.

'So she called you, then,' the man said. 'My name is Chris, by the way. Chris Nunally.'

'She?'

'The girl.' He paused, his mug in mid-air. 'She *didn't* call you?'

'Nobody called us,' Neilson said. 'We have a record of a phone call made to you on Sunday night from the telephone of a homicide victim. We hoped you might be able to help us.'

'I can't,' Chris said. 'I mean, confidentiality and all that, but in this instance I can't because I don't know anything. I took the call myself, Sunday night. It was a girl, hysterical, saying someone was dead, that it was all her fault . . . and so on. I got her calmed down a bit and told her she had to call the police. She said she would. She promised she would. But you say she didn't?'

'A neighbour called us,' Neilson told him. 'You say a girl?'

'She didn't give her name, and even if she had—'

'A girl, not a woman? Saying she'd killed someone?'

'No,' Chris explained carefully. 'She said "she" was dead and that it was all her fault.' He sighed. 'Look, we're not supposed to discuss our calls, though in this situation, with a homicide and all, I guess it's OK. But I don't know any names or anything like that.'

Neilson looked at his notebook. 'The call lasted about ten minutes.'

'They usually do.' Chris nodded. 'It takes time to get people's confidence . . . a lot of the calls are long silences while they get up the nerve to say what's wrong. We hear a lot of sighing and snuffling.'

'And in this instance?'

'It took time to calm her down.'

'But she didn't say her name?'

'No. I asked, but she wouldn't.' He looked reflective. 'I think she began regretting calling us, began to realize what she had said. The funny thing is, her voice sounded kind of familiar.'

'Familiar?' The coffee was terrible, over-strong and musty, but Neilson forced it down.

'Yes. I thought at first she was one of our regulars, but usually regulars say their names right away. She didn't. Maybe she just *sounded* like one of the regulars.'

'Some people call you a lot?' Muller asked, curious.

'Oh sure. That's what we're here for. Some people need a lot of help just to get through the night.'

'Are most of your calls at night?'

'I'd say so, yes. That's why there are only two of us on at the moment. Afternoons are slower. It picks up around supper time, then just keeps going.'

'You do a good thing.'

Chris shrugged. 'If it helps one person to stay alive it's worth it. It breaks your heart, but . . .' He leaned forward. 'They helped talk my mother out of suicide, encouraged her to get help. I do this for her. I should have been listening to her myself, but I wasn't. None of us was. But the Suicide Hotline listened, so . . . she's still alive.' He drank his coffee with every evidence of enjoying it. 'Here I am. I'm sorry I can't help you more.'

'You've been very forthcoming,' Neilson said. 'We appreciate what you've told us.'

'It wasn't much.'

'It was a start,' Muller said. 'A good start.'

'This changes everything,' Neilson said, as they clattered down the stairs and out into the breezy morning. They both buttoned their coats – it was a cold wind and a mischievous one. 'He said a girl called.'

'One of her students?' Muller suggested.

'Who else would be at her house?' Neilson asked. 'We'll have to talk to them again. I suggest we start with the Chinese girl.'

Muller sighed heavily. At least Neilson was consistent.

They managed to track down Chan Mei Mei at the university, away from the dour supervision of her parents. She was drinking coffee in the Student Union with a group of friends – none of them the Mayhew graduates – and when they appeared she looked apprehensive. 'This is harassment,' she said, standing up. Her friends looked interested and ready to object strenuously if she did. She was wearing a GSU sweatshirt and embroidered jeans. Her long, shiny dark hair fell down over her shoulders and her slightly tilted eyes were dark as molasses. Neilson fell in love all over again.

Muller seemed immune. 'Could we speak to you alone,

Miss Chan?' he asked, indicating an empty table in the corner.

'I suppose so,' she said cautiously. 'But I can't tell you anything else.'

'Let us be the judge of that,' Neilson said and could have kicked himself. Especially when she gave him a quizzical and slightly pitying look.

When they had settled at the round table, the girl said nothing, but waited. She had the gift of silence and used it. Both men were slightly disconcerted by the sense of patient waiting she exuded.

'We're still looking into the death of Professor Mayhew,' Neilson began.

'And you haven't solved it yet?' she asked. There was no judgement in her voice, just curiosity.

'Are you sure you didn't go back to her home later on Sunday night?' Neilson asked.

She smiled. 'Well, I would hardly tell you if I had, would I? What I told you was the truth – I was at home, with my parents, all evening.'

'But they are your parents,' Muller pointed out.

'And so would lie for me? Of course they would,' she agreed, quite unperturbed. 'But the fact remains, I was at home. I did not go back to Professor Mayhew's house. I did not kill her. I had absolutely no reason to kill her. She was my mentor and my friend. She understood the conflict of cultures in my life, she made allowances, she was interested. She gave me confidence.'

'As a good teacher should,' Muller said.

'Exactly,' she agreed. 'And now I am without her, I feel a bit lost. We all do. They have assigned us a new graduate tutor, but it is not the same. There is no friendship there, just what you might call technical support. By the book. No relationship.'

'And you had a relationship with Professor Mayhew?'

'We all did,' Chan said. 'Some of us were more dependent than others, but we felt she was in our corner all the way, interested in us as people.'

'You say some were more dependent than others—'

'Galumph was in love with her,' she said flatly. 'He didn't make a pass at her or anything, but it was plain how he felt. She treated him gently, never referred to it as far as I know. But she knew. Lois is just a dependent kind of person – clingy, needy, pathetic. Jerry Hauck . . .' she paused. 'His mind met hers, somehow. There was no physical thing . . . but they thought alike. She admired his brain. We all do. It's him we can't stand.' She grinned suddenly, showing slightly uneven teeth and a dimple. Neilson was completely lost. His mouth fell slightly open.

Muller had to carry on, recognizing his new partner's state of mind. Everybody in the squad room knew about it, even rookie detectives. It had happened before and it would happen again. Neilson was a good officer, a good detective. But every once in a while a woman would get to him and he became useless, totally useless. Muller, with his whole week of experience, was disdainful of this unprofessional attitude, but could see Neilson was beyond redemption.

'Do you think Mr Garrison could have been jealous of Elise Mayhew's husband? Taken advantage of his absence to make his feelings known to her? Been rejected? Lost his temper?'

Chan's eyes widened. 'That's an interesting scenario,' she said slowly. 'All possible, of course. Except if you knew him you would never believe it. I don't believe it.'

'But it is possible.'

'Well, anything is possible,' she agreed with a sideways glance at Neilson, who had closed his mouth but still wore a slightly vacant expression. 'Are you all right?' she asked him suddenly.

Caught out, Neilson jerked upright. 'Sure. Sure, I'm fine.'

She turned back to Muller. 'I guess you could make up all kinds of stories of what might have happened. About any of us. But they wouldn't be true.'

'Tell us about Lois McKittrick,' Muller said, glancing

at his notebook, where he had quickly jotted down details of that interview when Stryker briefed them earlier.

She shrugged. Neilson coughed, tried to get himself in order. 'She is a strange one,' she admitted. 'Very, very intense. But kind of silly, too. Personally I can't stand her, but she's part of the group so I do the best I can. She drives me nuts. I think she had a crush on Professor Mayhew, too. In a gorpy, teenagery kind of way.'

'And Jerry Hauck?'

'Is in love with Jerry Hauck,' Chan said firmly. 'He makes a perfect couple, all by himself.'

When Muller finally was able to drag Neilson away, he practically had to frogmarch him to the car. 'What the hell is wrong with you?' he demanded. 'Couldn't you think of anything to ask?'

'No,' Neilson said. His head was full of oriental magic.

'Jesus,' Muller muttered. He leaned against the car and looked at his notebook, taking in all that had been gathered about the four graduate students. One stuck out, of course. The only other woman. And the caller to the Suicide Hotline had been a woman. Or a girl, the guy had said. A girl. It seemed pretty obvious that was Lois McKittrick. But before they talked to her, Muller said he thought they ought to check out her alibi. McKittrick had said she had been with a friend – Nan Prescott. They'd located her home address but had not followed up the alibi yet. Nan Prescott was a student nurse, which meant she might be at work or at home, depending on what shift she was on.

They were closer to Prescott's home address than to the hospital and, as luck would have it, she was there, sleeping, when they rang her doorbell. After quite a while, during which they had almost turned to leave, she opened the door and stared at them blearily. 'This had better be good,' she said.

It was.

Abbi Waxman had prepared a delicious meal, and they

were now replete and happy. They sat round her dining-room table, a council of war – Kate, Liz, David, Dan and Abbi. Dan was staying with his brother and sister-in-law while recuperating.

'What do you plan to do?' Abbi asked.

Kate and Liz looked at one another. 'We're not quite sure,' they said, almost together.

'We could go and punch the guy out,' Dan suggested. Since his beating he had become very aggressive. He wanted very much to hit back. Someone, anyone, would do. But it was only a whim – underneath he was still a healer, not a hitter.

David drank some of his wine. 'We're still not absolutely, positively sure,' he said. 'You could go off at half-cock and have the wrong guy – followed by a nice big lawsuit.'

'I know,' Kate agreed. 'That's the trouble. The evidence – the matching that you did – is not admissible in court. They would only accept the evidence of a qualified technical expert.'

'It takes three years to qualify, by the way,' David said. 'I asked my friend.' But the friend, a qualified expert, had more or less confirmed David's nominee, although he would not go into court to testify unless he ran further comparisons himself.

'It seems a shame, after all the trouble you took,' Abbi said. She stood up, went to the kitchen, and came back with a large cheeseboard and another bottle of wine. After putting them in the middle of the table, she went back again and got the coffee. 'I mean, I suppose David saw it as an interesting exercise, but even so—'

'I called him back,' Kate blurted out. They all stared at her. She shrugged, knowing it was another example of her recent changes of mood. 'I just wanted to make sure.' She flushed suddenly. 'I snapped, OK? I'm sorry. I called him a stupid old fart. And then I hung up.'

'Oh Kate,' Liz said in a disappointed voice. 'You warned him.'

'Oh, I didn't explain and I didn't say who I was. I just called him that and hung up, like I said.' She grinned with an air of defiance. 'It felt good.'

'So now he has an obscene caller,' Dan pointed out.

Kate shook her head. 'I could have been a student. Students do stuff like that sometimes. He probably just dismissed it. But the voice was the same. I am sure it was the same. I was sure when I first rang him to get him on tape. But I waited until David confirmed it.'

'Ricky Sanchez was Torrance's prize pupil,' Dan said suddenly. 'It was Torrance who suggested to me that we give him a job.'

'Who is Ricky Sanchez?' Liz asked, curious.

Dan explained about Ricky being killed on French Street and his private co-operation with Pinsky.

'Why did Ned Pinsky ask you to do this?' Kate asked, puzzled. 'Jack hasn't mentioned anything about it.'

'I gather the others are working on a different case,' Dan said. 'Pinsky has taken leave to follow up on Ricky's death.'

'Oh dear,' Kate said. That was not good.

'You know this Torrance?' David asked.

Dan smiled. 'I was, in my time, his prize pupil also.'

'And what is he like?' Kate asked.

'Well, to be honest, I can imagine him making those phone calls,' Dan admitted. 'He is a very volatile man, very passionate about his work, and since his wife died he's got a lot worse. We used to meet for lunch a couple of times a year, but after last time I backed off.'

'What happened last time?' David wanted to know.

Dan took a deep breath, winced slightly and let it out. 'He was out of control,' he said simply. 'Practically frothing at the mouth because he was losing so many students to other faculties. Paranoid about it.' Dan looked at Kate. 'He was particularly nasty about the English department – not only were they poaching students from science, but their big new building cast a shadow on his office. He seemed to take both things as personal attacks.'

'So he is a nut case,' Kate said. 'I had heard rumours.'

'Could he have been the one who beat you up?' David enquired.

'Good Lord, no.' Dan laughed. 'He's a little dried-up guy; you could blow him over with a paper fan. Wonderful teacher, though,' he continued in his mentor's defence. 'Absolutely inspiring in the lab. Oh shit!' He snapped his fingers. 'I just remembered.'

'What?' they all chorused.

'He mentioned Ricky at that last lunch. He used him as an example. Said Ricky was thinking of dropping out of pre-med and going into something else. Something Torrance thought was a waste of time and talent.' Dan frowned. 'What the hell was it?' he asked himself. They waited. His battered face cleared. 'Bones,' he said triumphantly. 'He was fascinated by bones. He was thinking of switching courses.'

'To what?' David asked.

'Anthropology. Physical anthropology.'

TWENTY

'I THINK WE SHOULD PULL her in,' Neilson said.

'Tell me again what the Prescott woman said.' Stryker sat at the table in the police cafeteria, an empty plate in front of him, a still-steaming mug of coffee beside it. He was a fast eater. Kate was out at a dinner tonight with Liz. Something about a project for the university, she had said, and he hadn't felt like cooking for himself.

'She said Lois McKittrick was agitated all through the movie,' Muller read from his notes. 'She kept muttering to herself and didn't want to stop for coffee afterwards. She said she had to get something settled.'

'She must have known Prescott would say this,' Tos suggested. 'You told her we would check her alibi for the evening. Up to eleven o'clock, that is.'

Stryker shook his head. 'She might have thought she was acting perfectly normally. We don't always know what we project to other people – especially if we're caught up in our thoughts.'

'What was the movie?' Neilson asked. 'Maybe the movie upset her.'

'Valid point,' Stryker acknowledged.

Muller checked his notes again. '*American Beauty.*'

'Ah,' Stryker commented. 'About confrontation. Among other things.'

'Even so,' Neilson said. 'It all hangs together – her alibi for after eleven is no alibi at all. And the guy at the Suicide Hotline said it was a girl's voice saying "She's dead – it's my fault".'

201

'Yes . . . and she was very asthmatic the next day when they all met to discuss the situation, very stressed.' Tos was thoughtful.

'Well, her favourite professor had just been offed,' Neilson pointed out.

Stryker shook his head. 'It hangs together – we should talk to her right away.'

'The girl on the phone could have been Chan,' Neilson said hopefully.

Muller glared at him. 'Can you really picture her calling the Suicide Hotline? Or panicking at all?'

'No,' Neilson conceded. 'She's a cool one.'

'When we talked to McKittrick she was a very tightly wrapped little bundle of nerves,' Stryker reflected.

'So would you be if you'd killed someone.'

'We don't know that,' Stryker cautioned. 'But yes, it does look interesting. She was very edgy when we talked to her – but I thought it was just the reaction of a very timid person to being interviewed by two cops. Maybe it was more. Bring her in tomorrow morning.'

'My God,' Liz said, 'you don't suppose this Torrance killed the boy, do you?' They were still seated round the dining table at David and Abbi's home, staring at the empty wine bottles in the centre of the table, picking at the last bits of cheese.

Dan shook his head. 'I can't really imagine that,' he said. 'Torrance is a talker, not a doer.'

'He's a talker, all right,' Kate said. 'But you said he was out of control.'

'Only in a manner of speaking. He was obsessed, could see just his own point of view. He didn't use to be like that.'

'So he could be a killer,' Abbi said, wide-eyed.

Dan shook his head again. 'No, I don't believe that. There's no physical threat to him. Or there wasn't.'

'But if there's a chance,' Liz said. 'We don't want to mess with him.'

'I agree with Dan,' said Kate unexpectedly. 'I think this connection with Ricky is only a coincidence.' She had been growing steadily more stubborn about Torrance ever since David had revealed his name. She knew it was unreasonable, but she couldn't seem to stop herself. Knowing she was probably wrong only made her more determined, because . . . because . . . well, because. Nobody ever said she had to be sensible all the time, did they?

'But if—' Liz began.

'He values life,' said Dan. 'For its own sake. You don't have to worry about him attacking you.'

'Not if we go together,' Kate ventured. 'I think that would do it. I think we can scare the hell out of him, make him stop the calls. Threaten to expose him.' She glanced at Dan. 'He's not very big, you said?'

Dan grinned. 'No, small and skinny. You could handle him.'

'If he's sane, we could,' Liz agreed. 'I don't like this, Kate.'

'Oh, pooh,' Kate said dismissively. 'I vote we go to see him and nail him once and for all.'

'Better you than me,' Abbi contributed. She had drunk less wine than the others and was listening with a sceptical ear.

'I'd be careful if I were you,' David said.

'I'll go with you,' Dan volunteered.

They all looked at him.

'Well, why not? A male presence might strengthen your case. And I know him, remember. He likes me.'

'God knows why,' David muttered. 'You're not in very good shape to confront anyone, Dan – not even a small, skinny old guy.'

'I'll take a big stick.'

'How about a baseball bat?' Abbi suggested mischievously.

'Um – I think that would be against the law,' David pointed out, helping himself to more goat's cheese. 'Carrying a weapon with intent to do bodily harm.'

'I could be on my way to baseball practice,' Dan said.

'In November?'

'Winter training?' Dan offered.

'No, I'm determined,' Kate interrupted this flight of fancy. 'We can handle it. Dan, thanks for the offer, but I think it's up to us.'

'Who, exactly, is "us"?' Liz wanted to know.

Kate looked at her reproachfully. 'You don't want to come?'

'Well . . .'

'You have The Look.' David smiled. 'That should nail him for a start.'

'I don't know . . .' Liz hesitated. She looked at Kate, saw disappointment in her eyes. She understood her friend very well. She knew Kate was being backed into a corner. She saw confusion in her eyes, pleading, fear and stubbornness. Foolish or not, Kate was going forward, alone if she had to. And that Liz couldn't accept. But she made one last try. 'Now that you know, don't you think it's time to tell Jack? He could send a woman officer with you.'

'I hadn't thought of that,' Kate allowed. 'But Jack is very busy on another case and . . .' She trailed off.

'Oh, hell,' Liz said. 'All right. I'll go with you.'

'Good.' Kate felt free now to indulge her appetite for strong cheddar and black coffee. Everything tasted so good lately; she knew she was being indulgent. She reached for a cracker. 'Then that's settled.' She was so busy cutting cheese, she didn't see the dismay on the faces around her.

Lois McKittrick wouldn't come out of her room.

'We just want to have a word with you, Miss McKittrick,' Neilson said in his most winsome voice.

'Go away,' was the answer from beyond the locked door.

Muller glanced over his shoulder at the three girls clustered behind them. Lois McKittrick lived in a house near the campus and shared it with these other girls.

It was a shabby house but well-kept and clean inside. Typical student accommodation, where the landlord does as little as possible and charges as much as possible. But the girls had made it homelike and it was obvious they were a decent group. They seemed uneasy and puzzled by the presence of two police officers in their upstairs hall, and kept looking at one another with worried expressions.

Muller turned to them. 'Does she do this often?'

The plump girl, Lorrie, nodded. 'Not that we ever ask her to come out, but sometimes she stays in there for days. We know she creeps down at night to get some food and use the bathroom, but otherwise ... we don't see her a lot anyway.'

'She pays her rent on time,' said Ayo. She was a tall, beautiful black girl with bright eyes. 'She doesn't leave a mess in the kitchen or after a bath – the ideal housemate, really.'

'If you like living with a ghost,' said the third girl, small and thin and sporting the amazing name of Peaches Crabtree. She didn't have a southern accent, though she probably should have had with a name like that. 'The rest of us are good friends, but Lois ... just makes up the numbers, really. We've tried to include her in things, but she prefers to be on her own. She's not nasty about it, she just ... is very ... solitary.'

'How long has she lived here with you?' Neilson asked.

They exchanged glances. 'Three years,' Ayo finally said, after a little thought. 'Her junior and senior year, and now she's doing graduate school. So are we. I know she took her degree with honours, summa cum laude, but I only knew that when I read it in the programme. She never said.'

'Isn't her behaviour kind of ... off-putting?' Neilson asked.

The girls shook their heads. 'Everybody has a right to live the way they want as long as they don't hurt anyone,' Ayo said. 'Why should we want to change her?' She

shrugged. 'She is what she is. And she has to live somewhere, doesn't she?'

'Yes, but . . .'

'I can hear you talking about me. Go *away*!' called the
voice beyond the door again.

'Do you have a key to her room?'

They looked shocked. 'No, of course not,' said Peaches.
Neilson was looking at her in a way Muller didn't like.
Was Neilson deserting his crush on the oriental beauty
of Chan Mei Mei for this little fluffy thing, all blonde
curls and blue eyes? Muller detected a brain behind those
eyes and that name – Neilson didn't have a chance here
either.

'But what happens in case of fire?' Neilson asked.
'Suppose she fainted in there, or was taken ill? What
would you do then?'

Again they exchanged glances. 'It's never happened,'
Lorrie finally said. She was the plain one of the three,
but had a fantastic smile. Or had, when she first let them
in. Now none of them appeared to be very friendly. 'She's
not stupid, you know. She doesn't usually lock her door
anyway. Just closes it.'

'Ah. But she has locked it now,' Muller said. 'When
did that happen?'

They didn't know. They hadn't tried the door before
Muller and Neilson had arrived. Why should they? their
expressions said. It was only when Muller knocked and
then tried the handle that the situation became apparent.

'Don't you feel responsible for her?' Neilson asked.

They all shook their heads. 'She's not responsible for
us either,' Ayo said. 'We are independent women who
happen to share a house, that's all. We each have our
own lives to lead.'

'That we get along with each other is a bonus,' Lorrie
put in eagerly. 'But it isn't necessary. Not really.'

Muller knocked on the door again. 'Miss McKittrick,
you have nothing to fear. We only need to talk to you
about Professor Mayhew.'

'No,' was the unequivocal answer.

'If we want to drag her out we'll have to get a warrant for her arrest,' Neilson whispered. He eyed the three girls, all of whom were beginning to look irritable. They had withdrawn to the stairway and were muttering among themselves. He was especially worried about the one called Ayo – she seemed to have strong convictions and he would bet she knew what was what about every law in the land. 'McKittrick has rights.'

'But we only want to question her.'

'Yeah – and my mother sings with the Metropolitan Opera,' Neilson sneered. 'She's our best suspect and you know it. Come on. We'll pick up a woman officer while we're at it.'

They said goodbye to the girls and went down the stairs.

'Lieutenant Stryker is going to love this,' Muller said.

The three girls stood quietly in the hall until they heard the front door close. Then Ayo went to the locked door and rapped gently. 'Lois, they've gone. It's just us here. Would you like some coffee? We're just going to make some.'

There was a long silence. Then came the sound of the key turning in the lock and the door swinging back with a slight squeal from the hinges. 'I'm in bad trouble,' said Lois McKittrick, her eyes wide and wet behind her spectacles.

Ayo, Lorrie and Peaches drew themselves up and somehow together. 'We'll help you,' Peaches said. 'Won't we, girls?'

'Woman to woman,' Ayo said. 'Whatever it is, we're on your side.'

'But it's very bad,' Lois said again.

Lorrie looked puzzled. 'How bad can it be? It's not like you killed anyone or anything.'

'Well . . .' Lois began.

TWENTY-ONE

STRYKER STARED AT THE LIST of phone calls from Torrance's office and home phones. There it was in black and white. Torrance had been placing regular phone calls to Mayhew's home and to her office. Enough to count as harassment – or a love affair. Thinking back to Torrance's appearance, the latter seemed highly unlikely, but he knew attraction between the sexes often didn't make sense. Torrance was a widower. And Mayhew's husband was often away for days at a time.

But that wasn't what was bothering him.

It was another number that he recognized.

Kate's office number.

According to the records, Torrance had been calling her regularly and often for some time now. He hadn't noticed the number at first, but when he had registered it something inside him had turned over. What the hell?

Kate had come in very late last night and rather giggly from too much wine. After he had gently scolded her for driving in that state, she had owlishly informed him that Liz had been driving and anyway, she was a grown woman and could make her own decisions. In fact, she had said, she was in charge of herself, thank you.

It had been more of the same song she had been singing over the past week or so. He still didn't know what she meant by it. But neither of them was in any state for a discussion – it had been so late and he had been exhausted too. This morning he had left her asleep, and had put a couple of aspirin and a glass of water on the bedside table for when she awoke.

He had felt sympathetic and loving, for despite her recent bad tempers and moodiness, he loved her very much.

Now he just felt angry.

Was this what all the cold shoulders and prickly attitudes had been about? No affair, he was certain of that. But what was her connection with Torrance? And why hadn't she mentioned it?

He left the office and drove over to the campus, determined to track her down and ask for an explanation. Did this have something to do with the 'project' she and Liz were working on? Was Torrance a part of it or what? Some of his anger was fear – Torrance was obviously a suspect in the Mayhew killing and he didn't want Kate involved in any of that.

In the event, tracking her down wasn't difficult. She was in her office, drinking black coffee and looking miserable. He barged in without even knocking and glared at her. 'What are you doing with Albert Torrance?' he demanded.

Kate looked at him, shocked and dismayed. 'What?' she asked nervously. 'Don't yell, Jack.'

He swallowed and spoke more quietly. 'What are you doing with Albert Torrance?' he repeated.

'I don't know what you're talking about,' she said, drinking some of her coffee and hiding behind the mug.

He flung himself into the chair opposite the desk. 'Oh hell, Kate, stop the crap. I happen to know that Albert Torrance has been calling you regularly for some time. What's it about?'

She looked almost frightened, which puzzled him. Her eyes avoided his. 'It's nothing,' she said finally.

'I said, cut the crap.'

'What are you so angry about?' Kate flashed back. 'You come in here, yelling and crashing around . . .'

'I asked you a question. Please answer it.'

'I can't,' she said.

'What the hell does that mean? You can't or you won't?'

'All right then, I won't.' She had got her breath back and glared at him in turn. 'It has nothing to do with you; it's my problem and I will deal with it.'

'And does Liz know about this problem?'

'What if she does?'

'So you confide in Liz but not in me, is that it?'

'It's a woman thing,' Kate improvised quickly. 'It has to do with a biological survey. Professor Torrance . . .'

'Oh Jesus, Kate, cut it out, will you? I've met Torrance. As of right now he's involved in the Mayhew case.'

'You mean – you think he killed her?' Kate went a little pale.

'No . . .' He hesitated. 'But we think he may have been harassing her somehow. Has he been harassing you?'

She looked away.

He stared at her. 'Has he?' he asked more gently.

She felt herself wanting to cry at the concern in his voice, but managed to hold back. 'He . . . can be . . . difficult,' she finally allowed. 'He doesn't like other departments poaching students.' Suddenly she remembered something. 'Do you know about Pinsky and Ricky Sanchez?'

'Yes, I do. How do you know?'

She explained about Dan Waxman and meeting him at the Waxman house where she and Liz had had dinner the previous evening. She kept talking, quickly, hoping to distract him from asking any questions about what she and Liz had to do with the music department. 'Dan said Torrance talked about Ricky, that he was angry because Ricky was changing from pre-med to anthropology. Physical anthropology, which was what Elise Mayhew taught, wasn't it?'

'Yes,' he said. 'But . . .'

'Torrance was angry with me because he said I had poached Michael Deeds and Janet Linley from science, and apparently he was angry with Mayhew because of Ricky.

Maybe he killed her and Ricky, too,' Kate said, going as quickly as she could, hoping he wouldn't pursue the mention of Michael Deeds in her revelation. She drew a breath and took another angle. 'Ned Pinsky is on leave, isn't he?'

'Yes. I think I told you that – he was very upset about the boy's death.'

'Well, he's investigating it on his own,' Kate told him. 'He got Dr Waxman to help him, too. Somebody beat Dan Waxman up the other night. Maybe it was Torrance.'

'Where has Waxman been asking questions?'

'At the hospital, because Ned told him—'

'I know about Ned's theory.'

'You should be helping him,' Kate said. 'He's doing it all on his own.'

'His choice. Fineman made it clear he didn't want it taken any further and we were stuck with that.'

'Your Captain Fineman is a fool.'

'Not really.' Stryker almost smiled. 'But he has a lot on his desk.'

'Not in his head, obviously.'

'Look, Kate, nice try, but I came to ask you about Torrance.'

'I told you, he's mad because he thinks I poached Michael Deeds and Janet Linley from science to English. He's an old man with a grudge, that's all.'

'Well, stay away from him. Hang up if he calls again. He's got something to do with the Mayhew case – he was probably harassing her too and it may have led to her death. Leave it to me.'

Kate regarded him. 'If I had told you that I was getting annoying phone calls, what would you have done?'

'Me?'

'Yes.'

'I would have told you to call the phone company. Were they dirty calls?'

'No,' Kate conceded. 'Just . . . angry.'

'The phone company would have put a tap on your line, gathered evidence and dealt with him.'

'Dealt with him how?'

'I don't know. Depends on the situation. Did he threaten you physically?'

'No.' She didn't have to lie about that.

'I don't know, then. If he had threatened you or been sexually offensive they might have taken him to court, I suppose. On your behalf. Otherwise I suppose they might have just given him a warning . . . or cut off his telephone.'

'Yes. That's what I thought,' Kate said. 'So I didn't bother you with it.'

'Kate, I want you to bother me if you have problems.'

'Well, I want to deal with my problems myself,' Kate said firmly. 'I am not your child or your possession.'

'I never said you were.'

'Well, then – stop coming in here and yelling at me and telling me not to do things. I resent it.'

'Oh, you do, do you? Well, I resent your not being truthful with me.'

'I am truthful with you. I just don't tell you every little problem I might have at work. I am a grown-up, remember?'

'You could have fooled me.' Stryker stood up. 'Just ignore Torrance, all right? Stay away from him, do not talk to him. In fact, I forbid you to have anything to do with him. Leave it to me.'

Rage welled up inside her. 'My work, my problems.'

'Well, this is *my* work,' he snapped. 'My case and I want you out of it. Is that understood?'

She glared at him, arms folded across her chest, curls practically standing on end and eyes flashing. A bell sounded in the corridor outside and she stood up abruptly. Her voice was suddenly cold and hard. 'If you have finished issuing orders, I have a class to teach.' She strode out without a backward glance.

He sat there for a few minutes, off balance and confused, not quite understanding how he had come in full of righteous anger and had ended up in the wrong.

How did she do that?

How did they all do that?

'You can't come in.'

Muller looked at Neilson. Then he looked at the pair
of bright-brown eyes that peered at him from around the
corner of the front door. They were back on the front
porch of the house shared by McKittrick and the other
women. It was cold. He was getting pissed off at the whole
situation. There had been no woman officer available,
and he and Neilson had returned alone. 'We have to see
Lois McKittrick,' he said stolidly.

'I'm sorry, you can't come in.'

'We have a warrant for her arrest,' Neilson said.

'That may be, but you don't have a warrant to come
into this house,' said Ayo. 'It's our house, not hers. The
lease is in our names and we don't want you to come in.'

Muller sighed. 'We are authorized to use reasonable
force,' he said patiently.

'Go away,' was the reply and the door was firmly shut
in their faces.

'Oh, for crying out loud,' said Neilson. 'This is ridiculous.'

'She's got them on her side.'

'We can break the door down.'

'Is that reasonable force?' Muller wondered. 'That's
pretty drastic.'

'We could get a couple of boom boxes and play loud
music like they did for Noriega,' Neilson leaned his back-
side against the railing of the porch that ran across the
front of the house. He crossed his arms. 'I'm here to stay,'
he added.

Muller rang the bell again.

'Go away,' came a voice from behind the closed door.

'I don't think the neighbours will be very impressed if
I get an axe and break down your front door,' Muller
bluffed. It was hard to bluff when you looked like a kid,

213

but he gave it his best shot.

'Neither will we. We would sue you for criminal damage.'

'We are officers in the pursuit of our duty. You are obstructing us. We could charge you with obstruction.'

'Get another warrant, then.'

Muller turned to Neilson. 'We can do that, right?' he asked in a low voice.

'What, the axe or the charge of obstruction?' Neilson was still amused.

'Either.'

'Sure. I'm not saying Captain Fineman will like the publicity, but we could do it all right.'

'Shit,' said Muller, who rarely swore.

'I am going to call the Student Union,' came a different voice from behind the closed door. 'I am going to call the newspapers. I am going to get reinforcements.'

'Mexican stand-off,' Neilson said approvingly. 'Nice move.'

'If we do it fast, there won't be time for them to call the press,' Muller said.

'Oh, hell.' Neilson levered himself off the porch railing. 'Go on, then.'

'We're coming in,' Muller shouted. He glanced around. Already there were a couple of students from nearby houses on the sidewalk below, looking on with interest and some contempt. 'I hate students,' he confided to Neilson. 'While we're crapping around out here, this Ms McKittrick could be slipping out the back way. Maybe she already has.' They stared at each other. They hadn't thought of that. They should have.

'Maybe we should call for back-up.'

'They'll just about arrive along with the press.'

'Oh, shit,' Muller said again, establishing a new record for himself. 'Have we got an axe in the car?'

'Nope. Got a tyre iron, I think.'

They assessed the door. It looked pretty solid, but the lock was old. 'We can do it,' Neilson said, backing off a little. 'But if I get a dislocated shoulder out of this, you're

214

doing all my paperwork for the next month.'

'Kick, then,' Muller suggested. 'Kick first – the lock looks weak.'

'OK. On my count of three.'

'Why is it always three?' Muller asked.

Caught off guard, Neilson lowered his foot. 'I don't know. Does it matter?'

'I just wondered,' Muller said. 'It just occurred to me.'

'Have you a preference for something else?' Neilson enquired sarcastically.

'No. One, two, three will be fine,' Muller said. 'It just occurred to me to wonder, that's all.'

Neilson glared at him. 'One,' he said ominously. Muller sighed and lined up beside him, bracing himself. 'Two, three,' Neilson shouted and they both kicked the door at lock level. It burst open easily, revealing Ayo, Lorrie and Peaches on the other side. They all screamed and backed down the hall as Muller and Neilson fell through the open door, just managing to stay on their feet. The girls had been unprepared for the sudden access and clung together. Or rather, the smaller two clung to Ayo, who looked furious.

'We have reason to believe Lois McKittrick is on these premises,' Neilson said, a little short of breath, steadying himself on a nearby chair.

'This is breaking and entering,' Peaches informed him in a tremulous voice.

'Oh, hell, woman, where is she?' Neilson snapped. 'Still in her room? We'll arrest the whole bunch of you in a minute.'

'I'm here,' said Lois McKittrick, coming out of the living room to their right. 'They were only trying to protect me.' She sounded defeated. 'I'll come quietly.'

'It would have been a lot cheaper if you'd done that before,' Neilson said irritably. 'Now they'll have to get a locksmith.'

'We'll send you the bill,' Ayo said ominously.

'Fine, fine, send us the bill.' Muller was aware of some

215

voices outside in the street. They didn't sound like the happy voices of peasants at play. Students and neighbours were gathering, and the sight of them kicking in the door was obviously not to the public's liking. By now someone was certain to have called the police – and the newspapers. If the girls themselves hadn't already done so. It was just the two of them, without back-up, and if they didn't act quickly the situation could become ugly. Students loved any excuse for a demonstration. Especially one that involved the police. Muller had had plenty of experience with ugly crowds when he had been in uniform and didn't relish a repeat. He had thought detectives were past that. Apparently not.

'Let's go, Miss McKittrick.'

'I have to get my coat,' she said.

'Oh no,' said Neilson. 'I'll get your coat. You stay right here where we can see you.' He paused. 'Where is your coat?'

'In my room.'

Neilson sighed and, with a glance at Muller, who nodded, went up the stairs to Lois McKittrick's room. As he stepped through the door, his mouth fell open. One entire wall was covered with pictures of Professor Mayhew. Most were candid shots, obviously taken without the woman's knowledge. A couple were posed shots with other students – he recognized Jerry Hauck, Chan Mei Mei, and Morrie Garrison. One was a posed portrait, apparently enlarged from some publication, as it was very grainy. 'Holy St John Birchman,' Neilson said. He knew what it meant. It meant obsession. It meant psychiatrists. It meant complications. It meant trouble. He went to the cupboard and got a warm coat for their obviously loony arrestee.

He was a less than happy man.

Kate was an unhappy woman. She sat in her car, stuck in a traffic jam, and scowled at the other drivers around her. Inching forward in the lunch hour traffic, she wondered whether she felt like going to the gym or not. She was so angry with Jack that she wanted to ram the car in front of her, but it was a Mercedes and the bills would have been horrific. Maybe she could work off her annoyance at the gym – that had been the idea, anyway. Liz was meeting her there. They would have a workout and then some lunch.

She pounded her fist on the steering wheel and blew her horn quite unnecessarily at the car in front, whereupon the driver gave her the finger. He knew she was a bitch. She knew it too, but anger was destroying any common sense she'd ever had. She managed to stop herself from getting out of the car and confronting the man, but it was a close-run thing. She asked herself what exactly had made her so furious.

The word 'forbid'.

Red rag. Fighting word. The trouble was that she knew he was probably right. She and Liz had planned to confront Torrance and now she couldn't because Torrance had something to do with Jack's precious case.

She met Liz in the changing room and told her about Jack's visit.

Liz seemed very relieved. 'Well, then, that's that,' she said. 'I know you're probably disappointed, but it's for the best, Kate.'

'Best for whom?' Kate wanted to know, pinning her locker key to her T-shirt and heading for the weights room. 'I wanted to deal with Torrance myself. We went to all that trouble tracking him down, got David involved, and now . . . nothing.'

'That's better than getting killed,' Liz said mildly.

Kate glanced at her. 'You don't believe Torrance killed Elise Mayhew, do you?'

'I have no idea. I don't know any more than I read in the paper. I seem to remember there was some question of suicide.'

'No.' Kate explained about the gun being wiped of prints and the lack of contact powder burns Jack had told her about.

217

'Well, even a little skinny guy can shoot a gun,' Liz pointed out, grunting a little as she began her shoulder lifts. 'And if he caught Ricky from behind, by surprise . . . even if Dan says he's small and weak, he's also mean. We know that from the calls. And anger or madness is supposed to make people stronger than normal.'

'Well, I'm angry, but I don't seem able to lift any more than usual.' Kate dropped her hand weights back in the rack after struggling with shoulder presses.

Liz, relieved that Kate seemed to be more reasonable, nodded and reached over to replace her own weights. In doing so, she missed the look Kate gave her in the mirror.

It would have scared her.

They arrived back at Kate's office about an hour later, switching on the lights, as it was darkening early. A roll of thunder in the distance said cold rain was on the way. They had just settled down with coffee when the phone rang.

'Hello, Katie,' said the familiar hated voice.

'Hello, Professor Torrance,' Kate said and Liz nearly dropped her coffee. 'How delightful of you to call.'

There was a silence. 'So you know who I am.' The voice was, if anything, a little tighter, a little nastier than before. 'That is a shame.'

'Oh, really? Why?' Kate asked.

'Because now I really will have to go to see the Dean,' Torrance said. 'It's been fun, but it's time you were put in your proper place. I saw the picture of you in the student paper yesterday.'

'Not a good likeness,' Kate said through clenched teeth.

'No. But an excellent demonstration of what I have to tell the Dean.'

Kate closed her eyes. It had been an old picture of her at a Rag Week celebration, hugging a male student with enthusiasm. Not Michael Deeds, fortunately, but definitely a male student. The story had been on the history of Rag Week, presaging a light-hearted new book by another English faculty member.

'Can't we settle this between us?' Kate asked.

'Too late, Katie,' said Torrance and hung up.

Kate gripped the phone with white knuckles and looked at Liz. 'He's going to the Dean.'

'Stop him,' Liz said. 'Call him back.'

Kate rang the science department, but was told that Professor Torrance was not in today. 'He's at home.' Kate put down the phone. She reached for the phone book and began riffling through it for Torrance's home address.

'No, Kate,' Liz said.

'Oh yes,' Kate said. 'Oh yes.'

TWENTY-TWO

DAVID WAXMAN DROPPED HIS BROTHER Dan off at the entrance to the Emergency Room, where he was taking the late-afternoon shift. Dan was in no shape to drive comfortably. He was still staying with David and Abbi, and they were glad to be able to look after him. Dan worked long hours and it was hard, heartbreaking work most days. Worse to go home to an empty flat and have to struggle with those broken ribs.

Dan was still determined to help Sergeant Pinsky out in his investigations, even after the battering he'd received. David sighed and pulled back out into traffic. All this was getting a bit much, he thought. First the vicious phone calls to sort out for Kate – he admitted he'd enjoyed that. But it involved no physical confrontation. He was worried about Kate and Liz going to see this Professor Torrance. It felt wrong to him that they would have no male support. It was not a matter of not respecting their individual rights as human beings, nor of coming over all protective male. It just seemed ... unbalanced. And it was the same with Dan. The hospital was huge, it was full of all kinds of people, at least one of whom obviously had it in for Dan. Which meant Dan was getting too close to whoever had killed the boy, Ricky Sanchez. If only Kate and Dan weren't both so stubborn.

Two kinds of confrontation – Kate's face to face, Dan remaining vulnerable to another possible attack from behind – and David didn't like either of them. He himself required a peaceful life. He was not a coward, nor was he lazy or afraid of physical effort. He just liked a clear mind and quiet surroundings in which to make music.

All this emotional static was interfering with his work.

It definitely wasn't his kind of thing.

But it was all around him and he was getting edgy.

It felt like . . . thunder in the distance.

Lois McKittrick just sat there, tears rolling down her face, trembling from head to toe, but saying nothing. Absolutely nothing.

Neilson had told Stryker about the pictures in the bedroom and they agreed that it appeared as if the girl had had an unnatural obsession with her teacher, but further than that they couldn't go without some response from her. No matter what they asked, she just sat there in the grubby interrogation room.

Saying nothing.

'The arrest warrant was premature,' Stryker said, cross with himself for not overseeing the arrest.

'It was the only way to get her down here,' Muller protested. 'Those girls weren't about to let her come quietly – they were prepared to stand us off and make a splash in the press.'

'But what we have is purely circumstantial.'

'Why is it always "purely" circumstantial?' Muller wanted to know.

Neilson turned on him. 'What is it with you and this philosophical questioning of everything?'

Muller shrugged and turned away to hide a smile. He had found a way to bait Neilson and he was beginning to enjoy it. Little did they realize that under his little-boy exterior there lurked a demon born to torment the innocent. He would soon have them all licked into shape, he thought to himself. The Rookie from Hell.

Stryker continued. 'We know she has no alibi after eleven for the night of the murder, that she was close enough to the professor's home to reach it at a fast walk in twenty minutes or so, or a three-minute drive. We know there was an altercation at the house some time around eleven thirty and we know that a woman called the Suicide Hotline from Mayhew's phone at around midnight shortly after the shots were fired. But we have no prints, no witnesses, nothing.'

'We have that she was stalking Mayhew.'

'We don't know that. We only know she was obsessed with her.'

'Lesbian,' Neilson said with disgust.

Stryker eyed him. 'We don't know that,' he said quietly. 'And maybe she doesn't, either. She seems very immature for her age. It could just be some kind of crush.'

'Either way, it doesn't prove she killed her.'

Having given up for the moment on direct questioning, they were looking through the one-way mirror at Lois McKittrick, who sat in the interrogation room, with a woman officer watching her from a seat in the corner. Stryker frowned. 'I want a doctor to look at her anyway,' he said. 'Hear that?' The microphone in the room beyond the mirror was on, in case McKittrick said anything to the woman officer. 'She's beginning to wheeze ... the last thing we need is for her to have some kind of asthma attack while in custody.'

As they watched, Lois rummaged in her handbag. The woman officer started to stand up, but when the girl drew out an inhaler and used it, she sat down again.

'She's OK,' Neilson said with relief.

'For the moment,' Stryker conceded. 'The point is, now that we've got her, what the hell can we do with her if she doesn't say anything? We can't hold her for ever and we can't book her without evidence. Our only hope at the moment is a confession and that doesn't seem to be forthcoming.'

'She hasn't asked for a lawyer.'

'I think we should ask again whether she wants one or not. I think we should make clear just what we do have and why we suspect her of this murder.'

'She'll see right away it isn't enough to convict.'

'Maybe not,' Stryker said slowly. 'First we'll tell her the situation, *then* we'll get her a lawyer.'

'That is very sneaky,' Tos said. 'You're counting on her ignorance.'

'What else have we got?' asked Stryker irritably. 'Unless you want to call in the Chinese girl as well.'

'We could—' Neilson began.

'No point,' Muller interrupted. 'I doubt she has a picture wall of the professor, her parents wouldn't allow it, and I certainly doubt she is the type to panic and call the Suicide Hotline. The guy said the voice was a little familiar, remember, as if she were a regular. McKittrick strikes me as just the kind of person to call the Suicide Hotline on a regular basis.'

'They don't wear identification tags,' Neilson argued. But he knew Muller was right. They all knew it. The odds were that Lois McKittrick had killed Professor Mayhew. But they were only odds – they were not evidence.

It was very frustrating.

'Maybe we should try a woman detective,' Tos suggested. 'Who have we got?'

'No. How about getting that woman psychiatrist in?' Stryker said slowly. 'We've used her before and she's retired from her full practice, so she's usually available as a consultant. She can check McKittrick's physical situation and maybe get her to talk as well. What's her name again?'

'You mean Dr Maclaine, that white-haired old biddy in the tracksuit and trainers?'

'Yes, that's the one. We can brief her on the situation and she might be able to draw the girl out. We can tape from in here. It's worth a shot.'

'I'll get her on the phone,' Tos offered.

Dan tried not to breathe too deeply, but he felt like heaving a big sigh of exasperation. The pain in his ribs was restricting his movement, which in turn restricted his work. Even bending over to listen to a suspect abdomen was painful. He had taken some mild painkillers, but didn't want to impair his faculties. Can't make a good diagnosis when you're spaced out from here to Mars.

The staff were making allowances and doing all they could to make it easier on him, but so much depended on touching the patient, palpating organs, judging clamminess or dryness of the skin, feeling the temperature and pulses of injured limbs and so on. He was a hands-on doctor and always would be.

He straightened up and looked at Ann-Catherine, the nurse who stood on the other side of the patient. 'I think it's a hot appendix,' he said. 'Better get her admitted, stat. Better ring them to prep an OR, too.'

'You got it,' she said and moved to the phone on the wall.

He turned to face the patient, a frightened-looking woman in her late forties. 'Mrs Jenkins, I think what we have here is appendicitis and I think it would be best to have it taken care of as soon as possible.'

The woman gasped. 'I thought it was just that spicy sausage I ate,' she said.

'Then you have a better threshold of pain than I do.' Dan pointed to her taut abdomen. 'That must hurt like blazes.'

'They gonna cut me?'

'I'm afraid so. But it's a quick, routine operation. Leave it any longer and it could get a lot more serious. Fast.'

She closed her eyes. 'OK,' she breathed. 'Anything to make it stop.'

'Good girl,' he said, giving her upper arm a reassuring squeeze. He left the cubicle and looked around. 'Anything else?' he asked Ann-Catherine as she passed by with a handful of charts.

'Nothing we can't handle. Get yourself a cup of coffee or something, you look like hell.'

'Gee, thanks.' Dan grinned. But he was grateful for the break as there was something he wanted to check out.

* * *

'Hello, my dear. I'm Dr Maclaine.'

Lois looked up, didn't say anything. The woman who had entered the room was in her seventies, white-haired and benign-looking. Her hair surrounded her face like a halo, but was well cut and styled. She was dressed in a navy-blue tracksuit and bright white trainers, and carried a small black bag. When she came in she glanced at the woman police officer who had been sitting with Lois McKittrick and the officer left, closing the door behind her.

'The officers are worried about you, my dear,' Dr Maclaine went on, opening her bag. 'They've asked me to check you over, to make sure you're all right. Is that OK with you?'

Lois sighed and nodded. She held out an arm, as if offering it for a sacrifice. Dr Maclaine duly took it and counted her pulse. 'A little fast, but then, under the circumstances that's not surprising,' she said gently. 'I understand you're an asthmatic?'

Lois nodded. She fished her inhaler out of her bag and presented it to the doctor. 'Ah, yes,' Dr Maclaine said, reading the label and handing it back. 'I'd like to listen to your chest, if that's all right with you?'

Lois submitted to this. Dr Maclaine listened intently, then removed her stethoscope. 'I think another puff or two would be in order,' she said with an encouraging smile. 'I am getting wheezing in there, still.' She sat down beside Lois, folding up her stethoscope, and watched the girl take two puffs from her inhaler.

Dr Maclaine tilted her head on one side, like a wise old bird. 'And how do you feel in yourself?'

Lois looked at her and suddenly the slow tears became racking sobs. She covered her face and gave way completely. Dr Maclaine took a box of tissues out of her bag and put them on the table between them. She waited patiently. She knew what had happened – they had gone at the girl hammer and tongs, with no result. All men, all bigger than the girl, all angry. One kind word was all

225

it needed. One sympathetic voice. A woman's voice. Because although she might be over twenty-one, this was a child.

Dr Maclaine knew about children. She'd been a psychiatrist for forty years, specializing in children. Children of all ages.

As the sobs decreased in intensity, Dr Maclaine drew one of the tissues out of the box and held it where Lois could see it. Lois took it and began mopping her face, her chest still heaving with sobs and wheezes. The storm of emotion had done her asthma no good at all, but might have released other tensions.

'They're going to put me in jail,' she finally hiccuped.

'Are they?' asked Dr Maclaine. 'Why do you think that?'

'Because . . . because . . . I killed her.'

'Killed whom, dear?' Dr Maclaine's voice was non-judgemental.

'My mother,' was the answer. Taken aback a little, Dr Maclaine glanced briefly at the one-way glass and frowned. This wasn't what they had briefed her about at all.

'I kill everybody I love,' Lois went on.

'When did your mother die, Lois?' the doctor asked softly.

'When . . . when . . . I left home.' More sobs, dry sobs now, and wheezing. Dr Maclaine looked into her bag to make sure she had epinephrine in case this blew up into a big attack. She knew they kept oxygen in the building, but she would like to have had a nebulizer handy. Letting the girl go on like this was a risk, but it was important she got it out. All out.

'Then you didn't kill her,' the doctor said in a reasonable tone.

'She took too many pills,' Lois said. 'She didn't want me to go to college, she didn't want me to leave. He did. He liked the idea of me spending someone else's money and not his. He promised not to hit her anymore, but she knew when I left he would start again. I knew it, too. In my heart I knew it but I didn't want to admit it.'

'Who is this? Your father?'

'Yes. He . . . he . . .' She stopped, her chest obviously constricting. 'He's evil. And I'm evil too. He always said I was. He was afraid of me.'

'Surely not.'

'Oh, yes. If I'd stayed . . .'

'If you'd stayed he might have started hitting both of you,' Dr Maclaine said. 'If your mother was afraid of him, she could have left with you. But she stayed. It was her choice, Lois. Not yours. You have your own life to live. I understand you came to GSU on a full scholarship, all your expenses covered. Nobody could reasonably be expected to turn down such an opportunity.'

'I could have. I could have stayed. I should have stayed.'

Dr Maclaine waited until Lois's breathing was a little less laboured. She knew the police officers behind the glass were impatient, but there wasn't always a fast way through misery. 'But that isn't why they have arrested you, is it, Lois?'

'I don't know.'

'You don't know why they've arrested you?'

'Well, they said . . . they think I killed . . . Professor Mayhew. And I didn't. I didn't!' She looked straight at the doctor, her blue eyes bloodshot, the rims reddened. 'But she died because of me. It was my fault. I am evil, like he said. He said I was an evil child. Just like Daddy used to say!'

TWENTY-THREE

DAN WAXMAN WALKED ALONG THE hall and entered the ward
that broke everyone's heart – filled as it was with terminal
AIDS cases. There, at the far end, he spotted Ivan Sherwin
with his blood tray, doing the work of the phlebotomist
who was off sick. Gowned and gloved, he was gentle as
he worked, looking for the elusive veins under the tender
skin.

Dan stood and watched, saying nothing. When Ivan
finished, he looked up and started. 'Dr Waxman,' he said.
'What are you doing here?'

'Watching, just watching.' Then he turned on his heel
and walked away, reasonably certain of what he had seen.

Ivan caught up with him at the door. He was unusu-
ally chatty. 'I have to do a lot of this,' he said, walking
beside Dan as they went towards the elevators. 'Mary –
that's one of the phlebotomists – she has chronic kidney
problems. Loses a lot of time.'

'Kind of below you, isn't it?' Dan suggested with a wry
smile.

Ivan shrugged. 'We all pitch in because of Mary. She's
a good woman, she can't help being sick. And I enjoy the
clinical side of it, too. We can get a bit ivory-towerish in
the lab.'

'What are you looking for?' Dan asked, as the elevator
doors opened and they joined the people inside.
'Anything besides white and T-cell count?'

'Whatever I can find. You know I'm working on AIDS
research myself.'

'Yes, I know that,' Dan said carefully. 'How's it going?'

Ivan shrugged. 'Uphill, always uphill.'

The door opened and Dan got out. 'Keep at it,' he said casually and turned away as the doors closed behind him.

Then he leaned against the wall and tried to slow his breathing. The nearness of the big man had unnerved him. That, plus what he had seen. Or thought he had seen.

'Dr Waxman! We have a triple traffic smash-up on the way in,' called one of the nurses.

'Coming.'

Lois McKittrick had stopped crying, but she was wheezing badly and struggling to control her breathing.

Dr Maclaine waited. Finally, she spoke. 'Why do you say it was your fault Professor Mayhew died?' she asked softly.

'Because she was angry and upset.'

'Angry with you?'

Lois shook her head, reached for the glasses she had discarded, twiddled with them, not looking up. 'No. With the man on the phone.'

'What man was that?'

'Some man who had been calling her and saying bad things. I heard him. I took the phone away from her and told him he was disgusting and he called me . . . he called me . . .'

'An evil child?'

'Yes.' Lois emitted a small hiccup. 'Even he knew.'

'Why did you go to see Professor Mayhew that night?'

Lois sighed, as much as she could. 'She hugged Chan, but she didn't hug me,' she said sadly. 'In the movie, the man stood up for himself and I thought I should, too. She didn't listen to my paper, she didn't take time for me on Sunday, and I loved her so much and I knew it was a mistake and so I went to see her. I know that was wrong, now. It was late. She was so tired. She said her head felt like it was about to burst. But then the phone call came and she got so angry. She started yelling at the man and she was so upset, and I wanted to protect her, so I took the phone, but then he said ... what he said ... and I began to cry and that made her even angrier with the man and then she suddenly flopped down on the bed and said she'd had enough. It was too much, she couldn't go on any longer. She told me to leave and I started to, but then I saw her take a gun out of the bedside table. I thought she was going to kill herself.'

'Really?' Dr Maclaine sounded neither surprised nor unsurprised. Just interested.

'Yes.'

'Did you think she was serious?'

'Oh yes. Oh yes. She had the gun. I thought she was going to kill herself or the man on the phone.'

'She knew who it was?'

'Yes.'

'Did she say who it was?'

'No.' Lois frowned. 'She just said he'd been calling and calling, and saying she was wicked and that he was going to tell someone she was lying in her book – falsifying research, that kind of thing. As if she would. She said she was sorry he'd upset me.' Lois gave a convulsive single sob and hunched slightly forward. 'She was worried about me ... she cared about me ... she did, she did.'

'Of course she did. You were her student. Someone special.'

'Yes. She knew I loved her. Not ... not ... in a bad way.'

'Like you loved your mother?'

'Yes. Yes. Like with your whole heart, you can't help it. It just is there, and I wanted to tell her, but he called ... he called and it was all spoiled.'

Dr Maclaine took a deep breath and let it out slowly. 'And then what happened?'

'I knew if she went and shot someone she would be put in jail, so I tried to take the gun away. She wouldn't listen, she was in such a state, like nothing mattered any more. I'd never seen her like that. She was so tired and it was all too much finally. She said she was going to end it. I didn't know if she meant to kill the man or herself, then. But I knew she wasn't being reasonable. Maybe I wasn't, either. I wanted to stop her, to hold her, to protect her . . . and it went off. The gun went off.'

'And?'

'And she was dead. It was horrible. Horrible.' Lois was beyond tears now. Reliving the moment, her eyes wide with horror, panting as her chest constricted and she struggled to breathe.

Dr Maclaine took out the vial of epinephrine. 'I'm going to give you an injection to help you breathe,' she said and did so. Lois ignored her, showed no reaction to the needle, but after a minute or so she seemed easier. She was still staring at the far wall, seeing something where there was nothing.

'It was an accident,' Dr Maclaine said after a minute. 'The gun went off in the struggle.'

'But if I hadn't been there, there would have been no struggle,' Lois said in a surprisingly sane tone.

'Then she might have done something foolish.'

Lois shook her head. 'No. It was because I was there. Because of what he said to me. It made her snap. She was so tired, you see. And she had a splitting headache. And it all . . . it all . . .' She shrugged. 'If I hadn't been there she would have had no one to get angry for. She was angry for me. She cared about me. She wanted to protect me.'

'And you wanted to protect her.'

'I should have called the police when she was dead. I called the Suicide Hotline – they have always been so good to me. The man said I should call the police, but I was afraid to. I know how it looked. So I wiped off the gun and the telephone in the bedroom before I left. I'd been in the house before, but never in there, you see. Then, the next day, I should have said right away, I should have admitted it all. But I wanted to wipe it away like I had wiped my fingerprints off, I wanted to forget it, I didn't want to be there, I didn't want to have been there at all. So I pretended to myself that it had been someone else, not me. It worked at first, but . . .'

'But the police figured it out.'

'I guess. They arrested me, didn't they?'

'If you had told them what you told me, I'm sure they would have understood.'

Lois shook her head, her thin hair swinging on either side of her narrow face. 'But it was still wrong. Wasn't it? I will still have to go to jail.'

'I have no idea about that,' Dr Maclaine said briskly. 'I think it's more important that you get some treatment to help you get over this. It was a terrible thing to happen. You were wrong not to speak up, that's true. But you were frightened.'

Lois looked straight at her, then, and her gaze was clear and suddenly more adult. 'I was more frightened for myself. That is the bad part. I only cared about myself when I left home and I only cared about myself when Elise was dead.' She gave a sudden shiver. 'Daddy and that man are right. I am a wicked person.'

Dr Maclaine turned to look at the blank expanse of glass on the far wall. She shook her head. She placed her hand on Lois McKittrick's shoulder.

Beyond the glass Stryker, Tos, Muller, Neilson and Captain Fineman heaved a collective sigh. 'She's going to fight for her,' Stryker said. 'She's a tough old bird.'

'It was an accident,' Neilson said in an amazed tone. 'Why didn't she just tell us that?'

Captain Fineman cleared his throat. 'She's only a kid. Maybe one of us looks like her damned father.'

Two hours later they gathered in Stryker's office, although Fineman left them to it, claiming other duties. They could see he'd been upset by the girl's confession. They all had. They all wished they had been gentler, kinder – but it was too late for that now.

When you work on murder, sometimes you lose perspective.

'We'll have to charge her,' Neilson said. 'I mean . . . we will, won't we?'

'Let the DA decide,' Stryker said. He glanced at the Assistant DA who had joined them. He was named Bradman and he was fairly new to the DA's office. To the rest of them he looked about the same age as Lois McKittrick or Muller.

The Assistant DA shrugged. 'It's complicated – could go either way. I'll have to get back to you.'

Stryker tried to explain. 'She's in a pretty bad state. Dr Maclaine says she has apparently been mentally abused for years by her father. He's a fanatic "Christian". They live in isolation up north. He's a survivalist, too. She and her mother must have been in torment. The only reason he let her go away to college was what she said – someone else was paying for it. He would have liked that – getting the better of the system, a system he hated and feared. And that other stuff – about him calling her evil – it seems her mother had an affair and she was the result. He never let her forget it, used it as an excuse to beat and torture his wife. Said he kept Lois out of pity, to cover up her mother's sin. But there was something about Lois that scared him, too. Maybe he knew who the real father was, maybe there was something about that.' Stryker shrugged. 'It will take a long time. She lives half in a dream, half in the real world and can't seem to make a solid connection between the two. Poor Professor Mayhew – exhausted, faced with the girl and her fantasies, and then . . .'

Bradman pressed his lips together. He had seen Lois McKittrick through the one-way glass and he pitied her. But he knew he was supposed to be without pity, without judgement, and to go on the facts alone. Could they get a conviction? Should they try? 'I'll get back to you,' he repeated and left the room, clutching his new briefcase to his chest.

There was silence. Then Neilson cleared his throat. 'So, what about this guy who was upsetting Mayhew with phone calls? Is it Torrance?'

'Oh yes, I think so,' Stryker said. And he told them about Kate's calls. 'He set it off.'

One of the civilian aides came over. 'There was a call from a Miss Olson. She said it was urgent, but you were in the observation room.'

'I wonder what Liz wants?' Tos hoped this was a breakthrough in their relationship. He could use some good news.

'No, the call was for Lieutenant Stryker,' the aide said. 'I'm sorry, should I have interrupted after all?'

Suddenly afraid, Stryker picked up the phone and dialled Kate's mobile. 'Listen, Kate, about Torrance—'

'Oh yes, indeed, he's right here,' Kate said overbrightly. 'We're here together, having a nice talk.'

'I thought we'd agreed you wouldn't . . .' Stryker sat up, his chair lurching beneath him.

'We're here talking to Professor Torrance at his home. He's not a very happy person, you know, dear. He couldn't control his impulse to call people. I understand that now. He's sorry. But he wants to explain more. He doesn't want us to leave. We can't leave, Jack.' The brightness dimmed a little as her voice faltered.

'What are you saying?' Stryker demanded.

'Well – he has a big gun,' Kate said, as if explaining to a child. 'And he says if we try to leave before he explains—'

'He'll shoot you?' Stryker was horrified.

'No, not exactly. He says if we leave he'll shoot himself. So, you see, Jack . . . we can't leave him, can we?'

TWENTY-FOUR

PROFESSOR TORRANCE SAT AT EASE in a rocking chair. He gazed at Liz and Kate, who sat across from him, side by side on the sofa. His eyes were icy and a little wild, almost glittering as they darted from woman to woman in a kind of rabid satisfaction.

When they had first arrived he had seemed merely uncivil. He spoke through a slightly opened door, but Liz leaned on it and her sheer weight gradually overcame him. They went inside.

Kate faced him with her hands on her hips. 'What is all this crap about Michael Deeds?' she demanded in what was, at the least, a very confrontational attitude. Her challenge had not gone down well.

'Sit down!' he had thundered and they had – perhaps unwisely.

He'd glared down at them. 'Michael was one of my best students. Then he was flattered into thinking he could be a writer.'

'He is very gifted,' Kate said. 'But—'

'Do you know where I found him after you had thrown him out? Working in a car wash. In a car wash! It was disgraceful. He said it gave him time to think.'

'Good for him,' Kate said. 'He really should consider his options.'

'He has a responsibility to his abilities. When you had discarded him so cruelly—'

'I asked him to leave because—'

'Because you had become bored with him,' Torrance snapped.

'No – because he had become overfamiliar and taken advantage of her kindness,' Liz contradicted.

'Pah,' Torrance said and began pacing around the room. 'I told him that if he returned to his science studies I would aid him financially.'

'A bribe?' Kate asked. 'Very professional.'

'I can afford it,' Torrance said dismissively. 'Promising students get scholarships and sponsors all the time.'

'They earn them,' Liz put in. 'They don't beg for them.'

'You underestimate the boy,' Torrance said. 'When I reminded him that many physicians have been famous writers – from Conan Doyle to Michael Crichton – he realized he could achieve both goals. And he realized also that all Miss Trevorne's encouragement had been purely for her personal gratification—'

'That's a damn lie!' Kate shouted.

He ignored her and kept his eyes on Liz. 'Once he realized that, he agreed to my terms,' he finished triumphantly.

'Which were?' Liz asked through gritted teeth.

Torrance smiled. If he'd had a moustache he would have twirled it. As it was, he merely looked smug. 'I personally cashed the cheque Miss Trevorne had given him. I have it safely put away. He is now settling in to new accommodation and in the spring term will be resuming his studies. As a science major.'

'Oh, really?' Kate asked. 'And perhaps I should go to the Dean and say that you have an unhealthy relationship with Michael Deeds.'

He stared at her. 'What?'

'I could put the same interpretation on your interest that you put on mine.' Kate's anger overcame her common sense. 'He is a very pretty boy, after all.'

'How dare you?' Torrance gasped.

'How dare *you*?' Kate responded. 'If we want to have a foot race, I think I could get to the Dean before you,

Professor Torrance. We're pretty even on slurs, I'd say.'

'He is losing time,' Torrance growled. 'When I saw that, I saw what you had done to him. And that is why people like you should not be teaching in a decent university.'

'I think the shoe is on the other foot, Professor Torrance,' Kate said. 'You are unbalanced. You have been calling me, harassing me, threatening me . . .' She paused as he chuckled to himself, apparently relishing the thought of what he had done. 'And you have no place teaching in even a poor university, much less a good one. You are an evil and a wicked man, and I am going to make it my business to see that everyone knows what you are really like.'

That was when he had crossed to the desk and taken out the gun.

Stryker stood outside the house. It had begun to rain but he paid no attention. Slowly, steadily, his clothes became sodden as he paced and stared at the house. All was quiet on the street, but he had seen curtains stirring. The sight of police cars and uniformed men was better than daytime television. He had to assume Kate was still inside and possibly Liz, too. He knew Liz and so did Tos. She wouldn't have let Kate go alone, no matter how insane the situation.

One of the uniformed officers came over. 'There's a call for you, Lieutenant Stryker. It's Sergeant Pinsky.'

'Tell him I'll call him back,' Stryker said, his mind on Kate and whatever might be happening inside the house. He had to decide whether to rush in or wait it out.

Either way could be wrong.

Things had been pretty quiet since Kate had talked to Stryker on her cellphone. Torrance had kept the gun at his temple, grinning, and they had sat there watching him. Nobody moved. Nobody said anything.

'You don't belong here,' Torrance suddenly said to Liz. 'Get out.'

'No,' Liz said. 'I stay.'

'Go, Liz,' Kate instructed. 'Go right out. Please.'

'No,' Liz repeated firmly. 'I'm not leaving you here alone with this loony.'

'I am not a "loony" as you put it,' Torrance snapped. 'How dare you?'

'How dare I? How dare you threaten Kate, torment her with phone calls?' Liz demanded. 'If that isn't loony behaviour, what is?'

'I was making a point.'

'Which was?'

'There is too much poaching of students from serious studies to easy ones,' Torrance said. 'Michael Deeds, Janet Linley, Ricky Sanchez – they were all students with wonderful careers ahead of them, careers that would have brought benefit to the world. Instead, they were lured away to silly pursuits, poetry, archaeology and so on. It is a disgrace and it must be stopped.'

'Oh, for crying out loud,' Liz said. 'Students switch all the time in their first year.'

'Not *my* students,' Torrance said.

Dan beckoned to Ann-Catherine and drew her into the staff lounge.

She looked at his expression. 'Trouble?'

'I think so,' Dan said. 'I've kind of been . . . nosing around.'

'I noticed,' said Ann-Catherine, who didn't miss much. 'How come?'

'I think I know who might have killed Ricky Sanchez, and why. But it's so wild . . . I still can hardly believe it myself.'

'Maybe you better tell me,' she said without batting an eyelid.

'I've been going over and over it in my mind all day,' Dan went on. 'I have a couple more things to check out and then I'd like you to call Sergeant Pinsky for me.'

'Is that the one we called when you got beaten up?'

'Yes. Give me about half an hour, then call him and ask him to come down here.'

'Tell me first,' she urged. 'Just in case.'

'Just in case what?' He was puzzled.

Ann-Catherine sighed in exasperation. 'Don't you watch TV?' she asked. 'Don't you know that's always the way it goes – the hero or heroine knows something but doesn't tell anyone else and then trouble comes. Of course, if they did tell someone the programme would be twenty minutes shorter, but . . .'

Dan grimaced, but he knew she was right. 'OK. Here's what I think.' And he told her what he thought he knew.

She didn't believe him. 'That's crazy.'

'I know,' he agreed. 'That's what worries me.'

David Waxman had been working all day, shut away in his university office with his dog Milo for company. Milo enjoyed the academic atmosphere. David had been trying to catch up on the classwork he had let drop over the past week. Finally he was satisfied and sat back, tossing the last student composition on to the pile. Milo snorkled in his sleep and turned over in his basket.

David stood up, stretched, looked at his watch. Startled, he realized he was already late to collect Dan at the hospital. Where the hell had the time gone?

He was in his car five minutes later, Milo hanging out of the back window as usual, and when he pulled up outside the ER entrance he expected to see Dan waiting and annoyed. But he wasn't there. David backed out of the ambulance bay and parked as close to the ER as he could, which wasn't all that close, and walked back, leaving Milo in the car. No one would try to steal it with Milo in there, he thought. As long as they didn't realize he was really a pussycat in disguise.

He went in through the double doors of the ER and asked for Dan.

Nobody seemed to know where he was.

'But his shift was over twenty minutes ago,' David said.

Yes, the girl on the desk agreed, that was so. She would page him. A few minutes later she came back to reception, frowning. 'He doesn't answer his pager. That's not like him.'

'Would he turn it off after his shift?' David asked.

'No – he'd keep it on as long as he was in the building,' she said. 'Maybe he took a bus or something.'

'Not Dan.' David smiled. 'He'd rather wait and chew me out than actually get on a bus.' He, too, frowned. This was unlike Dan. He felt that something was wrong. They were very close, he and his brother, and the situation being what it was – could he be lying in an alley again, broken, bleeding?

He stood there, shifting from foot to foot, not certain whether to go outside to look or to start searching the hospital itself. But that was pointless. It was a huge building. He could be going up in one elevator while Dan was coming down in another. Why wouldn't Dan answer his pager?

He sat down in the waiting area next to a man with a bloodied towel round his hand. The man held it up. 'Nearly cut off my finger,' he said.

'Bad luck.' David tried not to look.

'Damn meat cleaver,' the man continued. 'Mind of its own.'

David said nothing, but attempted to look sympathetic. He shut out the drone as the man went on to describe the circumstances of the accident, the blood everywhere, the pain. There was real pride in the man's voice, as if nearly cutting off his finger were a great achievement. Maybe it was, in an otherwise dull life.

Where the hell was Dan?

Professor Torrance had been silent for a while.

'If you agree to stop the phone calls, we'll let it drop,' Kate offered finally. 'That's all we want, to stop the phone calls.'

'No – you'd tell on me anyway,' Torrance said almost childishly. 'And I could still tell on you.'

'No, we wouldn't,' Kate said. 'And I told you, there's no truth to what Michael Deeds said about me. None at all. I'm sure if I ask him, he'll admit that. Do you know where he is?'

'Bitches,' Torrance hissed, ignoring her question. 'Stealing all the good students for yourselves. Don't you realize the world needs scientists more than ever? Students shouldn't be encouraged to take the easy route.'

'And you think English is an easy route?' Liz asked.

'Did I call you?' Torrance snarled.

'That's not the point,' Liz said briskly.

'Oh, I think it is. What do you teach?'

Tell him you don't teach, Kate thought, trying to send the message telepathically to her friend. Then he'll let you go.

'I teach French and Spanish,' Liz said. 'I'm thinking of trying Italian, too.'

'Ah, languages.' Torrance leaned forward. 'But the easy languages – not technical like German or Latin. No good, no good at all.'

'People have to communicate,' Liz said righteously.

'I know. I communicate.' Torrance giggled. 'That's why you're here, remember? You don't like the way I communicate. Maybe I should do it in French. Ooh-la-la.' The giddy way he said it made it sound even worse. His voice had become strange, like a doll's: high and flat. It occurred to Kate that, having got them into this situation, he was now frightened himself. Liz had warned her about cornering people. Maybe he didn't know how to surrender the moment. Perhaps it was beyond him to go back.

Her cellphone rang and it was Jack. She reassured him, then looked at Torrance and held out the phone. 'He wants to talk to you.'

'I have absolutely no interest in talking to him, whoever he is. Turn it off,' Torrance ordered. 'No more calls.'

'What did you hope to achieve by all this? I'd really like to know.' Liz was trying to talk him down, Kate realized. If they could keep him talking it would give Jack space to manoeuvre. She was certain he was outside in the rain. She had heard cars arriving, people talking. She sensed his nearness.

'Would you, now,' said Torrance. 'Well, I'll tell you, as you asked. It amused me. That's all. It amused me. Since Margaret died I haven't had much amusement. And the thought of their silly faces at the other end of the line made me chuckle. You are useless, all of you females, taking up university space and time and money. Stealing students—'

'We don't steal students,' Kate repeated patiently. 'There are always shake-ups after the freshman year, students who switch courses until they find what they want. It's always been that way.'

'What they can get away with, you mean,' Torrance snapped. 'They're lazy, they want an easy degree, an easy life.'

'Then your argument is with them, not us,' Liz said.

Torrance looked at her, startled. 'They're children. They don't realize what they're doing, wasting their time with sonnets and finger paints. If they were challenged they could do great things.'

'Not all of them,' Liz said calmly. 'Not all of them.'

'More of them than we get.' Torrance's knuckles were white where they gripped the gun, which was now back in his lap. At least he was no longer pointing it at himself, Kate thought. Or anyone. He rambled on. 'Fewer and fewer opt for science now. It's all arts . . . and computers.' His voice twisted on the last word.

'Oh – you've been calling computer science teachers too?' asked Liz. 'We didn't know that. We thought only the English department was privileged to receive your calls.'

'Oh no . . . oh no. I spread my favours widely.' Torrance smirked. 'Although I must admit the English department is a favourite.'

Kate suddenly had a thought. 'What about anthropology – do you call them too?'

242

'Only one,' he said. 'Only one. But she's not a problem any more. She won't steal any more students like Ricky Sanchez.' He leaned forward. 'He was one of the best, the most promising . . . and he told me he was going to switch his major next term. Can you believe it? He had a gift, a real gift, and he was going to squander it on the past instead of the future.'

Kate felt a sinking sensation in her stomach. Ricky Sanchez. Had Torrance killed him? Asking about anthropology had been a shot in the dark, on her mind because Jack was so caught up in it. Had Torrance killed both Ricky and Professor Mayhew? If so, he wouldn't stop at killing them. He had nothing to lose – and neither did they.

'I think we're going to go now,' said Kate, starting to stand up.

'Fuck you,' Professor Torrance said. He glared at them. 'Fuck you, fuck you, fuck you.'

Neither of them showed any reaction whatsoever – they had agreed on that before they came. Whatever he said, they would not give him the satisfaction of the response he wanted.

Their impassivity seemed to enrage him. He spewed out a volley of filth, machine-gunning them with it. They sat still, impassive.

'I'm afraid that kind of talk won't achieve anything,' Kate said with heavy disapproval.

He lifted the gun and pointed it at her. 'Shut up,' he yelled. 'Little bitch.'

Kate stared at him and at the gun. She loathed guns and the little circle of the muzzle was like the black eye of a snake. 'This isn't getting us anywhere,' she said calmly.

He fired. Missed. The bullet went into the floor beside Kate's feet. He'd aimed for her legs. The noise was tremendous, loud and shocking in the otherwise cosy room. And it *was* a cosy room, with chintz on the over-stuffed furniture, friendly pictures on the wall, house plants and the dogs. He had shut the dogs out into the hall when he produced the gun. Now they were barking furiously. French poodles. They probably thought firing a gun was unfashionable.

'I thought you said you were a good shot,' she said, amazed that her numb mouth could speak.

'You're still alive, aren't you?' snapped Torrance. 'Therefore I am a good shot.'

And you only have five bullets left, Kate thought.

David looked up as a nurse approached him. 'You're Dan Waxman's brother?' she asked. Her name tag read Ann-Catherine Grant, Senior Staff. The picture on it didn't do her justice.

He nodded. 'Do you know where he is?' he asked.

'I think he might be down in pathology,' she said. 'He went down there twenty or thirty minutes ago.'

'He doesn't answer his pager,' David said, standing up.

'I know,' said Ann-Catherine. 'That's what worries me.'

'How do I find it?' David asked.

David found the doors marked 'Pathology' and pushed through them. The room was huge, long tables filled with scientific equipment. The neon lights overhead were extra bright and the whole room seemed sharp-edged and steely.

'Is Dr Waxman here?' he asked, raising his voice slightly.

'He was here,' one of the women standing near him said. 'I think he's in the morgue with Ivan.' She gestured. 'Through there.'

David did not like the sound of the word morgue. He crossed the room and went through the indicated door. If anything, it was brighter in there, and colder, and smelled of harsh chemicals and something . . . sweet. He saw the drawers lining the wall. One was slightly open, but he couldn't see inside. The steel tables were all empty. No one living was there.

If Dan had gone back out through the labs, presumably

the woman would have noticed him. There was another door on the far side of the room and David went to it, pushing it open. 'Dan?' he called.

The other side of the door in the morgue led to a long, dark passage. Big ducts twisted overhead into the distance and there was a steady humming of the big machines that kept the hospital above him alive. David took a few steps into the corridor, feeling grit on the concrete underfoot. The echoing of the tunnel and the thrum of the machines made a kind of music . . . a sound that would be hard to capture.

'Dan?' he called again more loudly.

'Here,' came a voice from the distance. 'Go away. Let me deal with this.'

'The hell I will,' David muttered to himself. And he started down the dimly lit corridor towards Dan's voice.

About thirty yards along, the corridor widened and there was an alcove. In it stood two people – his brother Dan and a tall, thin man with dark, penetrating eyes.

'Go away, David,' Dan said. His voice was weary, hopeless.

'What the hell is going on?' David asked, stepping closer and taking Dan by the arm.

'Leave him alone,' said the big man. 'We're working things out.'

'What things?'

'Life and death,' said the big man. 'We're doctors, that's what we deal with, life and death.'

'It's all right, David,' Dan said.

'It obviously isn't,' David contradicted firmly.

'Your brother is interfering with my work,' the big man said. 'I can't allow that.' He raised his hand, which had been hidden behind him. It held a hypodermic syringe. 'I've taken care of that.'

'He's injected me with HIV,' Dan said in a lost voice.

'Dear God.' David went cold with horror. 'Why?'

'Because I realized what he was doing,' Dan said. 'Just as Ricky Sanchez realized.'

'Ricky followed me. He was in the way,' Sherwin said impatiently. 'He started yelling that I was unethical, that I was immoral. But I know what I'm doing.'

'You killed him,' Dan accused.

Sherwin shrugged. 'I lost my temper. Little holier-than-thou smart-ass. He was going to tell and I wasn't ready. It was too soon.'

Dan looked down at his arm. 'Better you should have smashed my skull in than done this.'

'But I can cure you,' Sherwin said. He reached into his pocket and pulled out a small ampoule. 'I can cure them all now. Just a few more tests, just a few more . . .'

'Allow me to introduce Ivan Sherwin,' Dan said wearily. 'Pathologist and research scientist. They refused him a grant, so he's been going out into French Street and tracking down people we have on record as having HIV.'

'They're victims of society,' Sherwin said. 'They need someone to stand up for them.'

'Yeah, and you do, don't you, Ivan. Big time.' Dan looked bleakly at David. 'He injects them with genetically altered viruses, using them as human guinea pigs. He tells them it's vitamins, something new for their treatment. They believe him. Hell, they'll believe anyone who gives them a few bucks. When they end up in here – and they always do – he draws blood to see what effect his treatment had,' Dan said.

'I can cure them,' Sherwin said to Dan. 'I know I can. You'll see. You'll have to believe me now.'

Dan sighed heavily. 'He's been telling me all about it. Whenever he was supposed to be taking blood samples, he was also taking some extra, testing his treatment. If he didn't see the result he wanted, he would inject the patients again. Then, when they died – and they all died . . .'

'But mine take longer,' Sherwin said earnestly to David. 'It's working. It's going to work, as soon as I can get—'

'You bastard!' David shouted and without warning leapt at Sherwin. He hadn't even known he was going to do it himself, it just happened; suddenly he was at him, grabbing him, shaking him. The syringe and ampoule dropped to the floor as Sherwin struggled to defend himself from a whirlwind of fists and kicks. Dan, also startled, had enough sense to kick the syringe away and tried to help his brother. His ribs stabbed him with pain – already, in an earlier struggle in the morgue with Sherwin, he was pretty sure another one had been cracked.

Sherwin bellowed with rage and knocked David to the floor, then ran off down the long, dim corridor.

'He's nuts,' Dan said. 'He's lost it completely. His brother died of AIDS, so he's a man with a mission – at least, that's how he sees it. God knows how many he's killed with his half-assed "treatment". He told me all about it and it's crap, it has to be. He's gone completely over the edge.'

'Well, we'd better stop him,' David said.

'But—'

'Come on,' David said and he started off down the corridor too. He turned back. 'Where does this go?'

'Everywhere,' Dan said. 'It's a maze down here.'

David turned back and ran on. After a minute Dan went after him. Their footsteps echoed hollowly as the invisible machines thrummed on. All around them the hospital was breathing. The air rushed through the ducts above. They were in the bowels of the place, chasing a human virus that had infected the building with murder.

Dan was right, the corridors were a maze, some very old, some blocked and rerouted, intersecting, going off at angles, now hot, now cold. And they were infested . . .

David had stopped, winded. 'Who are these people?' he asked Dan, who had caught up with him. Every once in a while he had come upon one, curled up in layers of filthy clothing, huddling over bags of possessions.

'Homeless,' Dan gasped, his breathing uneven, ragged. 'They come in through the delivery doors at night because it's warm. Security throws them out, but they come right back. Mostly we just ignore them now.' He turned to one. 'Did you see a big man, running?'

The bundle of rags stirred and a hand emerged, pointing. David and Dan started off again, knowing they had been in some places before, losing their sense of direction. Abruptly they found themselves at a dead end, among shelves loaded with discarded equipment, a big room with no other exit, and in the far corner Sherwin crouched, breathing hard, leaning against the wall, his eyes wild and desperate behind his dishevelled hair. *Like the demented animal he is,* David thought with disgust. He glanced at Dan and nodded. The room was poorly lit, one overhead light, swinging slightly in the draught from the hallway and squeaking rustily. Bright, dark, bright, dark. It gave the place an odd, stroboscopic feeling. Like an old movie run on a broken projector.

David reached back and closed the door behind him. There was no key, no way to lock it. They had to stop Sherwin here. And now.

'Leave me alone,' Sherwin growled. 'You've got to leave me alone to go on with the work.' He looked at Dan. 'I can cure you, I know I can. Let me go. Let me go.'

They came at him from two sides, co-ordinating without thinking, without saying anything, no need. They were brothers.

When they jumped, together, Sherwin was ready and fought like the madman he was. Falling and rolling as they struggled, Dan was crushed beneath the other two and cried out in agony. He scrambled away, panting shallowly for precious breath. He was pretty sure he'd punctured a lung.

'No!' Sherwin kept shouting. 'You don't understand. You need me. They all need me. I can do it. I'm almost there.'

Blindly David fought on, though he was no fighter. He had no system, no plan, just wildly punching and kicking because he knew no other way, and rage for his brother was driving him.

Sherwin was like a huge spider, long arms and legs going everywhere. He bit, he fought, he screamed and cursed and twisted. Twice he nearly got away. Each time David brought him down, once by the neck, then by the legs, but it was getting more and more difficult. Sherwin was full of panic and it gave him great strength. 'You don't understand ... you're wrong ...' he kept saying, as he tried to get away, but David would not let go.

Grunting and gasping, they continued to struggle. The blows between them were becoming fewer, slower, lighter, and Dan could see Sherwin was getting between David and the door. David was going to lose him.

Dan looked around wildly, dragged himself to his feet, then grabbed an old metal bedpan and struck Sherwin on the back of the head. Once, twice, three times. Ribs or not, he put everything he had left into it.

Sherwin went limp and collapsed.

David scrambled up, panting, aching, half dazed, and looked down. 'He's finished,' he gasped.

Dan rubbed the place where Sherwin had plunged the loaded needle into his arm. 'So am I,' he said and slowly slid down the wall to sit on the floor beside the unconscious Sherwin. 'So am I.'

TWENTY-FIVE

STRYKER AND THE OTHERS WENT in through the back door.
Quietly they moved across the kitchen into the dining
room. They could hear Torrance still raving, his voice
quite calm but talking total nonsense, occasionally giving
a bizarre little giggle. He sounded tired, old and manic.

Stryker thought *don't do anything, Kate. Let him rave.*
Don't do anything. Leave it to me. For once, please, leave it to
me.

But in the cosy flowered living room Kate had made
up her mind. She and Liz were actually quite close to
Torrance – sitting like two birds on a telegraph wire,
motionless as he ranted on.

Kate had suddenly decided it was up to her. She glanced
at Liz and saw the same resolution in her eyes. If this guy
was a killer, they had no alternative, did they?

'On three,' Kate said very, very softly under cover of
Torrance's voice.

'He can only get one of us, Sundance,' Liz said.

Kate wanted to laugh, she was so strung up, but said
the numbers instead: 'One, two, three.'

They launched themselves at Torrance who, for once,
had been gazing at what was probably a picture of his
wife, as if he were explaining himself to her instead of to
them. The combined weight of Kate and Liz knocked
over the rocking chair Torrance sat in and the gun went
off – once, twice, three times. One, two, three. And a
scream.

Liz was lying across his chest and Kate was clutching

his legs when Stryker burst into the room, followed by Tos, Muller and Neilson, and some uniforms. Between them Muller and Neilson grabbed Torrance's arms and Stryker handcuffed him.

Slowly Kate backed off. But Liz didn't get up. She lay there, moaning, blood trickling from her arm and the other arm bent at an impossible angle. She was swearing steadily. Tos went and put his arms round her. 'It's OK, you're OK,' he murmured.

She looked up at him and raised an eyebrow. 'I'm leaking,' she said, looking down at herself. And passed out.

'Damn you, Kate,' Stryker said.

She turned to him. 'I love you, too.' She burst into tears.

Muller took the call. It was Pinsky again. He turned to look at the others as the ambulance took a heavily sedated Torrance and a semi-conscious Liz to the hospital. Tos went with them, ignoring Torrance completely in his concern for Liz.

Neighbours had gathered, drawn by the police cars, the shots and the ambulance. Standing in the freezing cold, they watched, they listened. Drama on your doorstep, courtesy of your local police department. For this you pay your taxes. Muller handed the cellphone to Stryker.

'They got him,' Pinsky said in a peculiar voice from the other end.

'Who?' Stryker demanded, his attention on the ambulance.

'The guy who killed Ricky. They got him. I wasn't even there and they got him.' Pinsky sounded stunned, relieved, resentful, weary. Somebody else had done what he was supposed to do. It wasn't fair, it wasn't right.

'What?' Stryker asked. 'Who got who? What the hell are you talking about?' He was jittering with adrenalin, holding Kate with one arm, walking her back and forth, back and forth.

'Those two brothers – the Waxman brothers. They figured out who he was, what he'd done. They got him. Jesus, they knocked him out with a bedpan, can you believe it? I got there just after. But he injected one of them with bad blood ... HIV ... before they brought him down. You'd better get down here.'

The man at the reception desk was tall, broad and angry. 'I want to see my daughter,' he demanded in a loud voice.

'I'm afraid that will not be possible,' said the receptionist, quailing a little as she consulted a list on her desktop. 'She is to have no visitors, on doctor's orders.'

'I don't care what a goddamn doctor says, I want to see my daughter,' said the man, even more loudly than before. 'I have a right to see my daughter.'

'Actually, you don't,' said a quiet voice behind him. He turned and saw a small woman in a red tracksuit and white coat regarding him. 'Your daughter is over twenty-one and has rights as an individual. She doesn't want to see you and I don't want her to see you. You have done enough damage already.'

'Who the hell do you think you are, you old bitch?' he shouted.

'I am Dr Maclaine. I am in charge of your daughter's health and well-being in this clinic, and she is to have no visitors. That is also the decision of the police, by the way. You will have to leave.'

He stepped forward threateningly. He was an ugly man, his expression brutal, his size intimidating. Dr Maclaine did not move.

'I come all the way down here to see her. They say she killed someone. No way, no way she has the guts to do that. She's a bad one, but she's no killer.'

'You would be surprised at the amount of courage your daughter has, Mr McKittrick,' said Dr Maclaine. 'And the charge against her has not been settled yet, but it is certainly not going to be a charge of homicide. What happened was an unfortunate accident. Her only real

252

crime was trying to hide it, from herself and everyone else.'

'Bullshit. Don't give me that psycho mumbo-jumbo. Do I have to get some damn lawyer to make you let me see her?' he growled. He was obviously unaccustomed to opposition and, had the two of them been alone, there was a good chance he would have added physical abuse to verbal. As it was, the lobby was crowded and the attitude of those people in it to the large, noisy, unattractive and, frankly, dirty man was hostile to say the least. There were murmurings, there was a security guard – and then there were two security guards. Then three. They all stood watching, prepared to move if they had to, but the little old lady in the white coat seemed to have it all under control. The angry man loomed over her, but she remained unmoved.

'You can get any number of lawyers, Mr McKittrick, it will make no difference,' said Dr Maclaine. 'Lois is not going to be bothered by you or anyone else. She has had a nervous breakdown and is physically ill as well. No visitors. Is that clear?'

He stepped back, brushed his long matted hair away from his scowling face. He was suddenly aware they had an audience. 'We'll see about that. I got rights too.'

Dr Maclaine managed a wry smile. 'Under the Constitution of the United States? The Constitution you profess to uphold against all comers and all sense? Yes, you do have rights, Mr McKittrick – but they do not include seeing your daughter in her present condition. Good day.' She turned and walked towards the elevators.

McKittrick stared after her. 'We'll see about that!' he shouted rather pointlessly. Glaring around at the other people in the lobby, he charged the outer doors like a bull moose and disappeared from view in the crowd beyond them.

There was a silence.

And then a little quiet scatter of applause.

* * *

253

Liz lay in the hospital bed, looking very uncomfortable. 'I figured he would get you, not me,' she said with a wry grin.

'Ah, and that would have been all right?' Kate asked.

Liz shook her head. 'Of course not. But it would have been justice – the whole thing was your idea, remember. Going there, confronting him.'

'I know, I know,' Kate admitted. 'I must have been insane.'

'You have been a little more goofy than usual lately,' Liz conceded. 'But here I am, not even able to scratch my own nose.'

'Do you need it scratched?' Kate asked with concern.

'Yes, as a matter of fact,' Liz said. 'Right at the bridge.' Kate leaned over and complied. 'Ahh,' Liz breathed. 'Thanks.' Both her arms were immobilized – she had broken the right one when she fell over Torrance and the rocking chair, and when his gun had gone off in the struggle the bullet had gone into her left shoulder. She looked down. 'I don't know what the hell I'm going to do now.'

'You'll be coming home with me,' said a voice from the door. It was Tos, looking determined. 'I will take care of you.'

'You mean you'll come and stay with me?' Liz brightened. 'What a great idea.'

'Better than that,' Tos said. 'I'm taking you home to Mama.'

There was a long and considerable silence.

'What?' Liz finally asked in a rather weak voice.

'All fixed,' Tos went on. 'I explained everything.'

'Everything?' Liz prompted.

'Well, about how brave you were and all, protecting Kate, here.'

'I wasn't protecting Kate,' Liz protested. 'I was trying to catch a madman.'

'I can look after myself,' Kate also protested, her last feeble words of defiance falling on deaf ears.

Tos gave a huge Italian shrug, hands wide. 'It amounts to the same thing.' He came further into the room, pulled over a chair and straddled it. 'You remember Machiavelli?'

'I taught him all he knows,' Liz said.

He ignored that. 'Mama is a sucker for a sick person,' Tos said. 'And a brave sick person is even better. She will cook for you, look after you when I am at work and she will naturally grow to love you because who could resist?' He grinned. 'Not me.'

'Oh my God,' Liz groaned. 'I don't believe this.'

'It will be easy. All you have to do is show an interest in recipes and agree to learn Italian,' Tos said, full of enthusiasm.

'I don't like cooking,' Liz interrupted.

'Pretend,' Tos continued. 'Look on it as domestic chemistry. Also some interest in the afternoon soap operas would help. Get on her wavelength, break her down.'

'And your sister?' Liz asked.

'Elvis,' Tos said.

'I beg your pardon?'

'Ask about Elvis Presley – listen to a few CDs . . . that's all you have to do.'

'All?' Liz's voice was a bit strangled.

Tos looked a little uncertain. 'It's the best thing I can think of,' he said. 'Best for you and best for us. See, when she knows you . . . becomes used to you . . . getting married will be easy. Mind you, you might gain a few pounds, but what the hell.'

Liz and Kate exchanged a glance.

'I think you've just been proposed to,' Kate said.

'Just what I always wanted,' Liz said. 'Two useless arms and an elliptical proposal in front of my best friend.' But her eyes were shining.

Kate stood up. 'I think it's time I left.'

'See you, Sundance,' said Liz, but her attention was all on Tos.

* * *

Kate walked slowly out of the room and down the corridor. It had been three days since the excitement, and during that time she and Jack had hardly exchanged ten words. He had been busy dealing with Sherwin's arrest and arraignment, and she had been wandering from campus to home and back in a kind of daze.

What a fool she had been. She and Jack had an unlisted number. There had been nobody living in her flat. So, because Torrance had always called her at the university she had considered it her business and hers alone. She had to cope with it herself, in her own cack-handed way, being the big strong person at the centre of it all.

Suddenly she realized how Jack felt – wanting to be a cop. He had been trained, physically and mentally, to deal with everything from murder to vicious phone callers. She hadn't. He knew what he was doing. She didn't. She had been proceeding on emotion, not logic or experience. She was the worst of both worlds – both amateur and pig-headed. More than that, she also finally understood the fascination of it – why Jack did what he did, why he was loath to give it up. When she had been pressing ahead with the Big Chase for the Bad Man – it had been an adventure. It had been fun. She had felt in control, sure of herself, sure she was right.

Without a legal leg to stand on, she had turned vigilante.

Oh Jack, she thought. *No wonder I drive you crazy.*

'It's the damnedest thing,' Dan said to David and Abbi, as he came back from the phone and plumped himself down on the piano bench.

'What?' David asked. Abbi just looked at her much-loved brother-in-law with huge, sad eyes.

Dan grinned. 'I'm clear.' He laughed at the expression on their faces – hope mixed with confusion. 'I'm clear!'

'But how can that be – you said he injected you with blood from that guy who died of AIDS,' David said, putting aside the pillow he had been hugging as if it were a life preserver.

Dan was looking a little stunned himself. 'But that's just it – he didn't die of AIDS,' he said in a voice filled with awe. 'They never do. It's Auto-Immune Deficiency Syndrome, remember? It means they have no resistance to infection. Mostly it's pneumonia they die of, or heart failure. A dozen things. But the HIV virus stays alive as long as the body is warm, so he was drawing blood from the cadaver to test against previous samples.' He took a deep breath. 'And there was no HIV present in the dead man's blood.'

They stared at him. Abbi laughed, gasped, laughed again. 'I don't understand,' she said. 'He was an AIDS patient. He must have been filled with HIV.'

'Uh-huh,' Dan agreed. 'He was when they brought him in. They checked the records – the results were clear, he was infected with HIV when admitted a month ago, but he was free of it when his heart gave out.'

David sank back into the sofa, staring at his brother.

'My God,' he breathed. 'You mean it worked? Sherwin's treatment actually worked?'

'We don't know that,' Dan said carefully, but he still looked stunned. 'Not for sure. All we know is that there should have been clear traces of HIV in the dead guy's blood and there were none. There were none in mine, either. They've gathered up all the patient's notes and all Sherwin's notes. They even found that ampoule that got kicked around in the basement. They're putting together what they can, but the research and experimental notes are in some kind of personal code and Sherwin is not exactly in a state to explain them. It could be a fluke and of course, they'll have to keep checking me, but . . .' He looked at them, a mixture of bafflement and amazement in his eyes. 'It could take years,' he said. 'To be sure of what he did, what in his treatment made the difference, how it was processed . . .'

'Meanwhile he's going on trial for murdering Ricky Sanchez,' Abbi said softly.

'There might not even be a trial,' Dan said, turning his back and playing a few random keys on the piano. 'He's confessed, he'll plead guilty.'

'And?'

'You tell me,' Dan said, facing them again. 'If it were up to me, I'd slap him in a jail with a really big laboratory attached and let him get on with it. But it's not up to me. And you know how the bureaucrats in the justice system mess things up. They'll never trust him. He'll probably be put in a psychiatric hospital and made to do jigsaws all day. Barney will go through his notes, other people will go through them and maybe they'll figure it out, but without Sherwin . . .' He raised and lowered his shoulders.

'Jigsaws,' David said with disgust. 'Doing jigsaws.'

'Isn't everything?' asked Abbi softly.

The cemetery was quiet. A light fall of snow covered the ground, put little shrouds on the gravestones. Ned Pinsky left the path and walked across the snow, leaving wet, dark footprints in the grass. He stopped before a new marker. The ground had not yet begun to settle over the fresh grave and it seemed as if there were a warm blanket mounded over the person within. Eventually a headstone would be erected there. Pinsky would make sure of that.

He stood, looking down, then bent and put a bunch of flowers by the marker. 'I didn't get him for you, Ricky,' he said quietly. 'I'm sorry. I wanted to be the one, I thought I owed you that. But he won't kill again. At least you achieved that and you should be proud.'

It had been galling to know two amateurs had caught the killer he had so wanted to arrest. He knew Stryker had been right to insist he leave Ricky's murder alone. He knew that his mind was clouded by emotion, that he might have been unable to reason coherently and could have botched it. But he had worked methodically, carefully, doing a good job and getting there.

Instead, the Waxman brothers had rushed in. When

he thought of how much danger they had been in he felt quite weak. He was a cop, he expected to be in danger, it was what he was trained for, paid for. It could have gone so wrong. And maybe it had. He would call the hospital later to see how Dan Waxman was. If he died from AIDS eventually, Pinsky would have to add that to his burden of guilt and regret. And it was already very heavy.

He stood there for a while, looking at the bright colours of the flowers against the white of the snow. There were still two Sanchez children left. He would do his best to help their mother when she needed support. He would watch over them, as Ricky had watched over them. He promised this to Ricky.

Then he walked away.

When Stryker came home that night, Kate was ready for him. She knew he had the next two days off, that he would need rest, but she needed to straighten things out between them. Now more than ever. She had been doing a lot of thinking, a lot of looking at herself in a cold, clear light. She'd been ten kinds of a fool and nearly got herself killed. She hadn't trusted Jack, when trusting him had been the most important thing all along.

She gave him his favourite meal, then waited until he had stretched out on the sofa.

She came to sit at the other end, taking off his shoes and rubbing his feet. 'I'm sorry,' she said, plucking at the toe of his sock.

'What about?' His eyes were closed.

'Everything. Going off on my own, acting so stupidly, getting so angry . . .'

He managed a smile. 'You sure were that.' He opened his eyes. 'What will happen to Professor Torrance?'

Kate shrugged. 'He'll be retired without fuss and probably sent to a clinic to get help. The university has been pretty generous about it. Since neither Liz nor I are going to press charges, they can just deal with it quietly. The Dean tracked down Michael Deeds, got the true story out of him. He said Torrance's judgement was affected by grief. One way of looking at it, I guess. There's a good medical plan, he'll get what he needs.'

'Which was not being confronted by two angry women,' Stryker said wryly.

She started to bridle, then had the grace to smile. 'True.'

They sat companionably together, and after a while Stryker reached for her hand and held it. 'How do you feel now?'

She sighed. 'Exhausted. But Jack . . .'

'What?'

'I think I understand, now, about your wanting to be a cop. About how it matters to get things straightened out, even to face danger doing it.'

'Really?' He sounded unconvinced.

'I . . . loved it,' she said in a small voice. 'Catching him. I loved it.'

He regarded her thoughtfully. 'I don't do it for fun,' he said quietly.

'No, I know that. I understand that too. It's to get things settled, to stop the wickedness, to make peace.'

'Powerful wampum,' he said, teasing her, but pleased that she was trying hard, obviously very hard, to understand his point of view. 'It's all of that. And sometimes exciting, I won't deny that. But Pinsky . . .'

'He got emotionally involved, like I did,' Kate said. 'Is he very upset that he didn't get the killer himself?'

'He'll get over it,' Stryker said. Pinsky had returned to find Muller using his desk. There had been words. Muller was now at a desk by himself in the corner. But Stryker had seen the look on his baby face and he realized there were some fun times ahead. Whereas Pinsky knew how to handle Neilson, Muller had found the chinks in Neilson's ego and could now rile him with a look or a comment. What's more, he obviously was made for mischief. There was a lot more to the boy than even he had suspected, and finding the right partner for him was going to be a ride and a half. But it seemed to him that Muller would be worth the effort.

More silence. Peaceful silence at last between them.

'It really was all connected, wasn't it?' Kate finally asked.

'It's like the man said – life is just one damn thing after another,' Stryker commented. 'All the violence had a common starting point, but we had no way of seeing it until it was too late.'

He held up a hand and counted off on his fingers. 'If Torrance hadn't called Elise Mayhew once too often, Mayhew would have taught her next day's class as usual. But Lois McKittrick was with her when he made his last call. She was begging for the attention she desperately craved, which Elise Mayhew was too exhausted to give. Lois took the phone and Torrance said God knows what to her, making her cry. When she saw those tears, Elise snapped, went for the gun to kill Torrance. It was an emotional moment, but Lois had enough sense to wrestle her for the gun, to try and stop her doing something so foolish. In the struggle, Elise Mayhew was shot.'

'Like Liz got shot,' Kate mused. 'Because of me.'

Stryker sighed, remembering Lois McKittrick as he had last seen her, broken, sobbing, temporarily beyond retrieval. Dr Maclaine had taken charge, worked with the DA, made it her business to see Lois was looked after properly.

He went on. 'Not quite. In a struggle, yes, but not for the same reasons. Anyway, as a result of Mayhew's death, her classes were cancelled. Without a class to attend Ricky decided to work an extra shift at the hospital the next night. Some time during that extra shift he followed Sherwin to French Street, saw what he was doing and saying to his "patients", confronted him.' He smiled slightly. 'From what I've learned about Ricky Sanchez from Ned, I don't imagine he was very sympathetic to Sherwin and let him know in no uncertain terms what he thought of him. Sherwin lost control and killed him to shut him up.'

'So it really started with Torrance?' Kate asked.

Stryker sighed, sat up and put his arm round Kate. 'I suppose you could say that. It's all been a matter of normally sane people losing control, one way or another. Speaking of which, how's David's hand?'

'Abbi says he'll play piano again, but it will take a couple of months of physio first. She also said David is quite proud of having broken three bones fighting for what he thought was his dying brother. And there's wonderful news there, too.' She told him about Dan and the strange, puzzling but splendid test results. Abbi had called her that afternoon to relay the details.

Stryker smiled with relief. It had been preying on his mind. It was bad enough to kill bad men – but to be the reason good men die was untenable.

When they had reached the hospital after a race from the Torrance house the Waxman Boys – as they would for ever be called in his mind – were the centre of attention in the ER, sitting on adjacent gurneys, getting treatment.

Stryker had opened his mouth to speak, but Dan interrupted, his voice strained. One of his rebroken ribs had grazed a lung, and he was still under the impression he was a man destined to die of AIDS. Shock had undermined but not totally unnerved him. 'It was my own fault,' he said. 'Ann-Catherine told me not to do it. She told me to wait until she called Sergeant Pinsky. But I was feeling like a hero. I caught Sherwin in the morgue and said more than I should have. I made my choice. I'll have to live with it.'

Now Stryker thanked God Dan had apparently been spared.

'They're quite a pair, those Waxman brothers.' Stryker grinned. 'They're hardly the first ones to spring to mind when it comes to bringing down a killer. A musician and a healer. And yet they did our job for us. We should never have dismissed Ricky's murder as a street crime. Fineman . . .'

'Do you mind?' Kate was amused.

'No. But Pinsky does. He wanted to catch Ricky's killer, you know. He wanted to deal out justice for the boy because he felt he had failed him by not paying more attention to what Ricky was worrying about. It became an obsession, made him risk his badge and his job. I think it will take him a while to settle it within himself.'

'I think we have some settling to do between ourselves as well,' Kate said. 'Things like who's in charge, when and why. I think we might have to start taking turns on that.'

'What – on alternate Wednesdays I have my way and all the rest of the time you have yours?' he asked with a grin.

'Maybe.' She got up and went across the room to her desk. She came back slowly. 'I've finally found out part of the reason I acted so emotionally; why I've been so moody and short-tempered.'

'PMT?' Stryker asked with a manly display of under-standing.

'Not quite,' Kate said and produced a small white stick from behind her back. She held it out. 'I'm pregnant.' She smiled.